Christopher

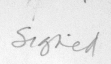

Christopher

Allison Burnett

Broadway Books New York

PRINTED IN THE UNITED STATES OF AMERICA

BROADWAY BOOKS and its logo, a letter B bisected on the diagonal, are trademarks of Broadway Books, a division of Random House, Inc.

Visit our website at www.broadwaybooks.com

First edition published April 2003

Book design by Ralph L. Fowler

Library of Congress Cataloging-in-Publication Data

Burnett, Allison.
    Christopher: a novel / by Allison Burnett.—Rev.
        p.   cm.
    1. Gay men—Fiction.   2. Seduction—Fiction.   3. Young men—Fiction.
4. New York (N.Y.)—Fiction.   I. Title.
PS3602.U8535 C48   2003
813'.6—dc21

                                                                    2002071121

ISBN 0-7679-1333-7

10 9 8 7 6 5 4 3 2 1

For Susanne Scheer

Old year, you must not go;
So long as you have been with us,
Such joy as you have seen with us,
Old year, you shall not go.

ALFRED, LORD TENNYSON

Christopher

Greeting

My story, which is not mine alone, but also that of a far finer spirit, takes place in 1984. As those of you alive at the time will surely remember, this was the most important year in the realm of the literary imagination since the death of God. The reason was, of course, Mr. George Orwell's notoriously unreadable *1984,* which warned of society's descent into an authoritarian hell, reeking of cabbage and old rag mats.

For decades, critics had bestowed upon Mr. Orwell's arbitrarily chosen title a profound significance, and so when the actual year finally arrived it was greeted with a collective exhalation of very bad breath. Sleeves were rolled up and typewriters shaken free of tobacco ash. In every periodical and newspaper, the novel was discussed, dissected, and reassessed. On television, pundits scoured the cultural landscape for any sign of Big Brother—a bootprint, a mustache hair, even a stray lump of scat. By spring, sales of *1984* had reached fifty thousand copies a day.

Of course, none of this meant anything. (So little truly signifies in the realm of the literary imagination.) For most people,

1984 was just another year: a ribbon of time marked by a seam or two—a birth, a divorce, a slow, stinky death—and as soon as it had passed it was all but entirely forgotten.

But I confess I am not most people.

For better or worse, 1984 changed me into something that quite closely resembles a human being.

—B. K. Troop

Christopher

January

On Sunday, January 1, 1984, Manhattan awoke to find itself buried under a cliché—a blanket of white. For the next few hours, before a million tires got hold of it, the streets of the City would look, dare I say it, almost pretty. I had a mad whim to fling myself facedown in Times Square and execute a flabby snow angel, but I resisted the temptation and set myself to the matter at hand—boxing up my life. The moving van was set to arrive at noon.

Packing was no small task. I had lived in that basement apartment for the past twenty-three years and had picked up, in that time, a vast embarrassment of rare and beautiful objects. If the choice had been mine, I would certainly have avoided this day forever, but, just a week before, my beloved friend and landlady, Sasha Buchwitz, had nudged me awake with the imaginary handle of an imaginary hatchet, explaining that Satan was standing naked on her fire escape, demanding that she cut off my head. (Hers had been a spirited twenty-year battle with paranoid schizophrenia and clinical depression; she was losing.) I scampered out the very next morning and, greasing a few

3

palms, secured for myself a one-bedroom apartment in a tenement just a few blocks away.

The doorbell rang as I taped shut the final box. I stood by with pride and watched as my life was whisked away on the shoulders of giants. The transition went off without a hitch—save for the queasy glare I was thrown by one of the removalists (a strapping, high-buttocked Dominican named Santos) in reply to my suggestion that he help christen my new digs by spending the night. His colleagues dragged him away by the elbows, and I set to work.

Sixteen hours later, just after cock's crow, I slid the last of my vast antiquarian library into its alphabetized place. What had once been an empty apartment was now a home. As I had yet to sleep a wink and am highly allergic to dust mites, I descended to the street, lost in a bleary, malevolent haze. My goal, a Denver omelet and Bloody Mary at my beloved Parnassus Diner, followed by a twelve-hour snooze.

I little suspected what the Fates held in store.

We nearly collided as he ran up the marble steps three at a time. He was of medium height with longish black hair and equally dark eyes. His head was large, well shaped. Our conversation was limited. "Oh, excuse me," we both said as we passed. It was only I, however, who glanced around for a peek—he was slender and strong all over. The fact that he did nothing to confirm that I was flagrantly neither all over, I took to be an ill omen, but one which I had come to expect whenever my fancy was stoked.

Our more substantial introduction came the next afternoon when I cunningly emerged from my lair at the precise moment that he entered his.

"Hello!" I said, stopping him in his tracks.

"Oh. Hi. I guess we're neighbors." He flashed the shy smile of an intelligent person who has just stated the obvious. And it *was* obvious—our doors were just three feet apart.

Christopher

"I suppose so," I replied cleverly. "My name is B. K. Troop. What's yours?"

"Chris Ireland," he said, extending a smallish hand. Even in the dim light of the hallway I could see that he was a nail-biter; thankfully, the kind in whom vanity trumps self-loathing, which is to say that his nails were short enough to lift my eyebrows, but not turn my stomach. We shook. His hand was cold. No surprise, Manhattan was in the grips of an Arctic freeze.

"The pleasure's all mine," I murmured. And it was. His features were fine and pretty, his complexion faintly olive, and his smile so pearly white that I, as one deprived of dental care until the age of fourteen, could only marvel.

"Rumor has it that there's a superb Greek diner in the area," I crooned. "Do you know where?" I knew exactly where the Parnassus was, of course (a playful snapshot of me was tacked above the cash register), but I wanted to prolong our intercourse.

"Sure," the boy said. "Right on the corner. But I'm not sure it's superb." Then he smiled at his door in a way that said, "Enough, ye pest, be gone."

I smiled back in a way that said, "You haven't seen the last of *me,* dearie. Not by a long shot."

I hurried off to the Parnassus, where, wolfing down a piping-hot Welsh rarebit, I told my dearest friend, Cassandra Apopardoumenos, all about my meeting with the fetching lad who lived next door.

A less worldly waitress would have said "good luck" or "fingers crossed," but not the Athens-born Cassandra, who, over the course of a rich and varied life, had become a veritable storehouse of signs, charms, divinations, and other quaint prospects of love.

"Do yourself a favor," she instructed. "Get yourself a four-leaf clover. When you swallow it, think of the kid, and you'll end up marrying 'im."

I choked, but passed it off as a laugh. Inwardly, I was seized by the oddest distortion. The thought of marrying anyone had always been anathema to me. There was no limit to my hatred of such a picture. And, yet, Cassandra's words had delighted me.

"*Marry* him?" I said. "Good God! I only want to seduce him!" She answered with a knowing smile. "Besides," I snickered, "where on earth would I find a four-leaf clover this time of year?"

Weeks passed before Christopher and I spoke again—which is not to imply that in the meantime I did not get to know him much better. The wall that separated our apartments was made not of brick or stone, but of some contemporary amalgam of plaster dust and spit. I overheard quite a bit of what went on in his cell. Plus, as a committed smoker of cigarettes, I left my front door ajar during waking hours, rendering me privy to a great deal of what Mr. Marcel Proust would have called *la vie d'escalier.*

The following is what I learned, or, to be more accurate, deduced. First, that my young neighbor was a reader. I rarely heard his television, except at seven o'clock on weekdays when he parked himself with a self-cooked meal before the grim journalistic stylings of Mr. Daniel Rather. The rest of the time, silence. And what else does a young solitary with flashing Mediterranean eyes, vivid with intelligence, do hour upon hour in a silent apartment but read?

Second, he was chaste. For not once in those weeks did he entertain a single visitor or spend an evening out. With one exception—every weekday afternoon teenagers came a callin'. Which led me to my third conclusion: Christopher was a tutor. I did not learn what sort of tutor until one afternoon when I met on the steps an icicle-nosed Medusa with big bosoms and hundred-dollar sunglasses (then, a hefty sum), who, as we passed, dropped a spiral notebook at my feet. I picked it up and handed it back, but not before I had glimpsed, inside, an alphabetized list: *ablution, abomination, abrogate.* The mystery was solved: Christopher prepared youngsters for the verbal section of their standardized college admittance tests.

"Thanks," the beast snarled.

"Don't mention it." I smiled, but my heart already ached for the lad. The only thing more dreary than teaching is teaching something useless.

Fourth, I guessed that my neighbor was an aspiring writer. One afternoon he lugged past my open door three reams of typing paper. The fact that there had yet to emanate from his apartment the clack of a typewriter brought me to my last deduction. He was, among writers, the most unfortunate sort: the hopelessly blocked. A storyteller without a story. Of course, it was possible that he wrote by hand, but I doubted it. He did not seem like the pretentious sort.

On Tuesday, January 24, I reached the limits of my patience and, unannounced, applied my knuckles to his door. In Manhattan, such an act is as rare and startling as a pheasant-sighting in Central Park. I heard a rustling of trousers and a slow, creaking advance to the peephole. I stepped closer and flashed my oyster-grays. A moment later, the door opened, sliding back a steel pole that extended from the lock to a metal divot in the pine floor.

"Hi," he said shyly.

"Good afternoon, Master Ireland. I would like to invite you to dinner. My place. Tonight."

I set my jaw, daring him to rebuff me. I saw it all—his desire to do exactly that, his suspicion that I would put up a fight, and his final surrender to neighborly civility.

"Oh. Okay. Sure," he said, "but I don't eat meat."

I twinkled archly. "Pity."

Before he could utter another word, I vaulted back into my apartment and set to preparing our meal; which is to say that I let my fingers sashay through the Yellow Pages until they stopped on a pizzeria which promised to deliver to one's door, for a modest sum, a mouth-watering spinach lasagna.

Christopher appeared at 8:01, wearing what I soon discovered was his daily costume: faded blue jeans, white leather sneakers, and a button-down Oxford. I swept him into the room and savored the moment when he beheld for the first time my *Bloomsbury aesthetic:* comfy antique furniture, gem-tone brocades, Persian carpets, exquisite oil paintings, and, jammed onto every shelf and into every nook and cranny, a multitude of great, dusty books.

"Wow," he said.

"Wow, indeed," I replied, then I popped the cork on a four-dollar Pinot Noir (high notes of black pepper; lament of trombone). I might have served better, but I lived on a fixed income. After letting it breathe, asthmatically, for a full ten seconds, I poured him a generous tumbler. He sipped, I gulped, then we retired to a walnut tea trolley and sank our forks into what I allowed him to believe was a delicious home-cooked meal.

Christopher proved to be a charming guest, never at a loss for words. When excited, which was most of the time, he spoke very quickly, gulping for air. The subject that riled him at present was the impending arrival of his mother, a psychiatrist from Milwaukee. Not only would her two-week visit disrupt his tutoring schedule, but his peace of mind, as well, for she was nothing short of a horror.

I repaid him with some candor of my own.

I told him all about myself.

He was naturally surprised that I had never taken a stab at creative writing myself. Flattered, I explained that while nothing would make me happier than a career in letters, I lacked the voice for poetry, the ear for drama, and the spigot for fiction. The spigot confused him. I explained that the great, horse-countenanced novelist, Ms. George Eliot, had once counseled, "Novels are easy. Simply turn on the spigot and let it run." Or something like that.

He chuckled. "Maybe that's my problem. I have a faucet, but I'm afraid to let it run."

"Of course you are," I said, "Every hour of every day we're bombarded with televised commands not to be a water rat. You've taken your civic duty to a ludicrous extreme."

He laughed.

He was lovely when he laughed.

For the next four hours, our conversation came as naturally as leaves to trees. We discovered that we shared a passion for the mighty dead of English verse. We compared geniuses. I showed him mine, he showed me his. After dinner, we retired to the living room, which was nothing more than a love seat parked six feet away. (Our apartments were more dog-runs than proper dwellings—typical of Manhattan, where every day someone brags about his fabulous new place, which is actually nothing more than five hundred square feet of crooked flooring with the sofa close enough to the fireplace on the opposite wall to toast marshmallows without leaving the cushion. This I do not find alarming; we swap comfort for culture. What I do find alarming is that so few of us know we've made the swap.)

Soon, the conversation turned even more intimate and Christopher spoke for the first time about his *wife*. I was astonished! I had been certain he was a homosexualist. Now it seemed I might be wrong. But I did not despair. I refilled his glass. Sexual preference is not and never has been an exact science.

Because he and his wife had split up only weeks before, the boy's wounds were still fresh, which meant he unburdened himself to me more out of compulsion than choice. In fact, the boy *did* have a spigot and I did nothing to stanch its mighty gush. As he spoke, his cheeks dampened and a single vein appeared between his eyes like an earthworm. Because every detail of Christopher's life is crucial to our story, I will share his tale of woe with you exactly as I heard it, but with less angst and far more economy.

Christopher had tied the knot a year before in a simple Yuletide ceremony on Cape Cod. Sadly, his bride was an aspiring actress, which meant that their union was doomed from the start. Unaware of this, Christopher cantered down the aisle with unbridled optimism. He realized now, looking back, that he and Mary should simply have lived together—there was nothing religious or societal to prevent it—but ours was a licentious age and their marriage was more public statement than private sacrament. They were saying to their peers, "Go ahead, screw yourselves silly, but we are building something strong, fine, and lasting." Whether or not anyone else believed it, did not matter. They proudly did.

After a two-week honeymoon in Antigua, the young couple settled into the flat where Christopher now lived. When Mary was not in class, completing her last year at The Juilliard School (the nation's foremost manufacturer of automata), she browsed junk shops, searching for affordable knickknacks to adorn their hovel. Her finest touch was a display of vintage perfume bottles. She also built a makeshift canopy bed and stitched a set of sheer, white curtains. She took up cooking, as well, which was unexpected, as she was also an aspiring anorectic.

It was only in spring, as graduation day loomed, that it dawned on Christopher that something had gone terribly wrong. Subsisting now almost entirely on a diet of rice cakes and mineral water, Mary spent hour upon hour in stony silence, reading entertainment magazines. She had become preoccupied with the lives of movie stars. (It was as though she believed that an intimate acquaintance with their climbs to the top would somehow ensure a swifter ascent for herself.) Also, their sex life had died. One morning, Christopher muttered over a bowl of oatmeal (self-prepared, for her generosity in the kitchen had ended as well) that he was masturbating more now than he ever had as a bachelor. Mary shrugged and asked, "What do you want *me* to do about it?" He answered eagerly, only to discover that the question had been merely rhetorical.

June came, Mary graduated, and they escaped to her family's empty beach house on the Cape, where all of Christopher's romantic disenchantment was sublimated into a passion for literature. He read ten hours a day, the Russians mostly, and at night planned his debut novel—a lofty account of first love, imaginatively entitled *First Love*. Mary spent her days fretting, jogging on the beach, looking in the mirror, and reading *Vanity Fair* (the magazine, not the novel). Once a week, she flew down to the City to meet with flesh-peddlers. By Labor Day she had secured one, a morbidly obese drizzlepuss named Esther Somethingstein who foresaw gigantic things in Mary's future.

Ten weeks later, Mary landed her first job. She had been waiting all day for Esther's call and when it came she pounced. As Mary took in the good news, a grin spread across her starving face, then she screamed with the sort of volume that in more civilized times was reserved for bad news from Guadalcanal. Christopher also screamed, but less madly, then flung out his arms for a celebratory hug. Her eyes flashed darkly and she walked away, plugging an ear. He stood, speechless, as she devoured the details. The role was Juliet at a regional theatre in Washington, D.C. Rehearsals began in three days. The pay was a whopping five hundred dollars a week.

When Mary hung up, it was as though her malaise of the past six months had never taken place. She was herself again, but with one important difference. On their wedding day, it had been their romantic future that had inspired her rapture; now, it was her own *professional* future. Within minutes, she had formed a plan. She would zip down to D.C. and begin rehearsals, while he stayed behind and tended to his students. In a few weeks, he would join her and, supported by her salary, begin writing, at long last, *First Love*.

It seemed ideal.

Three days into rehearsal, however, she stopped asking at the end of their nightly telephone calls, "And how was *your* day?" In fact, she asked him nothing at all. Instead, she banged on about her artistic director, her director, and her Romeo. They were like a little family, she said. (A little family with no other women in it, he grimly noted.) And when she hung up, she didn't say "I love you" anymore, but simply "Sweet dreams!"

Astir with dark foreboding, Christopher jumped a train the first week in December. For those of you who were not alive at the time or else are touched by meteorological amnesia, his arrival in Washington coincided with what experts were calling the New Ice Age. On the Mississippi, towboats and barges were frozen in place; in the Midwest gravediggers were forced to use jackhammers; by year's end, over four hundred souls—mostly those of the homeless—had joined the frosty ether.

"Appropriate weather for our reunion," Christopher said now, as he reached for the near-empty bottle of wine.

But at the time he had been full of stubborn hope. After all, he and Mary had pledged eternal fidelity to each other, not only before family and friends, but God himself. Their marriage was in trouble, no doubt about it, but it was the conquering of just this sort of adversity that separated true love from mere infatuation. (This well-meaning but fantastic notion was to be the theme of his novel.)

Mary, swaddled in cashmere, looking beatific and gaunt,

waited for Christopher on the platform. When he reached her, lugging his duffel, she did not kiss him. She merely looked him up and down.

"Hmmm," she said, "you're smaller than I remembered." Then she hauled him away.

At the theatre, he was introduced to Mary's new family. First there was Stu, the artistic director, who slurped coffee from a metal cup and wore a Stetson. Christopher was surprised to learn that, despite his Western twang and cowpoke manner, he was reared in New Jersey. Then there was Ken, the director, a Dubliner in his forties, with bloodshot eyes, no chin, and hips wider than his shoulders. The only hold Christopher could imagine such a sorry creature exerting over Mary was that he treated her rudely, as though he were sexy and could get away with it. Last was Phillip, her Romeo. He was younger than she was—his mind was silly and uncooked—but it was clear that he was already hopelessly in love with her. When he shook hands with Christopher, his cheeks rouged and he glanced away.

"Maybe some people can live without passion," Mary told Christopher that night, after having just performed on him a perfunctory fellatio, "but I don't think I can." Then, through anguished tears, she confessed all that she had come to realize about herself since the day she was hired. Marriage was crushing her spirit, she claimed. She feared that soon it would be too late. It would be as though her youth had never happened, as though as a teenage girl she had never made love on a moonlit golf course and on the front lawn at a graduation party and across her father's pool table. She would join the ranks of the living dead. Unable to suppress the bitterness in his voice, Christopher asked her why she had married him then. She said that she had felt she had no choice. Before him, there had only been cruel boys, each using her more selfishly than the last and each walking away with less regret. He had seemed like a miracle to be seized. If only she had known how much would change. She had landed a great role in a great play. She felt freer, younger, prettier—her extra pounds had simply melted away—and, most wonderful of all, men who before would never have approached her except as a potential victim now adored her in a way that verged on the religious.

The end came that weekend over at Mercutio's place. A cast party. Eager to mingle, Mary abandoned him at the door. As the room was filled with uninteresting strangers, Christopher contented himself with stalking her. He trailed her as she engaged her admirers, but they were too busy dancing and drinking to flirt, and, besides, with her husband present, what was the point? She grew peevish and disappeared through a doorway. Christopher waited a minute, then peeked in and saw her standing alone at a bedroom window, her eyes dull with self-pity. A blast of music shook the wall and Mary turned as though a glare from her might silence it.

"Jesus Christ!" she screamed when she saw him. "What are we, attached at the hip?"

She ran past him.

He followed, but by the time he had hacked his way to the front door all he saw was a flash of cashmere darting down the stairwell. He knew what she wanted. She wanted him to chase her, spin her around, crush her in his arms, and declare that he loved her madly and would never let her go. This was exactly the sort of romance she craved. Christopher rejoined the party, where he clapped along with everyone else when Hoboken-born Stu executed a boozy Texas two-step.

By the time Mary returned, the party was all but over. She found her husband in the breakfast nook playing poker. He knew it was repulsive to her, this custom among theatre-folk to break out the cards every time they found themselves together with more than a few minutes to spare. He watched as Mary gradually noticed what he already had: All three of her suitors were present. Stu faced the door, a filterless cigarette dangling between his cowboy lips; Ken downed a bottle of Celtic ale in greedy gulps; Phillip, her Romeo, studied his cards, then shot a worried glance at the ceiling like a schoolboy dividing large numbers in his head. He tossed in five dollars, calling Christopher's bet, and showed a pair of jacks. Mary winced as Christopher slapped down three aces and dragged in the pot.

"Excuse me," she announced. "I feel a migraine coming on. I'm leaving."

Everyone stared up at her blankly; they thought she had left hours ago.

"All right," Christopher replied wearily, gathering his winnings.

"No, stay," she snapped.

"Forget it. You'll get mugged."

"I don't care."

He thought about it, then shrugged. "Okay, feel better."

Her jaw stiffened and her eyes filled with spite. "What good would you be, anyway?" she asked. "You're a shrimp."

She held her ground. An embarrassed silence slapped like a wet net over the table. Christopher glanced over and saw Ken staring at him.

"Not safe for a lass to walk home alone," he muttered in a sloppy brogue.

"Better hit the trail," Stu recommended.

"You really should," Phillip said, nibbling his lip.

"Why don't *you* walk her home?" Christopher suddenly asked.

Phillip was unable to hide his happiness. Blood crept up his thick neck.

"Yeah, Romeo," Mary said, turning to him with a twitchy, little smile. "You're big and strong. You'll protect me."

Phillip rose slowly, grimacing, as though nursing an old back injury.

Hours later, Christopher was awakened by a burst of light from the bedside lamp. He gasped, terrified, then he saw Mary and settled back, rubbing his eyes.

"Where were you?" he asked.

"With Phillip."

"All this time?

"All this time."

"What happened to your migraine?"

"I never had one."

He continued to rub his eyes.

Impatient, Mary broke the news more brutally than she had perhaps intended. "I've been in his room for the past four hours. Making love."

Christopher took his hands away from his face and stared with blank amazement. She braced herself, expecting tears, profanity, perhaps even violence.

Instead, Christopher laughed—a patronizing little chuckle that ended with a snort. Indignant, Mary walked into the bathroom and slammed the door.

Ten minutes later, she emerged and slipped naked between the covers.

"Did you enjoy it?" Christopher asked, wide awake now, staring at the ceiling.

"Very much."

"Will you do it again?"

"Yes."

"Do you love him?"

"Very much."

Christopher laughed again.

She growled and rolled away.

A few minutes later, Christopher rose. He walked to the

dresser and began to stuff underwear into his duffel. She rose on one arm, slack-jawed.

"You're leaving?"

"Yeah."

"Why?"

Again, he laughed.

The elevator came quickly. They plunged together in ticking silence. When they stepped into the lobby, Christopher started to say good-bye, but Mary walked outside, wearing only slippers and a flimsy robe. He followed, lugging his bag, and together they carefully descended the icy steps.

The taxi driver opened the trunk.

"Be well," Mary murmured.

"You, too," he replied.

He kissed her sharp cheek and got in.

The taxi roared away. Christopher turned in his seat and saw, through a billowing cloud, Mary standing alone in the middle of the salted boulevard. She was waving good-bye. He wasn't sure, but he thought she might be crying.

Having finished his story with, I felt, a chilling excess of objectivity (as if he had not even been a participant), Christopher sat back. I could tell from the shy, sweet look he threw me that he expected words of comfort, but I am, if nothing else, unpredictable. I crossed my legs, flicked my ash, and asked casually, "And what did you learn from all of this?"

He shifted uneasily. "What did I *learn?*"

I nodded.

With reluctance, he began what proved to be, in the end, a twenty-minute dissertation on the perils of loving an actress. He claimed that actresses, in the marrow of their bones, despise themselves and, even more deeply, reality, because it is reality which entraps and wounds them. Their escape is fantasy. Although this is true of all artists, other artists render their fantasies abstractly with brush, chisel, or pen, but the actress's only tool is her stunted, malleable self, and so she is forced to *embody* her fantasies, which makes her life nothing more than a gigantic inauthenticity, a self-composed romance in which she has cast herself in the leading role. Mary had fled not because she was in love with Phillip, but because she was desperate to flee the collision with reality that marriage demanded. "Marriage is like being handcuffed to a mirror," Christopher observed pithily. It had forced her to gaze deeply into her own wretchedness. When the crucial choice had to be made between truth and lies, she had chosen the latter. Christopher exhaled heavily, rather proud of himself.

I frowned and shook my head.

"What?" he asked, confused.

I sipped my grape, torturing him with silence, then spoke with authority. "All of what you have said is not only true, but quite obvious. It is only your *conclusion* that I object to. It was not she who fled the marriage, but *you*."

He laughed. He thought I was joking.

I reached for another cigarette. "Mary had told you she was unhappy. You said yourself that at the party she longed for you to join her in her fantasy—chase her down and behave like a proper leading man. Yet you refused. You felt it beneath you. It would have lent, what? *Validation* to her fantasism. Am I right?"

He nodded.

"That's all well and good, but your wedding vow read, 'in sickness and in health,' didn't it? And the girl was clearly sick. It might have been temporary, who knows? Not you. You refused to follow her."

"But—"

I cut him off with a raised hand. "Yes, *of course*, on the surface it was she who ended the marriage, when she made sweet, sweet love to Romeo. You would certainly never have done anything like that. You're far too good. Far too cunning. Instead, you suggested Phillip walk her home." I took a pause and fed my glass the last splash. The air was charged. "You knew perfectly well what that would lead to. And when she fell into your trap, enacted the role just exactly as you had scripted it, what was your response? You packed your bags and hightailed it outta Dodge. It was you who ended the marriage, my boy. *You are the adulterer*."

I smiled and fell silent. With the orange tip of my cigarette, I began to rearrange the ashes in their hammered-copper tray.

Christopher said nothing.

Then, with more than a hint of shame, he muttered, "You're right."

"I know," I whispered softly. I released sexy tendrils of smoke from both nostrils, then leaned in close. "But *why*, Christopher? *Why* did you want out? What did you crave that Mary wasn't giving you?" I squinted and subtly pursed my lips, doing my best to look like the sort of older man whom one might flee marriage for the chance to plunder.

"God, I don't know," he sighed dejectedly.

A minute later, he was gone.

I awoke the next afternoon with a jolt. My first thought in the sober light of day was that I had gone too far. I had fed the boy difficult truths. Was he the better for it now or did he despise me? I received my answer when I opened my door and reached for my *Post*. Trudging up the steps was a kaleidoscope of cystic acne.

Christopher's door swung open.

"Hey, Lori," he said. Then he turned to me, smiling with good-natured sarcasm. "Hello, sunshine."

Sarcasm it was, because my eyes bore a Morphean crust, my lips were flecked with spittle, and my sparse hair stood on end like a troll doll's. But his greeting filled me with relief, because in that instant I knew I had not offended him. Clearly, he possessed what I consider to be the rarest and most appealing of all human traits: *the ability to learn from me.*

"I am not a morning person," I croaked. Then I smiled coquettishly and retreated, leaving my door ajar.

Christopher

February

On the afternoon of Wednesday, February 7, I was scraping dog-dirt off the sole of my cordovan loafer when I heard a car door slam. I turned and watched as a pockmarked Hindu moved to the trunk of his frozen taxi and removed a fat, green suitcase. A moment later, a creature emerged from the backseat. It was Christopher's mother. How I knew this, I do not know. He had never described her. Beholding her now, I understood why.

Before lifting the veil on a comic grotesque unmatched in Western literature since the debut of Pantagruel, allow me to state that while most novelists ward off potential litigants by declaring up front that their characters bear no resemblance to any actual persons, living or dead (which is, sadly, so often the case), I choose to render my hero's mother with such painstaking accuracy that, even if she were objective enough to identify her portrait in these pages, she would be far too embarrassed to admit it in a court of law.

She was short: today, in my imagination, from the vantage of over a quarter century, just under two and a half feet; in reality, just over five. Her hair, dyed blond, was hacked into a short-in-front, long-in-back number that at the time might have been charming on a Methadone-addicted salesgirl working in an East Village boutique, but was strikingly pitiful on a squat Midwestern psychiatrist wearing a down jacket and aviator shades. Her forehead was high, her schnozzle undistinguished, her upper lip adorned with a subtle shading of Sicilian fur. She took off her glasses. Her boggy eyes were those of a severe depressive.

Ever a gentleman, I stepped forward. "You must be the divine Grace Ireland," I purred. "I've heard *so* much about you."

"You have? Who are you?" she asked, flashing a brown snaggletooth.

I smiled back, savoring one of those rare moments when I have no reason to be ashamed of my enamel.

"B. K. Troop," I replied, with a solemn nod of the head. "A *dear* friend of Christopher's." I grabbed the handle of her bulging bag and was already on the landing before I added, "Allow *me*."

"What's with the Christopher?" Grace asked, as we scaled the dizzying heights. "Everyone calls him Chris."

"I am not everyone," I huffed.

"You say you're dear friends? That's weird. He's never mentioned you."

Whether she knew it or not, and I doubt she did, she wanted to hurt my feelings.

"We met thirty-six days ago," I explained. "But, let me assure you, we have quite a history."

Amused, she aimed her snaggletooth at me. "What, you mean in a *past life?*"

"That's right. We were cellmates in an all-female Victorian debtor's prison. Until one day, in a moment of premenstrual pique, he traded me for a thimble."

She burst out laughing. And for a moment, I felt dread. "Oh

no," I thought, "she appreciates my saucy wit. What if we become friends? The lad will never forgive me."

My worries were laid to rest a moment later.

"My son in a women's debtor prison?" she spewed. "That's ridiculous. He's *very* responsible about his bills."

She giggled. Another bit of malice masked as flippery. My knuckles grew white. I loathed and feared her. I dropped her bag with a thud at his door.

"Special delivery!" I sang, then I knocked loudly.

Christopher somehow understood, because when he opened the door he was already wincing.

"Safe and sound," I declared brightly, while offering a subtle, complicit scowl.

As I descended the steps, she gave his cheek a smacking kiss, then exclaimed, "Yuck! What's that awful smell? Oh, shit, don't tell me you've started *smoking!*"

In the next week, I spotted them only twice. First, through the front door of Arabia, a tiny restaurant in the middle of our block. He ate a salad, head down, silent, while Grace, sitting across from him, brandished a meaty kebab and prattled crazily. Her eyes (all three) seemed to move independently of each other. And then, two nights later, I noticed them amid the swarm of human flotsam that circles Bloomingdale's. He walked with his fists dug deep in his pockets and his eyes on his sneakers. Grace scurried at his side, chattering a mile a minute, her breath shooting out like exhaust from a plump, winded dragon.

It was only after Grace had been gone for a full three days that I learned, back in my lair, over a superb "home-cooked" Chinese stir-fry and an apt Chardonnay (languid and colonial; whiff of the Yangtze), the particulars of the boy's ordeal.

"It was horrible," he said. "She wanted to go places, *do* stuff. Museums, restaurants, plays, shopping. God! I would have refused, but I knew she'd never go out alone, and being stuck with her in my apartment's even worse. There's no place to hide. She follows me everywhere. If I go into the kitchen to . . . I dunno . . . make some tea, she stands over me the whole time. If I go into my bedroom to read, she pokes her head in and starts yapping. I can't even go to the bathroom. She follows me to the door and the only thing that stops her from coming in is not my fly unzipping—it's the door locking in her face. Finally, I just give up and watch TV. But this time even that didn't work. She pulled up a stool, sat right on top of me, and babbled the most inane shit."

Grace's new favorite subject was the breakup of her son's marriage, her insight into which was especially galling to Christopher because she had been divorced herself, three times, and had never once turned her analytic eye inward. And for good reason: introspection might have led her to seek counseling, and her only professional accomplishment to date was that she was the only psychiatrist in the Western world never to have spent a moment on the leather herself. She claimed it would be a waste of time and money—therapy is for people with problems.

Her other favorite subject was poetry. Her own. It seemed that for the past six months the multiuntalented Grace, although newly menopausal, had been enjoying a particularly fertile period as a poetess, or, as she preferred to be called, a poet. (She did not understand that just as the occasional writing of verse does not make a woman a poetess, the onset of menopause does not make a poetess a poet.) Although she had never been published—even the vanity presses shunned her—she believed herself on the verge not only of being discovered, but hailed. She had brought along two dozen new works and, from time to time throughout her visit, she honored her captive host with a reading.

Was her work any good?

In the spirit of fairness, the boy allowed me to judge for myself. He unfolded a single sheet of paper on which were arranged the following words, spelled exactly this way:

POEM OF MYSELF

All summer the lilies
March in like saints
Around my big house,
And I sit above them,
Just as splendid,
In the highest window,
And I ride my Speed-Bike,
And I speed!
(though stationery).
In front of me is only the
Great blue head of the sky
And the green lap of the park;
Below is my Secret Garden,
A conclave of blossoms in
Triumphant congregation.
I petal and petal for nearly an hour!
(though stationary)
And I am in All-Earth-Gladness,
Happy to be a Woman,
A Freed Mother,
And still able to ride so quickly,
Heart pounding!
Legs aching!
(though stationery).

—Grace Volpe-Ireland, M.D.

I handed back the paper, then, as a sanitary precaution, wiped my hands on my trousers. He nodded emphatically, and, also fearing contagion, quickly set it down. (After he left, I slipped it into a folder, which I marked *Malignant Narcissism*, and locked it in a cabinet.)

You might wonder why Christopher had endured it. Why he had not simply clapped a hand over her mouth and shoved her out the door. I did and I asked. He explained that he had been afraid to, because beneath her bravado there lurked an immense fragility. When faced with criticism or rejection of any kind, she simply fell apart. But then, before her adversary even had a chance to qualify his words, soften the blow a bit, she would reintegrate and attack. "The weapons of the weak are always too violent," Christopher explained. Grace had inspired the maxim, because her counterassaults were so cruel as to be almost unimaginable. She struck back where one was most vulnerable, slashing and burning blindly. Most healed in time; many did not. His geneticist father had drunk himself to death before his fortieth birthday. Her next two husbands had simply vanished.

"You know, I used to think I hated her," Christopher said, wiping a fugitive sprout from his luscious lower lip. "But I don't. Hate doesn't mean anything anymore. People use it all the time, about everything. Carrots . . . humidity . . . racism . . . I need something more specific. When I find the mot juste I'll let you know."

"I can't wait," I said, smiling sincerely.

And he smiled back.

I wanted him to kiss me.

Which brings us, gracefully, to the subject of seducing straight boys, or, as in Christopher's case, boys who *believe* themselves to be straight. Whether by accident of birth or gift from the Gods, I had always possessed an uncanny knack for being able to cull from the heterosexualist herd the lame straggler.

Christopher

In the thirty-five years between my first day of puberty and the day I met Christopher, I had managed to pull off seven of these difficult seductions. Once, after a remarkable streak that included, in a single sultry August, my summer-school tennis coach, a married bus driver, and a neighborhood bully, I had even toyed with the idea of writing a how-to manual. *A Pocketful of Prunes*, I wanted to call it.

In the case of Christopher, however, there were going to be challenges. He was young and pretty; I was old and ugly. His life was solitary; mine was lonely. I yearned for him; he did not yearn for me. Et cetera. But, on the other hand, we did have a magnificent rapport. Plus, he was chaste and sometimes tippled, and, as we all know, young men are capable of anything when they have slept alone for too long and are in the grip of the grape. Also, I was not too proud to lie and manipulate. In the final balance, I was optimistic.

The first step was a proper date. And, so, before parting I asked him out for the night of St. Valentine's day. As I was the furthest thing from a romantic, my choice was self-consciously ironic (a private joke to myself which made me chortle), but it was also shrewd, because, a month before, I had reserved tickets for that night to a performance of *La Ronde*, a play written by the now-all-but-forgotten Austrian scribe, Mr. Arthur Schnitzler.

For those of you unfamiliar with the play, I offer the following brief summary:

The action unfolds in a series of ten short dialogues. In scene 1, a Soldier and a Whore meet by chance on a bridge in Vienna. She propositions him. They embrace against a railing, the lights dim, and the audience watches as their silhouettes enact a dumb show of violent, hasty lovesport. Then they part ways: he quite satisfied, she hurling curses at him for not paying. In scene 2, the Soldier reappears, but this time hand-in-hand with a Parlor

Maid on the darkened pathways outside an amusement park. She protests feebly, but eventually yawns her flanks on the midnight grass. In scene 3 it is the same Parlor Maid, but this time she is coupled with a bored Young Gentleman, her employer. Just as he achieves climax, the doorbell rings. He waves her away, telling her to answer it at once. After all, it's her job. On and on it goes. Each dialogue introduces a new character and sheds an old; each features a seduction and a parting. The final scene brings a Count and a Whore together—and, guess what, it's the Whore from the first scene. They rut and the daisy chain is complete. An ingenious structure. Like a snake devouring its own tail. When acted with dash and verve, it is a most diverting evening in the theatre.

Now, what made this production unique, and a brilliant choice for my first proper date with Christopher, was that the story was set in present-day Manhattan and the cast was *all male*. The Whore was the Boy Hooker; the Parlor Maid was called House Boy, and the Young Wife, although quite male, remained the Young Wife. Not only would this bold reimagining give us plenty to discuss, but it would be a touchstone by which to gauge the lad's deepest feelings about the sort of love that in olden days dared not speak its name, but in modern times all too often shrieks it. What was *not* ideal was that I had reserved *four* tickets. Of course, I might have ripped up the other two, as they were free, but, being poor, I was frugal to a fault. So, I invited along my mentor, a professor emeritus of German literature named Wolf Zeller, and asked that he bring along a guest.

When Christopher and I arrived at Wolf's door in a sterile highrise on the outskirts of the West Village, Wolf was there to greet us, his arms flung wide, his smile tipsy.

Christopher

"My dear!" he said to me. "Oh, my dear, my darling boy!"

This was, of course, absurd, as I was forty-seven at the time and about as darling as mashed potatoes. He kissed me once on each cheek, then shook Christopher's hand. Wolf was a tall man, his legs skinny, his stomach flat. His round Bavarian cheeks bore deep symmetrical creases and his nose was tinged a permanent red. His ears, bearing twin hearing aids, were as long and loose as warmed scrota.

He escorted us into his immaculate living room. Christopher plopped down in a scoop chair and crossed a sneaker over a knee of the other. I hurled myself onto a poof. Within moments, Christopher was introduced to more of Wolf's speech—loud and Teutonic, each syllable clipped and grindingly pronounced.

"Time travels quickly!" Wolf boomed, gazing down at me with cloudy eyes. "And as one gets older, it seems to travel even *more* quickly, positively treading over one's lagging body. And how much of it has there been, B.K.? How much time since last we met?"

"Two months, three weeks, and four days," I tarted, lighting a cigarette.

(In case you haven't noticed, I am particular in time and dates.)

Wolf laughed, impressed, and, after handing us each a glass of expensive Zinfandel (intent on world domination), he began to regale Christopher with the circumstances of our first meeting. It was a story which, for some mysterious reason, he never tired of telling, especially to me. As he spoke, Wolf paced, stopping only when he felt a detail required the emphasis of a gesture or pause.

"A colleague informed me," he began, "that I must look out for a singular young man who had recently come to his attention, a stripling by the name of B. K. Troop. A first-year student possessed of a fine mind and an Etonian manner, both cultivated, God knows how, in the tundra of South Dakota."

"*North* Dakota," I corrected.

"Well, I did as I was told, keeping a watchful eye, as I lectured, on the great mass of students before me. When a young man would pose a question, I would think, 'Could this be Mr. Troop? Or perhaps it is he.' But, alas, I had no way of knowing. Until, *until!* the day I found a note in my box. You have no idea how surprised I was. It was a chastisement! Yes, of course, it was! Don't argue with me!"

I had not argued, then or now, but, as I was eager for the story to end, I threw up my hands in total surrender.

"The writer *scolded* me for my method of teaching! He felt it *reprehensible of me* to divulge in my lectures the entire plot of the novels in question, the knowledge of which destroyed, he said, his pleasure in discovering the great works of the syllabus. His note ended with a question: 'Dr. Zeller, why should I scale the perilous heights of *The Magic Mountain* if you insist on describing for me, beforehand, the view from the summit?' "

Christopher chuckled and glanced at me. He was proud to know me. I blew a cocky smoke ring.

"*Well!*" Wolf roared. "I recognized at once a formidable intelligence, so, when I spotted at the bottom of the letter the signature of B. K. Troop, I was hardly surprised. Ah, you laugh now; you did not then!"

In fact, I *had* laughed then and did not now.

"I might have answered your letter privately, but instead I addressed it publicly, so that all could benefit from our dispute. I told my students that I had seen perhaps nine productions of *Oedipus Rex* and that it was the most recent I had enjoyed most. The same could be said of great *prose* fiction. One does not read for plot! The value of narrative is derived from the *presentation of the moment*, and, if the telling is born of truth, there will al-

Christopher

ways be an attendant *significance*. The sophisticated reader has no more love of plot than does a lover of trains for a particularly sound mile of track." He wheeled toward Christopher. "And, so, young man, that is how Bryce Kenneth Troop and I began our friendship. To the continued health of our disagreements!"

He toasted, splashing grape. Before we could toast back, he teetered off to prepare our dinner, grabbing on to furniture as he moved, as though at any moment he might crash into a chair or collapse altogether.

I turned to my date. "Adorable, isn't he?"

He smiled and nodded, his eyes darting to the wall behind me.

"Go ahead," I urged, lighting up again, "rummage."

He rose. Wolf's library was full of dust mites, but spectacular in scope. As Christopher worked his way through it, opening and closing volumes with an expert eye, I listened to the riotous clatter of pots and pans from the kitchen. It was a music I knew I would miss when Wolf was dead.

When I turned back, Christopher was staring, slacked-jawed, at a handwritten inscription to Wolf, scrawled by Mr. H. L. Mencken in the fly leaf of a book of his Prejudices.

"Let it be a lesson to you," I said.

"What?" he asked, puzzled.

"Wolf's read every single one of those volumes, but what good has it done him?"

"What do you mean?"

"He's deeply unhappy. In material point, he's a virgin."

"*What?*" Christopher slid the book back into the shelf.

"Prune intact. At eighty-two. Can you imagine anything more tragic?"

"How do you know?"

"He told me. Just last year. After downing a half bottle of sherry. And I believed him. Imagine——" I sat back and drew my words wistfully from the bluish smoke that spiced the room. "Never having lost one's identity in the throes of passion. Never having lain . . . cloaked in black shadow . . . and felt the vast power of the darkness outside . . . and how it and every other night suggests death . . . and how it draws one more deeply into the heart of one's beloved." I could hear the insincerity in my voice, but I doubted he could. I sighed. "Poor Wolf. The life of the mind is glorious, certainly, but it's a sad substitute for *truly* living. Truly *loving*."

I looked over, smiling dreamily, straining every fiber to look like one capable of, or even interested in, romantic love. Before Christopher could react, the moment, if there even was one, was shattered.

"*You like shrimps?!*" Wolf bellowed.

He held a Bavarian tea tray laden with three steaming dishes. We rose and met him at a small round table laid with mono-grammed linen.

"You have your salad. Here is a spoon for the shrimps. Here is more wine. You have your napkin? Salt, pepper? The rice is here. And . . . what? What have I forgotten?"

"Silverware," Christopher said.

"What?" Wolf put a hand to one of his big deaf ears.

"*Silverware!*" Christopher shouted.

He looked. "Yes! You are an astounding young man! Our utensils! I shall fetch them at once!"

Wolf talked throughout the meal, pausing only to refill his wine glass. He was getting quite a bun on. Christopher listened in awe, as literary figures known to him only in books sprang vividly to life.

"I remember Auden and I were sitting together," Wolf be-gan, "in a café in Brooklyn. He was about to depart on a tour of Germany as a poet-lecturer, and he knew that everywhere he traveled he was sure to be asked about Rilke. He asked me for *my* opinion. And, without thinking, simply off the top of my head, I replied that I considered Rilke to be the greatest lesbian poet since Sappho."

Christopher burst out laughing.

Wolf grinned happily. "Ah, you like that! Well, here is one you will no doubt enjoy even more. Auden came home from school on holiday with a young chap in tow—the first time he had ever brought home a lad. After a short time, his guest excused himself to go to the loo. Father Auden, left alone with his son, reflected for a moment, then inquired calmly, 'Wyston, are you *queer?*' 'Yes, father,' the boy replied. The old man lifted his tea cup. 'Yes, I thought so.' And the subject was never raised between them again!"

Wolf roared with laughter.

Christopher grinned.

Promising, I thought.

Later, gesturing with his fork, Wolf approached a similar theme. "Thomas Mann and I had some contact, but I never knew him well. He was known to very few. Just yesterday a colleague asked me if it was true that the protagonist of *Death in Venice*—a work which interests me quite a bit at present—was based on Gustav Mahler. I told him not to be ridiculous!"

"I'd heard that, too," Christopher said.

"No, no, no, this is a misconception suggested by the film."

"Vicious gossip," I muttered dryly.

"You see, when Mann sat down to write the story he wanted to write of a man very much like himself—a genius of letters, displaced from the everyday run of humanity and full of a powerful yen for beauty . . . for immortality . . . in the form of one particularly splendid, young boy. He had to describe his hero, of course, and he wanted, for obvious reasons, to give him a face other than his own. When Mahler died they had published in the newspapers a photograph of his death mask, and so,

Mann, out of respect, used *his* face in his description of Herr Aschenbach. But, you see, that is where all connection ends, despite what that dreadful film implies."

"I guess you didn't like it," Christopher said.

"I suppose if I were an illiterate I might have found it very pretty, but I found it poor, indeed. The central error, of course, was the boy. He must be unself-conscious. A young sea god. The young actor in the film had the look in his eye of a tawdry prostitute."

By this time, Wolf's shirt and lap were spotted with sauce and littered with crumbs. He rose with effort and made his way to Christopher. He stood behind his chair and dropped his gnarled paws to the lad's shoulders. They tensed visibly. Wolf lowered his mouth and kissed the part in his hair.

"A delicious melon," he muttered.

Christopher threw me a scared glance.

I smiled, to reassure him that Wolf was harmless.

"We have spoken at length about many great men," Wolf sighed, "all of whom had homosexual leanings. And I think now you must speak to me candidly about how you fill *your* bed."

It was all too perfect. Wolf was doing my dirty work.

"Alone," was Christopher's honest reply.

"Certainly not!" Wolf's hands flew up and he steadied himself. "You would have little difficulty in finding a bedmate!"

"I haven't really looked."

Wolf, confused, put a hand to his ear.

"*I haven't really looked!*" Christopher shouted. "*I just separated from my wife! I'm getting a divorce!*"

"I see, I see." Wolf zigzagged over to the couch. "You require a period of mourning, of course. But, my dear, when you are ready again to reenter the world, you must not hesitate. Time flies fast. And if, like my friend Auden, you discover that you are *queer*, then by all means you must choose a good man and settle down!"

I struck a match, feigning casualness. In fact, I could hardly bear the suspense. I lifted the burning match to my fag, but, waiting for his response, did not light up.

"I'm going to write a novel," Christopher answered.

"Eh?"

"I'm going to write a novel!"

"Ah, yes, of course. Now, we must be off!" He abruptly spun around and pointed at me. "B.K., preen yourself! You have dandruff!"

From blocks away, the white arch of Washington Square glimmered against the black of the winter sky. I sat on the cracked vinyl of the taxi cab and ruminated on my prey's evasiveness. *I'm going to write a novel.* What on earth did that have to do with Wolf's suggestion? Had the lad simply declared himself to be an unambivalent lover of the fair sex, it would certainly have thwarted my plans to seduce him, but at least it would have eased my distress, for a dashed hope dies as quickly as one fulfilled.

Wolf cocked his wristwatch toward the window, then leaned back and patted Christopher's knee with a heavy palm. "Very good! We are on time. It is highly objectionable to be late to the theatre." Then he leaned into the boy's ear and whispered loudly enough for even the Ethiopian cabby to hear. "Tonight you will meet my goddaughter! I have three, but Blandina is by far the loveliest."

When we arrived, the girl in question stood under the small marquee, half-frozen, shifting her weight from foot to foot. Wolf had lied to us; she was not lovely; in fact, she was a vision of frowningness. Her hair was a sandstorm. Her features were delicate, but not unique. She was dressed like a vagrant. Yet Christopher studied her with interest. After hasty introductions, we hurried to our pew. (The theatre was housed in a remodeled church.) Wolf sat on the aisle, then came Christopher, then the awful Blandina, then I.

The stage went black.

As the action unfolded, Christopher flipped restlessly through his program. Wolf watched the stage with a vacant smile, head tilted back, like a senile general surveying his troops. Blandina grimaced the first time two men kissed and her scowl never entirely faded. As for me, I admired the production's courage, inventiveness, and lavish display of pectorals.

At intermission, I slipped outside and savaged three cigarettes with a ferocity that even I found alarming. Wolf did not accompany me; he was sound asleep in his pew, head back, neck unhinged, snoring like a sated beast. From where I stood, through the wide front window, I spotted Christopher and Blandina chatting in the little lobby.

Curious and panicked, I slipped inside and, using the milling crowd as a shield, ducked behind an artificial plant. It gave me a full-frontal of Christopher and a profile of my rival. Despite her youth, there was something jaded about her. She wanted a hot bath and a sound spanking.

"Honestly?" I heard her say, in that nasal whine so prevalent among American girls, but unthinkable on the Continent. "I know he's a genius, but he's so deaf it wears me out. Seriously, I get a sore throat. I think his hearing aids were made in, like, 1967."

Inexplicably, Christopher chuckled and flashed a look that can only be described as *charmed*. I felt a stab of jealousy. A plastic leaf trembled.

"So where'd you get a name like 'Blandina'?" Christopher

Christopher

asked, giving voice to the query on the minds of all who met her.

"From my mother. Who obviously hates me. I go by my middle name. Joy."

"Oh, that's much nicer," he said, flashing a gorgeous smile. "And *much* more fitting."

My God, was he actually *flirting?!* I struggled not to intercede. I fought back a molten reflux of shrimp.

Her cheeks pinked in an unsightly way, then she stepped closer. "So tell me something about *you*."

I leapt out from the plant like a drunken prankster and shouted something inspired along the lines of "Boo!" The girl spilled coffee on her blouse. Christopher dropped half his chocolate chip cookie.

We returned to our pew in tense silence.

Act 2 was something of a surprise—not the actual story, which was just as Herr Schnitzler had written it—but the epilogue, which the director had devised. After the final line, instead of fading, the lights began to climb until the stage was flooded with blinding, white light. The entire cast, brazenly naked, strode out on stage with a haunting minimum of expression. When they were lined up in front of us, one of them, the House Boy, told us that over one thousand people had died of AIDS since the disease first appeared. Then the Chicken told us how many cases had been diagnosed in all. Another, the Drag Queen, explained that AIDS is now believed to be a virus, transmitted through the blood. The Young Wife talked about the slowness of Uncle Sam to respond. And so on—a dire litany. But these were not the actors who spoke to us; it was the *characters*. The director's intention, I thought, was to imply that each of these characters had eventually died of the disease and that they spoke to us now from a sort of afterlife. The implication, of course, was that their deaths had been as a direct result of the circle of their sexual relations. As the last sad fact was recited, the ensemble bowed. Before our applause had died out, the stage crashed to black and they were gone forever.

We all left the theatre a little shaken, except for Wolf, who indignantly denounced didactic theatre, insisting that if it is not done well it can only be done dismally. He grabbed my arm and attacked Socratically. He said that although it was a unique evening, an erotically diverting evening, I didn't think, did I, that it was actually a *valid* evening? Before I could answer, he changed tack and began to decry the very notion of concept-oriented theatre—modern-dress Antigones, Wild West Cyranos, Othellos set on Jupiter!

Christopher, walking a few yards ahead us, glanced back from time to time. Was his attention drawn to Wolf's diatribe or to my more-than-obvious unhappiness? When our gazes met, it seemed the latter. His raven eyes were full of a desire to please me. Or so it seemed. I looked back at Wolf and suddenly remembered that he had a disturbing tendency to end evenings with a guillotine. I also knew that he hated to cab it home alone. I understood only too well what this might mean, and, sure enough, when we reached the corner, the old tyrant declared, "Enough! I am tired! B.K., take me home!" He gestured imperiously and a taxi cab screeched to his shoes.

I shot Christopher a soft, inviting stare.

"Joy and I are gonna hang out for a while," he said.

My heart plopped to the sidewalk like a tin can, but I refused to let him see. I shrugged with indifference and climbed into the car. As it pulled away, I asked myself how the evening could possibly have ended any worse. Wolf answered by clapping his hands to his knees, bracing himself, and fluttering out a stream of flimsy gas.

When I got home, I unscrewed a bottle of stubborn Chianti (a surprise touché of fig and cholera) and hurled myself in front

Christopher

of the television. On Channel J, a knock-kneed stripper, dressed as a cop, flopped his member like a rabbit's ear. It was one thing to lose my date to a rival, I brooded, but to lose him to a *female* rival to whom *I* had introduced him seemed the height of Olympian injustice. I tippled straight from the bottle. Goddamn Blandina. She'd ruined everything. No more subtlety, I vowed. Farewell to finesse. I would stay awake until Christopher came home, then go for the golden ring.

My vigil was not long. Two hours later there were three quick taps on my half-open door. I leapt to my feet, stumbled, fell, and, when I looked up, there he was, smiling down at me. He helped me up, settled me on the couch, and shared the details of his evening. He and *Joy* had gone to a tavern. He was unsure why, but he found himself immediately revealing all to her. He told her that he felt (and had since his escape from Washington) "lost." Before the word had even left his lips, he feared she would not understand, but he forged ahead, anyway, describing for her his heartbreak, his inability to write, his feeling that his future, once so vivid and secure, was now vague and treacherous. He was afraid to love again, he said, to trust anyone. She listened, but was it real listening, he wondered? Generous and receptive? Or was it the more common sort, where the person lets you speak only because he wants something in return, often just to speak himself?

Hearing this, I nodded, doing my best to look generous and receptive. Meanwhile, I endured a wave of Neapolitan nausea and it occurred to me that I might be drunk.

When Christopher had finally finished summarizing for Joy his catalogue of woe, he realized with a shock that it had been unfair to doubt her. Her eyes were moist. Her face was open with compassion. He felt a rush of relief. But then she moved close, until her pouty lips were just inches from his, and whispered, "Sleep over." He was crushed. She had not understood at all. This was precisely what he did *not* want; in fact, could not even imagine. He told her as much. She sat back, her cheeks red with embarrassment.

A minute later, he hailed her a taxi.

He said with a consoling smile, "Maybe we'll meet again."

"I hope so," she answered distantly, looking away.

Then he added, "When we do, you're gonna be older, but I'll be a lot *younger*."

She twitched as though he had just rattled off a sentence in Esperanto, then she ducked into the car.

End of tale.

I attempted to console the boy, but no matter how vehemently I blamed the girl's youth, unsightliness, and lack of generous receptivity for his denial of her offer, he held firm, insisting that *I* was not listening either. *There was no one on earth he would sleep with right now.* In fact, Joy was smart and beautiful and had simply wanted to ease his suffering, but he was wrecked, and the thought of intimacy with anyone filled him with dread. He said that obviously neither she nor I could comprehend a pain so deep that not even sex could allay it. I argued with passion that one must never turn one's back on physical intimacy, that no matter how repellent the thought of it might seem, one must do it, anyway. To deny the exigencies of one's loins was a crime against nature! A crime against one's very self! He smiled in a strange way. Was he tempted? But then his face changed and he stood.

I walked him to the door and, judgment impaired, I sucked air, lurched, and captured him in a mighty embrace.

A tussle ensued.

Then he was gone.

Later, lying on my back, pajama bottoms at my knees, walls spinning, a swan of tissue pasted to my chest, my brain all of a doodah, I groped for consolation. Anything. I finally found it.

Christopher

He had rejected me, yes, but not because I was old and repulsive; it was because of the play. Its message, especially that of the epilogue, had made, at least for the time being, a first homosexual liaison unthinkable.

Certain that my life had been affected for the first time by the emerging scourge of AIDS, I lifted a righteous fist to the ceiling and cursed its existence. Looking back today, knowing the far dearer toll the epidemic was to exact from millions, I shudder with shame, but at the time, like a spoiled child, I saw it only in terms of my own boundless needs. As I careened off to sleep, too tired even to yank up my pj's, I regathered my resolve. Fantasy was not enough. Soon, I would have the boy. Or, not to put too fine a point on it, *he would have me*.

March

Christopher and I did not speak to each other for the next three and a half weeks. I might have suspected suicide, were it not for the fact that every day I heard him entering and exiting his apartment. Yet, never did he walk the three feet to my open door and peek in. And I never poked my head out. The reason for my shyness was that my memory of our last encounter was dim. I had embraced him, yes, but had I also kissed his ear? Patted his rump? Lifted an exploratory knee? Just what was it that had incited the scuffle? Rather than jump to any dire conclusions, I forced myself calm and clung to my glorious rut. I read, I smoked, I tiffled, I dozed, I watched Channel J, I dreamt, then read some more. On Saturday mornings I browsed the local flea market. Since moving in, I had already picked up a pair of eighteenth-century bronze doorknobs, a carte-de-visite of Mr. Algernon Charles Swinburne, and an Alpine shepherd's prod (horn handle, cherry shaft, rusty point).

On the night of Saturday, March 10, I dined at the Parnassus with my ex-landlady, Sasha Buchwitz, who had recently returned from the bughouse. Over a sublime osso bucco and a

Christopher

side of curly fries, she told me all about her remarkable recovery—the result of a new wonder drug. Beelzebub still appeared on her fire escape from time to time, but now he was entirely clothed and had not a single nasty thing to say about me. Convinced that my head was no longer in danger of being separated from my shoulders, she insisted that I move back into my basement lair at half the original rent.

I gently demurred.

Our waitress, the sapient Cassandra, eavesdropping, almost dropped her pencil.

"Are you nuts?" she roared. "That's one helluva sweet deal!"

I explained that while I, as one living on a subsistence trust and a modest disability check from the federal government, rarely looked a gift horse in the mouth, neither did I change one in midstream. I had met Christopher. Until he was mine, purse be damned!

Cassandra smiled. Again, a sly Attic smile, fraught with concealed wisdom. Did she know something about me and the boy that I did not? Was such a thing possible? I demanded she come clean. She jammed her pencil behind her ear and walked away, tossing a cryptic chuckle over her shoulder. Then she muttered, mostly out of earshot, a phrase ending with the unsettling words, "—always the last to know."

I returned to my lair in a veritable swivet. I popped a California Merlot (acceleration of fast cars and cacti; no finish) and sank into my morris chair with a volume of conjugal odes penned by that masterly hypocrite, the twice-married, Mr. Coventry Patmore. Another lonely night loomed. I heaved a bolstering breath and opened the book.

I heard a creak.

I looked up and what did I see, peering in from the doorway? My neighbor's face, slick with sweat, a bit more olive than usual.

"Busy?" he asked brightly, trying to hide his anxiety.

"Of course." I jumped to my feet and hauled him in, offering him a glass of wine.

Tempted, he sniffed the bottle, but opted for tap water.

We spent the next few minutes killing time with small talk.

How *about* this weather, indeed.

My patience buckled.

"Cut the shit, dollface," I snapped, "you're upset about something."

He smiled. My God, his teeth were white, and so cute the dimples that appeared on either side of his bow-shaped mouth.

"Well, the night I was here after the play——" he began.

I nodded calmly, but fear battened every valve. At last, the moment of my humiliation was upon me. Yet, like the advent of all things dreaded but inevitable, it was, in a perverse way, thrilling. My thighs tingled, as with ants.

"Well, when I got home," Christopher said, "there was a message from my mother on my machine. She said to call her no matter how late it was. So I did."

"Big mistake," I noted crisply, but inwardly I was cutting capers. *His long silence had had nothing to do with me!*

"Well, I knew immediately that something was wrong. She wasn't as frantic as usual. First, she told me how much she'd enjoyed our time together and how wonderful it was to spend time with her parents. That's where she went after she left here. To New Haven. For a week. To see my grandparents. They're Italian. Well, finally, I asked her if something was wrong. She told me I was very intuitive."

"You are," I replied.

But I thought, "And so am I, *usually*, but not this time."

"She said it was her mother. She had just hung up with the doctor and it looked like her mom wasn't out of the woods yet. I had no idea what she was talking about. I freaked out and told

Christopher

her to start at the beginning. She said that when she got to New Haven, only my grandfather was there to meet her at the station, which was weird because usually they both come. Turns out, Grammy had stayed home because she wasn't feeling very well."

"Grammy?"

"That's what we call her." His brow blackened. He was daring me to mock this blatant Rockwellianism.

I gestured graciously for him to continue.

"Anyway, they had fun, laughed, ate zitis."

"Ziti," I corrected.

"Yeah, that's what *I* said."

"Great minds think alike."

"Anyway, everything seemed normal. But, later, while they were watching TV, Grampy turned off the set and said there was something they had to discuss. Grammy got pissed, didn't want to talk about it. But he ignored her and told my mother the whole story."

"Which *was?*" I coaxed, growing impatient.

"Well, Grampy had taken her in for a physical a coupla days before and the doctor had found cancer in her gallbladder."

"Oh, dear."

"He said that either they could leave it alone, in which case anything could happen . . . with old people you never know . . . she might live for years . . . or else they could remove it and hope they'd caught it before it spread. He claimed it was a pretty basic operation."

"No such thing," I murmured, refilling my glass. I remembered only too well the removal of a testicular cyst that had left me sore and weepy for weeks.

"That's what *I* said. And then I reminded her that Grammy is prone to infections."

"What do you mean?"

45

"I won't bore you with the details."

"Oh, I insist, Dr. Johnson."

He chuckled. "Well, they met at a dance when Grampy was nineteen and Grammy was twelve. He fell madly in love with her, and, within, like, ten minutes, he told her he was going to marry her someday."

"Today, they'd toss you in the clink for that."

"A few months later, she fell down a flight of stairs and splinters from her spine got lodged in her body. They got infected and for the next six years she was in and out of the hospital. She kept getting reinfected. When she turned eighteen, even though the doctors said she might not live very long and would definitely never have kids, Grampy married her, anyway."

"Lovely," I said, and I suppose in some strange way I actually meant it.

"So, of course, when my mom told me the operation was basic, the first thing I thought was that Grammy was prone to infections. Well, my mom obviously hadn't, because she spent hours convincing Grammy to have the surgery. Grammy didn't want to. She was scared to death. Finally, she gave in, but she said that if anything happened to her it was *my mom's fault*."

"Uh-oh."

He took a fast nibble at a thumbnail. "Anyway, she finally had the surgery a few days ago and, guess what, no cancer. Her gallbladder was just inflamed. But because the surgeon had been told to expect cancer, he poked around and ended up damaging her pancreas. It's infected now and she's in Intensive Care. She's got a really high fever. A hundred and four."

"Yikes."

"I went to New Haven as soon as I heard. When I got there, my grandmother was lying under this, like, *bower* of tubes and bags. She tried to say something. Grampy cut her off. He said,

'You're gonna be all right, Rosa. I'm gonna take you home soon. I can't have my girl away too long.' She frowned at him like he was nuts, then looked over at me and rolled her eyes. I cracked up. She stared at me for a really long time, then said, 'Write your book.' "

Christopher saw that I was puzzled, so he explained. "She's always believed in my talent. She was worried when I got married that I'd never have time to write." He shrugged his shoulders. "Anyway, that's it. She's been unconscious ever since. My mother called an hour ago. She keeps saying how it wasn't her fault, that all she had to go on were the *data,* and if the *data* were wrong, well, that was the *doctor's* fault, not hers."

"And what do *you* think?" I asked.

He reflected for a moment, then his face hardened. "I think she's fulla shit."

I nodded. I had nothing meaningful to say, so, by way of experiment, I said nothing. Inwardly I was scolding myself. "Silly man! You actually thought he was fretting about *you* all this time? Such grandiosity! How do you live with yourself!" But then I remembered that I do *not* live with myself, but merely with my *idea of myself*—an altogether more appealing companion.

After a silence, during which the boy's eyes grew inky, he muttered to one of my rare Persian carpets, "She's always been my favorite grandparent. If she dies, I don't know what I'll do."

I wanted to give him a hug, but, as I did not trust myself to keep it clean and could not bear a repeat of our earlier fiasco, I spoke instead. I told him I was terribly, terribly sorry. It sounded heartfelt, even to me. Perhaps it was.

He nodded gratefully.

A moment was gathering force.

"You blame your mother for what's happened, don't you?" I asked, touching his shoulder.

"Damn right. She's an M.D. She should have known."

He rose abruptly and moved to the door. I put up a fight, telling him that he looked positively spectral and offering to order him some vegetarian Indian. He refused, explaining that he had to be up early.

"Back to Connecticut?" I asked. "Would you like me to come with you? I might be helpful. You know, I went to medical school." (How do I come up with these things?)

"No, I just got back and there's really not much I can do for her. And since I'm not really writing . . . and since the primary's in a few weeks . . . I've decided to volunteer for Gary Hart."

I masked my profound horror beneath a bemused smile. "Come again?"

"I *like* him. I think he's got a really good chance to win the nomination."

A chunk of veal crawled up my esophagus. I took a good long look at the lad. What on earth could explain this sudden dive into the mire of national politics? His words had been upbeat, but his eyes were swirling now with anguish and alienation. It was then, Patient Reader, that I realized what I ought to have known sooner. Christopher was the most unfortunate of all earthly bipeds, with the possible exception of penguins: He was an idealist.

Christopher again absented himself from my life, but now that our bond had deepened, nothing would have been easier for me than simply to knock on his door and ask, in the vernacular of the day, "What's up?" But I did not. It would have been a strategic misstep. I had shown too much of my hand already. No, the boy must come to me.

I initiated a rousing game of Cat and Mouse.

Three days passed.

It is impossible to play Cat and Mouse alone.

I settled on another plan: I would go to him, but in such a way that he would think the Fates had brought us together. On the night of Wednesday, March 14, I ventured out, under a nearly full moon, to Arabia. I knew that Christopher ate there quite often. I had never tried the place for the simple reason that months earlier at the Parnassus, while reading the Terrible Sonnets of Hopkins over a robust shepherd's pie and a Tom Collins, I overheard a pair of old biddies pecking over certain rumors; namely, that Tarek, Arabia's owner, hated Jews, rubbed elbows with Mafiosi, and served rotten meat. Back then I was bothered, now I was not: Seduction is not a game for the faint of heart or tummy.

Little of Arabia's interior was visible from the street—a wall of hanging plants obscured the storefront window—so when I stepped inside I had no idea what to expect. What greeted me was more an opium den than a restaurant. Everything was rusty gold, from the cement floor to the ornate tin ceiling. On every wall hung dark shelves. Tucked along their shadows, like a family of nocturnal animals, was a shiny array of foreign objects—brass urns, ancient bottles, satin pillows. The only thing that reassured me I was still in postbicentennial America was a trio of samplers above the cash register: a white farm-house, a clown with pigtails who waved as she rode by on a uni-cycle, and a wedding scene that read "August, 1982, Chico, California."

When the door closed behind me, Tarek, a light-skinned Egyptian behemoth, was in the process of berating in fierce whispers his American waitress. Not only was she his wife, I later learned, but the genius behind the samplers. I found a corner table and ordered a chicken souvlaki sandwich, a side of couscous, and a domestic lager.

As I dined, I thumbed through my beloved Browning (Elizabeth Barrett, of course; not her knotty husband), and waited for Christopher to show. The window grew wintry white. The radiators hissed and clanged. Tarek's friends began to trickle in. They gobbled spicy meats and waved foul cigarettes. Tarek joined them at their table, where they argued world affairs. The rumors, it turned out, were absolute poppycock: It wasn't Jews they detested, but Zionists, the mob was never mentioned, and the meat was fresh. Later, they mulled over their financial woes. As I was leaving, they sang the praises of American women and their sluttish ways. Although I had betrayed the Parnassus and the good witch Cassandra, and although there was little in terms of flesh or ambiance to recommend Arabia, I knew I would return. Not only did Tarek serve a fine souvlaki, but I was sure that sooner or later my quarry would flutter in the door.

He did.

On my fifth consecutive night at Arabia (Sunday, March 18), the bell tinkled, I looked up, and there he was in all his youthful glory. He smiled, sat across from me, and we picked up exactly where we had left off. His disappearance was quickly explained. It seemed that the Hart campaign, within minutes of his darkening their threshold, had dubbed him Co-Coordinator of Manhattan Volunteers, an honor which entitled him to work twelve hours a day without pay. Plus, there were his tutees to attend to. Plus, he had spent hours filling out forms at Divorce Yourself, a discount concern that promised to end his marriage with ruthless dispatch. Plus, on weekends he escaped to New Haven to visit Grammy. In short, he was a busy beaver.

As we supped, I noticed that no matter how interesting my

chitchat, Christopher's eyes bounced intermittently off mine and landed on something across the room. At first I thought he was merely having trouble looking at me. I am, after all, on the sensual plane, an undeniable challenge: My epidermis tends toward the ashen, my teeth you know about, and my eyes are a smidge hyperthyroid—as though as a toddler I had been startled by a flashbulb and never quite recovered. But I sensed something else was afoot. A drip of tahini on my chin? No, he would have told me. I dropped my fork and, as I reached for it, spun around dramatically. There stood my answer: Tarek's American wife. Stringy blond hair, shattered blue eyes, big bosoms, *jambes anglaise*, basketball sneakers.

"What?" Christopher asked, smiling, fingers of scarlet clawing into his cheeks.

"She's taken, you know."

"I'm just looking."

"Well, you'd better not. She might start looking back. Then her husband will notice. Have you been introduced to the brute? He'll rip off your trousers and jam you on a spit. Which, despite its obvious allure, could prove painful."

"Tarek's okay," he chuckled. "We're friends."

"Don't be so sure."

He ducked back to his falafel.

Let me state that I had absolutely no interest in politics. As a pup, I had worshipped (no doubt the influence of my adoptive mother who hailed from Blue Springs, Missouri) that feisty haberdasher, Mr. Harry Truman, whom I believed to be the salvation of the planet. Imagine, then, my surprise when, not long after, he vaporized a considerable chunk of it. Ever since, I had left the business of vote gathering to mindless undergraduates, bored housewives, and the Irish.

That spring, however, politics was in the air. Not only did we have, coming up, a presidential election (described by the candidates, as all elections are, as "watershed"), but the United States was, as Christopher felt compelled to remind me, conducting illegal incursions all over the globe, but nowhere as shamelessly as in Central America, where, in the name of democracy, we were arming every thug we could lay our filthy hands on. Now, in an effort to mask our sins, we were rigging a free and fair election in El Salvador. Dipping lumps of falafel into a bath of sesame, the boy spoke of that election and of the sacrifices that would be required of voters. Government death squads terrorized the populace. For many, to vote was to risk a bloody death. He felt it incumbent upon U.S. citizens to honor these brave souls by becoming involved in *our own* electoral process.

Attempting to end the discussion, I yawned like a lion, but I discovered that my apathy only incited the young zealot. I listened for a full half hour as he sang the praises of Mr. Gerald Hart. For those of you who do not remember him, this daring reformer was a self-dubbed New Democrat. Chock full of fresh ideas and free of all ties to special interests, he would save the party from itself. As if that alone were not enough to make a grown man long for the days of Tory rule, he was also young, handsome, and Kennedyesque—but for his cowboy boots and his shirts with mother-of-pearl snaps. Fittingly, Hart's eventual downfall came as a direct result of glandular similarities to JFK (and I'm not talking about Addison's disease), but this was still years away.

Christopher regaled me with the triumphs of his week. His volunteers had papered a subway stop and a student union, even organized a small rally. From the pride he took in his work, it was clear he actually thought these sorts of things *mattered*—as though television had never been invented, as though grass roots could spring through asphalt. Tragically, as I listened to the boy beat his gums, his hysteria approaching that of his wicked mother, my interest in him never waned. In fact, I grew sexually aroused.

Yes, the boy actually *believed*. He had become a swallower of slogans. But why? I stared deep into his eyes, probing his very anima for the cause. In the end, I came back to his chronic idealism. Thwarted by the ruination of his marriage and finding no outlet in creative work, it was driving him toward folly. It did not matter that the cause was shallow and futile, or even that he had little understanding of politics beyond the headlines of the *New York Post* and the playground platitudes of Mr. Daniel Rather; what mattered was that each day he woke up with something high-minded to do. As ridiculous as I found it, it gave me hot pants. I don't know why.

When we parted at his door, he wagged a playful finger at me, warning that he would convert me yet. "You'll vote for Hart on April sixth, just you wait and see!" I could not bring myself to tell him that the last time I had voted I wore a Nigel Bruce mustache, a Beatnik beret, and sweet, old Ike was in office.

As Election Day neared, Christopher fell more deeply and hopelessly under the spell of his baby-kisser. A few nights each week, he would plop down across from me at Arabia and tell me all about his labors. He spoke mostly of an organizer named Mr. Del Ramsay. His anecdotes were so vivid they belonged in a short story, one of his own making, but I doubted that that would ever occur to him, as it is the nature of the young writer to search for his subject matter everywhere but where it actually dwells and flourishes—right before his unhappy eyes.

He had met Del on the second week of the campaign, when he saw a light blinking on a phone bank. The phone volunteers were always beleaguered, so Christopher grabbed the call himself. A man with a thick Hispanic accent asked for Del Ramsay in Scheduling. When Christopher found Scheduling, there was only one worker there—a mad, freckled Celt. She looked confused and sent him to the Press Room. The busy Press Room was made un-inviting by a wall of smoke.

"Del Ramsay!" Christopher called out. "Call on line four!" He made sure to sound impatient. He wanted everyone to know he was a messenger only out of courtesy. Del, a tall man smok-ing an unfiltered fag, moved through the crowd with long strides and picked up a phone just a few feet away. Christopher, for no good reason, stayed to watch. What followed startled him. Del listened to the caller for a few minutes, until his face turned bur-gundy, then he dropped his cigarette to the carpet, squashed it with a twist, and unleashed. He called the man various un-friendly things, including a "rotten hood" and a "slimy shit," then he said that he knew that that wasn't *olive oil* on the man's hands, either. He hung up and picked a fleck of tobacco off his tongue.

When Christopher, as shocked as he was impressed, asked who that was, Del said, "A corrupt son of a bitch who thinks we owe him a favor." The old party guys, Del explained, were the most contemptible bunch, worse than goddamn Republicans. "We don't need them. We already have good people up in Span-ish Harlem. There's a kid named Torres up there who makes this crew look like a buncha taco peddlers."

Christopher was electrified by Del's candor. He felt that this was exactly the sort of organizer Hart needed—the complete opposite of the smug corporate types that filled the office now. And, so, whenever he had a moment free, Christopher would find Del and glug at the fount of his brave wisdom. The old man's breath might be sour and his hands shaky, but he never failed to inspire.

"I've been in politics for thirty-five years!" Del would de-clare, "and the reason I'm workin' for our boy is that he's cleaner than the old crowd. Lot smarter, too. And a few million people in this country seem to agree. Like you, like him, like her! Like anyone with a brain in his head and a heart in his chest, huh? That's why I collect good people. In Harlem, I got a black kid from Columbia Law. I got people in the gay community. In Chinatown. And I'm tellin' you somethin'! We can get this nomination! We can beat old Fritz!"

Del had a habit, when he spoke, of looking across a crowded room as though it were a raw, rich frontier.

"This goddamn election's wide open," he would say. "Our man knows it, too. Hell, it's *got* to be open! The people haven't decided. They're not like the polls, huh? They wait and watch and think. I got a list that long!" He held his hands up two feet apart. "Full of places our boy's gotta visit, huh, corners he's gotta stand on. And if someone listens to me——" He broke into a hoarse whisper. "Somebody around here *wakes the fuck up* and gets Hart to follow my lead, we're gonna hit this city right where she lives!"

These rousing speeches only reinforced the boy's belief that their cause was both worthy and winnable. I did not rain on his parade, but I certainly could have. Already, I suspected Del was a kook, a barely tolerated oddity in no way integral to the campaign. His hire was probably a favor to someone. (I suspected he might even be a chicken hawk suffering from tertiary syphilis.)

One night, Tarek's wife, Patty, joined us at our table. We were her most loyal customers, so it was only a matter of time. The only hint that Christopher had a desperate crush on the wench was his sudden shyness within moments of her plopping down, across from him, her prodigious udders and shanks. I could not imagine what he saw in her, unless it was her potential as a sex object, but how he could even *guess* at that was a mystery as well: She kept her ample curves hidden beneath a formless robe—the Egyptian cousin of the Hawaiian muumuu.

"Who's this guy you're always goin' on about?" she asked, smiling in a sweet, dopey way.

Christopher gave her a little background on his idol, then

began to recite another chapter in their emerging friendship. That morning, Del had slammed the *Times* down in front of him and pointed with a yellowed fingernail to a small article, which said that a lobbying group that published policy statements on Middle Eastern affairs had recently met behind closed doors with the two leading Democratic candidates, but it had yet to announce its endorsement. When Christopher found nothing of interest in this, Del became agitated.

"Sure, there's nothin' wrong with a candidate meetin' with these guys, huh? Trouble is, this is *our* boy who's doin' it. He's supposed to be different! He tells special interests to go to hell, remember? Isn't that the whole angle behind this operation?"

Christopher nodded.

"So, what the hell's he doin' behind closed doors with these canaries? Tellin' 'em to go to hell? That doesn't take two hours! Makes our boy look like a goddamn *hypocrite!* That's what I'm gonna tell 'im, too, first chance I get. Shit, you don't pop down to Chinatown and eat an egg roll! You wanna be the Asian voice in Washington, you gotta walk down Mott Street with an interpreter. You gotta go up to Harlem, see the prices they pay. Some voter says he's votin' for Jesse Jackson, find out why! Maybe he's got a point!"

I would be lying if I did not confess that tales of Del had begun to bore and rankle me. I did not like sharing Christopher with anyone, but especially not with a peer. Every moment he spent discussing the old gerrymanderer was a moment stolen from me, and, more important, from the creation of a sweaty, writhing, *us*. In the end, I decided not to take it personally. Clearly, the lad saw in Del the image of his own drunken daddy—a man whose moldering shoes I could not, and would never care to, fill.

The next week, Christopher relayed one final anecdote about Del which he found disheartening (pun intended), but which I found ominous, not only for the campaign, but for the future of Christopher's mental health. It was the day before Hart was to arrive in the city. Del Ramsay escorted a pair of Asiatics to Christopher's desk and introduced them as Drs. John and Ellie Cheng. He said that they had a request, then he walked away. The Chengs were not Siamese, which was surprising as they spoke at the same time. They were Chinese and both great fans of the candidate. Their idea was to rent out a restaurant in Chinatown, at their own expense, and, if they were guaranteed that Hart would attend, they would guarantee the presence of at least twelve Asian newspapers and three cable television companies. Christopher, excited, asked the Chengs to wait, then headed down a short corridor and knocked on a half-open door. There were two people inside, both men, both young and pudgy. One of them wore glasses and sat at a desk. The other, balding, sat on a couch stirring coffee.

"Hi," Christopher began. "Del just referred me to something I think you should be aware of."

The man at the desk asked what.

Christopher took a deep breath. "Well, I just spoke with a couple. I guess they're pretty respected in the Chinese community and—"

"Wait a sec. *Del?* Who's that?" the man at the desk asked.

Christopher, flustered, pointed to the wall, and said Del Ramsay from Scheduling.

Both men drew blanks.

"Who's the couple?" the first man asked.

"John and Ellie Cheng. They're doctors. They want to organize a press conference."

"Don't know 'em. Do you?"

Christopher turned around. The bald man was intently dunking a doughnut into his java. He shook his head.

"What are they, club people?" the first man asked.

Christopher turned back. "I don't think so. I think this is pretty much their own idea."

"Lemme tell ya something," the bald man said suddenly, in a weary voice. "Every year we go down to these clubs in China-town, okay? The Wings, the Wongs, the Woos, they get all ex-cited and tell us how great it's gonna be. Big event they tell us! And I swear to God, you know what it turns out to be? Every goddamn time?"

Christopher shook his head.

"A big *this*."

The man curled his fingers and masturbated the air.

April

Rain not only cleans the streets, but it humbles the inhabitants. Day after day, chasing schedules, brows in knots, falling into taxis and out of trains, scuttling between purchase and sale, the foul denizens of our fair city inevitably lose sight of anything larger and more enduring than themselves. Being drenched by Mother Nature reminds them of how puny they really are.

The rain that fell on Election Night was not a surprise. It had been falling for hours, just as the experts had predicted it would. Yet, when Christopher and I stepped outside, neither of us was carrying an umbrella. Mary had taken Christopher's to Washington, and I find them effeminate to the extreme. But I, at least, wore a sturdy Victorian surtout and a Donegal tweed cap, while Christopher was clad only in a paltry windbreaker. By the time we landed on the sagging vinyl of the taxi, he was already soaked to the marrow.

The driver was a black dandy, about my age, wearing a white shirt and an emerald paisley scarf. Too-large eyeglasses sat crookedly on his licorice nose. When he heard Christopher say the name of the hotel, he looked into the rearview mirror and asked him a question, but got no reply. The boy's head was down and he was scraping his fingers through his dripping locks. After the driver had pulled into traffic, he asked his question again, this time revealing a Caribbean accent. "Will you tell me where that is, please?"

I did.

Outside Christopher's window, a pin-striped Protestant dashed out of a doorway, holding a briefcase over his head and hailing frantically. When we drove past, he lifted a fist and hurled an oath. Christopher noticed him, too, then, realizing why he was angry, he leaned forward and said, "You forgot to turn your meter on."

The driver laughed and pulled down the small red flag. "And my friends back home ask why I don't return with more money. I don't want to tell them the truth, that I forget to turn on my meter!"

Christopher chuckled politely, then sat back and watched the passing show. The neon was jeweled by rain. Despite the fact that he was shivering, he began to whistle a gay, little tune.

The driver looked into his mirror and smiled. "They say a man who whistles is a happy man."

Christopher met his eyes in the mirror. "Where do they say that?"

"Jamaica."

"Well, in my case it isn't true."

"Oh, too bad." He stopped at a light, then turned and offered a big black hand whose palm was almost as white as Christopher's. "Kenneth Gill."

"Chris Ireland," he said, as they shook. "This is my friend B. K. Troop."

"Don't wear it out," I said, dramatically flinging my scarf over my shoulder.

Christopher

"Are you a U.S. citizen?" Christopher asked him, as we roared away.

"No, I am here only to work. Why do you ask?"

"I wanted to know if you voted today."

I rolled my eyes. The boy was relentless. He didn't actually think *every* vote counted, did he?

"That's why we're going to the hotel now," Christopher explained, bringing a curled hand to his mouth and scraping a cuticle. "To watch the results come in. It's a sort of victory party, I hope. I've been organizing volunteers for Gary Hart for the past three weeks."

"Let me tell you." Kenneth gestured gracefully. "I have never involved myself in politics. I would vote here if I were an American, of course, but I do not invest my time or money. Never. And I'll tell you why."

I had feared he might.

"Because, by profession, I am a photographer and I have many projects which I wish to complete, and each requires quite a lot of money—and so I drive a taxi, which allows me to do the work that I love."

Christopher opened his mouth to speak, but Kenneth was not finished.

"Yes, I have become rather ruthless about my creative work. My brother and his wife tell me that I have turned selfish. Perhaps. But I have many projects in mind and only a limited amount of time to complete them."

"Turn here!" I barked. The tires screeched and slipped for a moment, then caught. Christopher was thrown against the door.

"Well done," I muttered.

Kenneth laughed, shook his woolly head, and stated the obvious. "I am a very bad driver!"

"So tell me about your projects," Christopher said.

"You're *interested?*"

Aghast, I glanced over and saw that, indeed, he was. In those days, I was curious about another person's life only when he was young and toothsome.

"I would like to make a book of black men," Kenneth said. "I would photograph only their faces. With a great abundance of detail."

"Who would you put in it?"

"Robert Mugabe. Nkomo. Nelson Mandela, if possible. And Bishop Tutu. Do you know these men? They are from Africa."

"I know Mandela. Would you also include writers?"

"Yes, of course. James Baldwin."

"Wole Soyinka?"

"Yes, the playwright!"

"And Derek Wolcott. From Trinidad."

Kenneth nodded and showed his teeth. "A fine poet! It's *remarkable* that you know him!"

"Chinua Achebe from Kenya."

Kenneth hit the steering wheel and laughed. "Another one! *How* have you heard of these men?"

"He's a freak," I explained. "He reads."

Minutes later, Kenneth pulled the cab to the curb and turned off his meter. "I have delivered you safely."

Christopher went for his wallet, but I reached across and handed Kenneth a tight fold of cash.

"Keep the change," I uttered grandly.

Christopher smiled, "Consider it our contribution to the cause."

(The change was fifteen cents.)

"But it is *not* a cause," Kenneth said, taking the money and staring intently at Christopher.

Christopher

I looked over to see what he was seeing: The boy's eyes were dismal; a half-moon of white showed beneath each pupil.

"Oh, you are very sad," Kenneth whispered. Christopher tensed. "You are very much a human being. That is a rare thing, so you must not let politics upset you too much." He laid a hand on the young man's shoulder. "Enjoy your celebration. But, when you get home, read something beautiful before you fall asleep."

The words hit the boy hard. He sat as though paralyzed, unable to speak. He was realizing, at long last, how the campaign had distracted him from his purpose, dropped him flailing into the great welter of the day-to-day—the very mess-pot he had become an artist to escape.

Finally, he braced himself and jumped out. He ran splashing through puddles and I nimbly followed. He stopped short, just a few yards shy of the hotel awning. In front of him, a trash can was stuffed with dozens of Hart leaflets. Christopher turned and looked. Hart's craggy mug lay on the sidewalk, folded, mangled, and marred, all the way to the end of the block. The boy understood only too well what this augured, but he fought the knowledge.

We were thrown by a revolving door straight into a quarrel. A young woman was holding forth with great passion about something irrelevant. Her skin was ghostly pale with a skid of pink at each cheek, and her long golden hair swept in wriggling snakes past her stupid, haunted face. She was too tall and would one day be fat.

"Her name's Celia," Christopher explained. "We worked together. She's a pretty successful model."

I found that hard to believe, but then, again, I have a tendency to judge my rivals harshly, and I knew at once she was a rival. Sure enough, when she noticed us, she stretched out her arms to Christopher and made a beeline for his kisser. She applied a stranglehold, smooched hard, and whispered, "We lost."

"*What?!*" the lad ejaculated.

"Can you believe it?" Her eyes grew moist. "We're losing in every category. Even Jackson's almost beating us."

Horrified, Christopher tried to pull away, but she held him fast. He glanced over at me, expecting, I think, to see some sign of schadenfreude. Instead, I pouted, saucer-eyed and sweet, like Mary Pickford. I had no choice; I was a guest. (In point of fact, the only reason he had asked me along was that I had stopped him in the hallway and, quite literally and repeatedly, refused to take no for an answer.)

Christopher spotted a silent television perched on a high stand. The screen showed a frantic car chase. A clutch of volunteers watched it blankly, muttering in funereal tones.

"I don't believe it," Christopher said softly.

"I know," Celia said, freeing him from her death-grip.

"Has he conceded yet?"

"Nope."

"Where is he now?"

"Philly."

"Is he coming here?"

"Maybe. But, listen, I've got some news. Only you have to be cool about it. Duff didn't want me to tell you till it's definite, but——" She lowered her voice. "It looks like they want us to stay on with the campaign."

My heart seized.

Christopher's eyes widened and he smiled. "Seriously?"

"It's a huge honor. They're not sure where they wanna send us yet. Maybe Texas, maybe Wisconsin. If it's Wisconsin, we'd have to leave in a coupla days. It's pretty urgent. There's no primary, only a caucus."

"That's so soon."

Christopher

"It certainly is!" I interjected, startling Celia.

She threw me a crazy glance, then looked back at him. "So? It'll be fun. We'll sublet our apartments and take off. Who knows, if we hang in there, we might even get to be alternate delegates to the convention."

Christopher considered the prospect, then his brow darkened a shade and he threw me a glance. "Let's get a drink."

At last, a moment of clarity.

As Christopher led me away, I spun around and stuck my tongue out at Celia. Childish, certainly, but effective. Next time, she would think twice before coming between B. K. Troop and his prey.

Suddenly, a loud shushing. In every corner, volunteers turned up the volume on the televisions. The pug-dog visage of Mr. Daniel Rather appeared on every screen, announcing that Mr. Walter Mondale had been projected the overwhelming winner in New York. Hart was ahead of Jackson by only two percentage points. He then began to explain how significant a victory this was and what it meant for the primaries ahead. Christopher slouched away, shaking his head. I trotted after. We passed a frantic, dappled woman, hugging a clipboard and a stack of press passes. (The mad, freckled Celt?)

"Maureen," Christopher said, stopping her by the arm, "have you seen Del?"

Two deep lines formed between her green eyes. "*Who?*"

"Del Ramsay from Scheduling."

Her brow unbent. "I don't know him. And I know *everyone* in Scheduling. Get dry or you'll die of T.B."

She bustled away. Christopher did not move a muscle. I was beginning to wonder if Del Ramsay even existed. We climbed a steep staircase to the mezzanine. At the top lay a dark saloon. As we entered, I spotted a scarecrow sitting at the bar, head down, staring at his hands, which rested on a pool of scattered papers.

One held an empty shot glass, the other an unlighted cigarette. I glanced over at Christopher—his face had gone slack and reverential.

Del Ramsay existed.

Christopher took a stool at Del's side. I took the next one over. The old man did not notice us. He was afloat in a woozy world without periphery. Chris ordered a mineral water; I a dago red.

When Christopher finally found the courage to speak, his voice was gentle. "Del? Are you all right?"

Del's head turned on a rusty swivel. His gaze was murky, his mouth coarse and listless. His white hair fell forward in sloppy bangs and his cheeks were salted with stubble.

"Still pissin' out there?" he growled.

The lad nodded.

"I tell ya . . . after I voted today . . ." Del shook his head and swallowed dryly. "When I saw that sky, I said, yup, the whole bunch of 'em—they're not gettin' away with nothin' tonight." He reached slowly for a wooden match. He struck it brutally three times on the waxy bar, leaving a red mark, then lifted it to his unfiltered cancer stick. "I said, yup, everybody loses today. Our man loses. Which means the country loses. Even Mondale loses, 'cause he's gotta face Reagan in November." He dropped the match, still flaming, into a plastic ashtray. "Hell, even Reagan loses, 'cause what's the point of a landslide, if it's just to beat a whiny old boob like Fritz?"

Christopher sipped his drink. I finished mine. I gestured to the barkeep for another. Del had not even noticed me yet, thank heaven—it allowed me to observe freely.

"You don't look too happy," Del said, smiling. "You thought we were gonna win, didn't ya?"

Christopher confessed that he had, or that it would at least be close.

Christopher

"Close is nothin' . . ." Del swirled the papers around in front of him like playing cards. "Close is for losers."

The bartender asked if he wanted another drink.

"No, no!" Del waved him away. "Don't take advantage, huh?"

"So, where've you been the past few days?" Christopher asked. "I looked for you everywhere."

Del turned over his shot glass. "You know what they did, kid? They . . . uhhh . . . Those bastards. They— Shit! There's a word for it . . . good word, too."

"What does it mean?" Christopher asked.

"The ax, the ax! It means . . . show the door . . . the old heave-ho, huh?"

"They *fired* you?"

"Fancier word'n that. But, yeah."

(I believe the word he sought was "cashiered.")

"How could they do that?" Christopher asked.

"Easy. Hell, they weren't even payin' me."

He collected his papers with two sweeping hands.

"Is that your list?" Christopher asked. "Did they ever see it?"

"I told 'em, I said, I got every street corner, every church. But somebody'd already drawn up the schedule. I dunno who. Some Washington punk." He smacked his hands together. His eyes were lunatic. "I saw the end comin' a long time ago and I coulda jumped ship, but I didn't! I got no illusions! I'm not some college kid, signs up 'cause he likes our boy's hair, the cut of his clothes! I came to serve my country! Only . . . only—" He gestured futilely. "The captains, they didn't want me. No, sir. Chucked me overboard. And you know when I knew it was over, huh? When I saw the end?"

Christopher moved so far forward on his stool that he slipped out of it and his feet settled on the brass rail.

"At the debate?"

"No! Shit!"

"The polls?"

"Wrong, wrong, wrong!"

"When?"

"Day we put up that first poster. I saw that fancy computer-writing and that sexy picture, and I said, this may fly for a while, but it's bullshit! This Kennedy stuff, that's not who our boy is. Know who he is?"

"Himself?"

He placed his words in the air. "Likeable . . . honest . . . smart as hell." He dragged his tongue over his dry lips and smiled. "Abraham Lincoln."

Christopher smiled, realizing, as I did, that Del was absolutely right.

"They shoulda let 'im talk. Let 'im educate. But, no, they tried to make 'im new and improved. Like fuckin' soap."

A huge cheer rose from downstairs. Christopher and I walked over and looked down. A crowd swarmed through the lobby. At the center of the chaos stood Celia, holding forth again. Suddenly, as if by magic, she looked up and met eyes with Christopher. She screamed excitedly and beckoned for him to join her. His face twitched as he shrank back into the shadows.

Del held his head in his hands now. "He's here, huh? Hell, he *had* to come. He didn't, folks'd think he was givin' up."

"Maybe we should listen to him speak."

Ignoring the suggestion, Del leaned back and stretched his arms, his hands in fists. "I hate this rotten game," he said, his voice trembling.

"Chris!" Celia was just ten yards away, galloping toward us.

Christopher knew what was coming and he was embarrassed that Del was going to be forced to witness it.

"Duff wants us in Texas!" she cried. She grabbed his hands and pulled him off his stool. "Then California! The convention!

Christopher

They're giving us expenses! You've gotta come! *Please?!*"
Christopher shot a glance at Del. "Come on, don't be a sore
loser!" she said. "We're gonna win in the West! It's Gary's home
turf! What's wrong? Don't you wanna come?"

"I'm not sure," Christopher muttered at last.

"Oh, you're just sad 'cause we lost. But that's why Gary's
here. To tell us not to give up! Come hear him talk. You'll feel
better. *Come on!*"

He removed her hands from his. "I'll be down in a second."

She was puzzled, her zeal draining. She slowly walked away,
then turned back with worried eyes. "Just a second, okay? You
promise?"

Christopher nodded.

She hurried off.

After Christopher had regained his stool, Del chuckled.
"You're a celebrity, son."

For a long time, neither of them spoke.

Finally, the corners of Del's mouth twitched. "What do you
do, anyway? When you're not hangin' 'round here?"

"Write novels," he lied.

"Artsy type. Yeah, I figured. Well, if you ask me, it's a lousy
idea for you to be listenin' to bullshit. But, if you disagree, you
go down there and listen to some more. Me, I'm goin' home."

"Are you sure?"

Down below, a robust roar from the crowd.

Del turned and listened with a wry smile. "Know what I did
this morning?"

"What?"

"Threw away my Hart button."

"*Really?*"

"Yup. Then I voted for Jesse Jackson."

Christopher's face fell.

Del burst out laughing, then gave him an affectionate slap on the shoulder. "You better get down there, kid. You might miss something. One of them new ideas."

Christopher was smart enough not only to know a lost cause (once it had already been lost), but one which had deserved to lose. Much to the chagrin of Celia (on whom I later learned the boy had developed quite an urgent crush) and to the delight of yours truly, Christopher rejected the campaign's offer of further involvement. But now that his hip bath in the bog of electoral politics was finished, where did that leave him? The answer was, of course, right where he had started—crushed by his own thwarted idealism.

At the time, it was easy for me to see that there was nothing wrong with the lad that a nervous breakdown wouldn't fix. I knew this from bitter experience. I had missed my college graduation, locked in my dorm room, keening like an Irish widow—not for the loss of a husband at sea, but for the loss of my innocence, my first love, my hair. I emerged eight days later, renewed, even joyful. But I was lucky. Resurrections like these are rare among the young, living as they so often do in a state of stubborn, prideful myopia. Refusing an easy, liquid surrender, most opt for a stony, compacted depression. Christopher was no different.

On Tuesday night, April 10, a week after he had quit the campaign, Christopher suggested (after I had discovered him brooding alone over a vegetable kebab), that we retire to his cell for a game of chess. I hate the game; not only am I a poor player, but for me it is a busman's holiday. I am *always* plotting my next move. Yet, I dove at the offer. It would allow me not only to view, for the first time, his habitat, but to study his sad, pretty face while he studied the board. Before the slaughter commenced, I slipped over to my apartment, to primp, perfume, and grab a bottle of cheap rosé (lemon nose; skunk tail).

Twenty-five minutes later, sitting in his clean, ordered cell, lined with books, where he had already thrice beaten me, he reached across the chessboard, without asking, and slipped one of my generic cigarettes from its soft, white pack. He grabbed my lighter, snapped, heaved a good suck, and immediately gagged. I pounded his back and then, ever a Virgil among the shades, I taught him how to inhale. Within minutes, he was a master. It was a wonder he had not succumbed sooner to the Divine Leaf.

Before I knew it, we had ourselves a little ritual: two or three nights a week we would dine in near silence (his depression was deepening), during which he would stare longingly at Patty's bosoms (imagining no doubt his noggin parked between them while she maternally raked her stubby fingers through his hair, murmuring, "There, there"), then we would traipse up to his cell and, tippling the grape and huffing the leaf, play five games of chess, all of which I would handily lose.

In no time at all, the boy went from one glass of wine to four, from two fags to ten. (A heartbroken idealist is a dark and fearsome creature.) While I was perfectly aware that this was nothing more than a glacially slow suicide attempt, I liked what it implied. He was open to a change in habits. Was it not possible, then, for him to abandon his predilection for the fair sex and reach for me?

I thought so.

I thought wrong. One night, I merely reached for his hand and he pulled it away as though from the jaws of a lizard.

I waited for his depression to get even worse.

The day after Easter, I returned from a court hearing. I had been accused two Saturdays before, at our local flea market, of shoplifting. I had put up quite a fight, of course, but when the constable found, tucked into a hidden pocket of my herringbone, a pair of Roycroft candlesticks and a carte-de-visite of Louisa May Alcott, I pantomimed that I wished to speak to my attorney. Walking on air now, happy to have beaten the rap (a year's probation), I found Christopher sitting on the stoop, sucking down a fag, looking every inch a portrait of infinite sorrow.

He had just gotten back from Connecticut, he explained, and could not even find the will to climb the steps. He had known the visit would be nightmarish, because his mother was there, but he had gone, anyway, because this time she had brought along a hostage. His sister, Anna, whom he adored. I plopped down next to him (the sides of our knees touched for an instant) and begged him to tell me all.

Grace and Anna were waiting for him when he stepped off the train. Anna looked exquisite. At nineteen, she was at the age when womanly beauty is beginning to rise in slow chiseled degrees out of the dough of a child's face. It had been over a year since he had seen her, and he was bursting to ask her about her new job and her new boyfriend, but before he could even speak, Grace lunged and grabbed hold of his arm. As they descended the steps to the street, she relayed, in a breathless stream, every detail of their trip from Milwaukee, as though it had been not a two-hour flight, but a hacking push through a tropical jungle. He felt rage rise in his chest, but when he opened his mouth to give it voice, it was drowned beneath a wave of numbness.

In the car, he and Anna listened from the backseat as Grampy shared the latest news. "Her doctor called this morning. He wants me to give up on her! Is that how a doctor should talk? These guys're gettin' paid!"

Grace was ready with a sensitive reply. "Well, Daddy, the

important thing now is that she get well. I mean, what if she survives and ends up an invalid . . . some kind of vegetable? You don't want that. Remember it's quality of life, not quantity, that matters."

"Yeah, I guess so," he muttered, but Christopher knew he had no idea what she was talking about.

It had been ten days since Christopher's last visit and as he walked into the hospital he feared the worst: Grammy lying in bed, bathed in blood, or sprawled on the floor, wrapped in tubes. The reality was almost as bad. He knew the face immediately. It was the same one he had seen on the face of his dying father. The cheekbones stand up sharply and the eyes have retracted into the hollows of the skull—an ideal place for pennies. Because Grampy had traveled the slow, daily gradations of his wife's decline, he was blind to its steepness. What preoccupied him now was his wife's graying hair. He had brought along some auburn dye and wanted Grace to apply it.

While the dyeing took place, Christopher escaped to the smoker's lounge. Minutes later, Anna joined him and burst into tears. (It was her first visit.) Although Christopher refused to cry himself, he was not uncomfortable with Anna's grief. He sat with his arm around her and the strange idea came to him that he was a ventriloquist and that it was his own wails that flowed from her mouth. When she finally blew her nose and spoke, he was surprised to learn what was upsetting her. It was not their dying grandmother, but their all-too-living mother.

"God, you should have seen her! Grammy's gonna die and all she can talk about is herself!"

"I know, I know," Chris said, drawing her closer, resting her head on his shoulder. "She's a monster."

"You know, it wouldn't be so bad, the way she's being, if . . . if she really *loved* Grammy, you know, and was just too scared or screwed up to feel it." Chris knew that she was talking about *him*, but he was not at all offended. "But she doesn't even *like* her!"

"What do you mean?"

"She *hates* her! She always has!"

With a shock, Christopher thought back to family gatherings when Grampy would tell corny jokes for hours on end, but when Grammy dared the slightest interjection it was immediately squashed by Grace with a scornful glance or angry shush. Once, she had even slapped the old woman's hand.

Anna continued: "And, you know, God *damn* her! She basically . . . Do you know what she did? No, no, forget it. What's the use? There's no point."

Christopher, sensing that something important was on her mind, took her hands in his, and said, "This is *not* the time to be discreet."

Surrendering, Anna shared her theory. She began with the evidence that had led to it. The first disturbing fact was that their mother never talked about her own childhood. Odd in anyone, but downright chilling in a psychiatrist. But, at the same time, it was obvious that she hated her mother and was madly in love with her father. "That's why she destroys every man she marries," Anna said. "Because none of them compare to Grampy. In fact, Mom told Grampy just last week that if Grammy dies, she wants him to move to Milwaukee and live with her."

The blood drained from Christopher's face. He sensed where this was leading. He reached for another cigarette.

Anna's theory was that when Grammy had fallen ill, or, to be exact, when her doctor had *thought* she had, Grace's long-buried hatred for her mother had at last reared its ugly head, which is why she had shoved the old woman toward the operating room.

Christopher

"Matricide," Christopher thought. *"Of course!"*

Within two hours, he was back on the train.

His tale finished, Christopher dropped his head and shook it. Anna's theory was still rattling around inside him. His pain was intense. I wanted to give him a hug, but this time a proper *mother's* hug. I felt no lust, only compassion. I fought this unfamiliar sensation. We climbed the steps and stopped at his cell. He refused my offer of a drink.

Hours later, feeling anxious and not knowing why, I forced myself, while playing the sedulous ape to Onan, to imagine myself naked and entangled with someone other than Christopher. My fancy sputtered. I could not. Alarmed, I called an ex-lover of mine named Claude, a strapping Quebecois television repairman who lived with his maiden aunt on Staten Island. Thank heaven he was home. He hopped the ferry and, for a mere forty dollars (American), he came over and ravaged me. Just what the doctor ordered. I drifted into sleep with a smile on my face, feeling refreshed, adorable, and as free as a bird. I might have hired Claude on a more regular basis, but his hair smelled of marijuana and his misuse of the objective case made pillow talk impossible.

May

At high noon, Wednesday, May 2, Christopher sat on the stoop, reading his daily horoscope, which strangely failed to mention the sleepy old catamite, who, at that very moment, right behind him, blinded by the sun, was about to plant a cordovan penny loafer into the curve of his delicate spine. Fortunately, a cloud moved, the light shifted, and disaster was averted. Fingering my dilating pupils, I plunked down next to him and, indulging in a bit of New Wave idiom, asked him "how it was hanging."

He said, "A little to the left," smiled impishly, then offered me a bit of unsolicited Chaldean insight (applicable only to me and a half-billion other unique Scorpions). It was something about avoiding airplanes, seeing relationships as they really are, and having faith in psychic hunches. As he read, I noticed a terrible gleam in his eye—terrible, because my latest psychic hunch was that Christopher, finished now with political activism, was going to grasp at some *new* distraction from his despair, thus avoiding the complete neural collapse that would not only lift him from depression but force him to question every aspect of his life, including his sexual attachment to the fair sex.

Christopher

My hunch proved correct when, after closing his *Post*, he announced, with a brazen lack of embarrassment, that he had enrolled in an enlightenment course at a place called The Center. The weekend, imaginatively called The Weekend, was the brainchild of a Tampa-born guru named Cameron Jaspar and it was guaranteed (with no money back) to "knock each student flat on his ass." Spiritually, that is.

For those of you too young or too old to remember, these were the years when the newly dubbed New Age movement had at last slipped the railings of Malibu swimming pools and Marin County hot tubs and begun its slow saturation of the national consciousness. Aquarians were conspiring on every street corner. Courses like The Weekend were springing up everywhere. How they worked was a mystery, because mere language was inadequate to spell their wonders; you simply had to trust the graduate who signed you up. In Christopher's case, it was a long-lost casual acquaintance named Andre Something, a herpes-addled Polish cinematographer who lived with his bulimic girlfriend in a squalid Alphabet City walk-up.

It was not Christopher's fault that he was drawn to The Weekend. He was, after all, miserable and craved relief, and, as he was unwilling to turn inward, where else was he to turn? Traditional religions offended his intellect, and psychotherapy scared the daylights out of him, being, as it was, the domain of his wicked mother. He might have turned to me, of course, who had enlightenment to spare, but he questioned my motives. (Perhaps he overheard me at night.) Plus, Christopher was a product of the times and, as I have said, the zeitgeist was awash with New Age initiatives.

By way of evidence, I cite the case of Fairfield, Iowa, on which, just a few months before, seven thousand followers of the Maharishi Mahesh Yogi had converged for an event dubbed a "Taste of Utopia." Its purpose was to heal, with a concentrated emanation of energy and love, our suffering planet. Healing was, after all, in order—the doomsday clock was poised at three minutes 'til. I thought that if the boy were to sample even a soupçon of the Taste of Utopia, he might back out of the course, so I set to force-feeding him the cautionary tale.

Upon arriving in Fairfield, event organizers requested that the local airport be shut down. They planned a laser show, they said, the highlight of which would be the projection of the Yogi's humble, straggly visage onto the unsuspecting Midwestern clouds. Their request was summarily denied. Undeterred, the faithful fell to their mats and began their mighty labor. Three weeks later, when the event concluded, leaders labeled it a huge success. The facts were undeniable: Local hospital admissions had fallen, the stock market was on the rise, and the United States had improved its relations with Laos. My message was clear: The New Age movement brimmed with frauds and idiots.

Such, however, is the arrogance of the young idealist in search of answers that Christopher ignored my warning. Two nights later, on the eve of The Weekend, I watched with dread as he filled out his Goal Sheet. His three Personal Goals were to forgive Mary, forgive Grace, and stop smoking. His Professional Goals were to drum up more students, read *Moby Dick*, and begin writing his long-postponed novel. (Since the dissolution of his marriage, it was no longer to be about first love and entitled *First Love*. Now it was about the demise of first love and entitled, after Byron, *Love's Sad Archery*.)

I spent the weekend of The Weekend fretting like an overprotective mother on her daughter's first night at sleep-away camp. Who would walk in my door on Sunday night? A moon-eyed robot? A babbling proselyte? Or simply my darling Christopher with a little less money in the bank?

My answer came within moments of his return, when I ac-

Christopher

costed him on the landing. He was a little of each. There was a new light in his eye and a new exuberance in his speech (this, despite the fact that his larynx was shredded—a result, he said, of so much cheering and shouting), but he still looked vaguely dolorous. I escorted him into my lair and demanded every last bean.

He spoke at length of all that he had realized during The Weekend. Because it is crucial that you do not lose respect for our young hero, I will not recreate his monologue for you. Sadly, it was peppered with words like "love," "power," and "clear," and jargon like "being present," "breaking attachments," and "coming from a place of truth." He had discovered that he was unlimited, that miracles were his for the asking, and that he was responsible for every single thing in the entire universe. He had also picked up a few smaller things: that he was extraordinarily passive, controlled by fear of abandonment, and all too often put the needs of others before his own. The effect of all this was that he had never felt better. He was ready at last to embrace his future.

To test the transformation, I offered him a cigarette.

He declined.

These profound changes in Christopher were no doubt real, but only in the sense that a melting snowflake is real. They would not last, of course, but I could not tell him. It would have been cruel, so I swallowed hard and asked, feigning happy astonishment, how he had come to realize so much so darned fast. In keeping with the code of Zen-omerta, he said the only way I could find out was to sign up for The Weekend myself.

"We'll see," I purred.

"Fat chance," I thought.

Over the next several days, we still dined together at Arabia and still discussed what we were reading. (I was rereading *Tristram Shandy;* he was delaying his harpooning of Melville for

Krishnamurti's Journal.) And, as before, we finished off each evening hunched over a checkered bloodscape of slain knights and assassinated bishops. Yet a chasm had opened between us, made manifest in myriad tiny ways. There was the school-marmish glance he threw whenever I tossed a wicked bon mot, the frown whenever I touched flame to leaf, the patronizing shake of the head whenever I implied that I or he or anyone else on the planet was in any way limited. Also, he had quit drinking alcohol. (This, a serious blow to my machinations.) But, most disturbing of all, he no longer tolerated my intense and irrational dislike for Tarek's wife. His interest in her had taken an alarming turn for the protective. He no longer hankered to bed her; now he simply wanted to "be there" for her, "support" her, and sign her up for The Weekend. It seems that Cameron had assured the Graduates that the only way to give oneself The Weekend all over again, in one instant, free of charge, was to sell it to others.

One night, when I was unable to dine with him (emergency boil-lancing), Patty joined him at his table and he began the enrollment process. Graduates were told that rather than get straight to the point it was best, first, to make an emotional connection. It took a little while, but soon he had Patty wistfully recalling the day when, as a child in Seattle, she and her beloved "Pops" had climbed Mount Constitution and got caught in a downpour. Soaking wet, they ate their lunch under a tree and watched as their golden retriever, Honey, ran around catching raindrops, dancing like a crazy Indian. (Thank God I was in the emergency room; at this point I would certainly have up-chucked my kebab.) Tears flowed as Patty told him of Pops's poker night when she used to pad down the hall, little and skinny in her flannel pajamas (the ones with the grinning moons on them), and squish between the wall and the open door to

Christopher

watch the game through the crack. Her aria ended on a high note, with a harrowing blow-by-blow of the night Pops had beaten Moms with a wiffle bat, packed his bags, and never come back.

Moved, Christopher pulled out an Enrollment Card. He touched Patty's hand, stared deep into her eyes, and told her all about The Weekend. He knew that Tarek treated her badly, but all that could change, he said. The Center was a place of unconditional love and absolute honesty, where she would be safe to discover, maybe for the first time, her beauty and unlimitedness. He handed her a ballpoint pen.

Patty looked tearfully at the card. Just when she was about to sign it, she smiled and veered wildly off course. When she met Tarek, she said, she had been working in a little Seattle crafts store, selling her handmade wares. Tarek and a friend stopped in and Tarek laughed at one of her embroidered pillows, her best seller, the one that said "Home Sour Home." Tarek and his friend stayed three days, and, when they left, she left with them. She and the brute were married a week later in Chico, California. No church, no wedding dress. On the phone, her mother had begged her not to do it, but she did it, anyway.

Patty reached into her basketball sneaker and pulled out a wad of damp twenties. Christopher was thrilled. The moment was at hand: his first enrollment. But the cash, it turned out, was for an air conditioner. What with summer coming and all, Arabia would need it. Tarek would be so surprised! She sniffled and refilled Christopher's iced tea. He sat back, deflated. This would take some doing.

The Weekend did, however, effect one change in the boy which I found encouraging. A few days after graduation, he drafted a letter to Grace, telling her that in the future, when she visited New York, she was no longer welcome to stay in his apartment. (She had recently taken to calling it her pied-à-terre.) When I asked him what had inspired this bold step, he said, of course, "Cameron."

It seems that in the first year after the great man had founded The Center, he had called his mother in Florida every week, urging, pleading, sometimes simply commanding her to fly up and take The Weekend. Her refusals were blunt. One afternoon, after a particularly unpleasant exchange, he told her that he had had "enough of her shit" and would never speak to her again. That night, Cameron announced to his squad of volunteers, his "Helpers," that he had broken one of life's most pernicious attachments—the Attachment to Mother. Soon, his decisive act had become a paradigm for the group. Now, no Helper ever remained in close contact for very long with any parent, sibling, or friend who refused The Weekend.

The day after Christopher penned his emancipation proclamation to Grace, he called Cameron. Before he mailed it off, he wanted to run it by the man who had "sourced" it. But Cameron was not interested in the letter. Instead, he wanted to know exactly what had happened when Christopher had called to enroll his mother in The Weekend. The boy stammered, confessing that he had not even bothered to call her, because he knew what she would say: These courses, like therapy, were for people *with problems*. She had no problems. In fact, she could *teach* The Weekend.

Dismayed, Cameron said this, his unwillingness to confront Grace, was an obvious sign that he had not yet committed himself to The Center. How could this be? the boy wondered. After all, he had never been more confident, never worked harder to come from a place of truth. He had even worked a few miracles. Why, just this morning, within seconds of his letting go of his Attachment to Control, the uptown 6 had pulled into the station.

Christopher

When Christopher told him this, Cameron asked why he hadn't signed up to be a Helper then.

"Well . . . I don't really have time," he explained. "I'm going to begin my novel."

Cameron laughed—a series of loud, crude barks. He explained that books are fine, but that no one ever learned anything from them. People change only because of an *experience*. Hell, he could have been a great painter or maybe an architect. He was born with the eye for it, but instead he taught The Weekend. How come? Because it *worked*. People got healed. Someday, after *everyone* had done The Weekend, there would be plenty of time to kick back and read. The world would *need* art again. But right now they didn't. He demanded that at the next Guest Night Christopher stand up and commit to a year-long Tour of Duty.

Christopher's head spun for days. Was Cameron right? Was he a flake for not volunteering? Was he being limited and selfish? And what *about* books? If they made no difference in the world, then his entire purpose, all of Western culture, in fact, was essentially meaningless. He might *as well* be a Helper. Finally, in a moment of despair, Christopher appeared at my door and asked what *I* thought. I replied, tactfully, that I believed Cameron to be a rank sociopath. Christopher said something along the lines of "very funny," then shuffled in and collapsed on my sofa. Moments later, as I wrestled with a bottle of stubborn Chianti (literally; the cap was stuck), he suddenly let go of his Attachment to Approval, popped up like a weighted toy, and reached for the phone. He asked if it would be all right if he called his mother.

I hurried over and hit the speaker function.

For the next few minutes, I watched as the brave lad, heaving deep breaths, told Grace all about The Weekend and how much it would mean to him if she trusted him enough to take it herself. His hands trembled as he waited for her reply.

"Oh, sweetheart," she sighed wearily, "these groups are for young people who are confused and unhappy. I'm a mental health care professional, for God's sake. I could *teach* the course."

He hung up, spirit broken.

The next day, Saturday, May 19, at six o'clock, my door creaked open. I had spent the past eight hours crouched on the carpet, pasting my vast collection of literary cartes-de-visite, chronologically, into a gorgeous, brand-new, Morocco-bound scrapbook I had pinched on Madison Avenue. When I realized that I had skipped Dr. Matthew Arnold (he had somehow fallen between seat cushions), I was forced to tear out everything from 1870 onward. A hideous chore. And so, when I looked up and saw Christopher's timid face peering down at me, I was un-characteristically curt.

"What is it?"

"Well—"

"Well *what*? Can't you see I'm busy?"

"Are you coming?"

"Right now? Heavens no. If I were, you'd know it. I become flushed and break into 'Take Me Out to the Ball Game.'"

In the old days, he would have laughed, but the first symptom of New Age enlightenment is the death of one's sense of humor.

"Come on, you know what I mean," he said. "To the Guest Night. It starts in an hour. Are you coming or not?"

He had told me about these events. Spread throughout the year, they were an opportunity for Graduates and Helpers to sign up their friends and family. The assumption was that once they had beheld Cameron's magnificence they would lunge for their wallets and purses.

"I haven't been invited," I replied, feigning hurt. But it was

Christopher

true. He had discussed inviting everyone but me. They must all have declined.

"Well, I'm inviting you *now*," he said with a sweet smile. "Please? It'll be fun. Cameron's gonna lecture on Interactive Sexuality."

"What's *that?*"

"I'm not sure."

"Sounds vile. Not to mention sloppy."

"I'm sure you'll get something out of it. He's a brilliant guy."

How could the boy have known that there was nothing on Pan's green earth this charlatan could possibly teach me about sex? I had experienced the Swingin' Sixties in the full flower of my manhood. I had soul-kissed a Black Panther, taken a bubble bath with one of the Weathermen, been fed an acid-soaked Communion wafer by a boy-mad priest named Father Corky.

"Will I be surrounded by grinning zombies clamoring for my hard-inherited lucre?" I asked superiorly.

"Sure, but just say no."

I threw a hand on my hip. "Thank you, Nancy Reagan."

He laughed. I grabbed my best silk herringbone and we slipped into the night.

At this point, Uneasy Reader, allow me to pause (using the time it took me and Christopher to rocket downtown on an eerily prompt express) to answer the questions which have no doubt been rioting in your brain for fictive weeks now: Why were you so generous with the boy? Why did you devote so much time to what was, after all, nothing but another seduction? Was he not, to say the least, a highly elusive quarry? Why were you so immersed in the details of his life? Are you sure he even liked you? In other words, where was *your* life?

The answer to all of the above is: I had not the foggiest. At the time, I was as aware as anyone that my desire for Christopher had turned into what Grace and her soul-forcing ilk would label an "unwholesome obsession." Not only had I made physical sacrifices (bad sleep, a boil), intellectual sacrifices (distraction from my studies, impaired fantasy life), and social sacrifices (staying home for nights on end hoping Christopher would pop by), but a *financial* sacrifice, as well, i.e., turning down Sasha Buchwitz's generous offer of my old digs at half the rent. (The fact that poor Sasha, just weeks after her offer, had seen her wonder drug turn ordinary and had been carted back to the cackle factory, screaming for the head of Mr. Delmore Schwartz, was irrelevant; I could not have foreseen this at the time I refused the offer.) Yet, despite my awareness of all this, I was resolved that the hunt would not end until one of us moved away, married, or died. In short, the boy possessed me. Exactly why, I hoped would reveal itself in the fullness of time. And it did.

The Center was housed in a downtown loft. The area had once been home to countless theatres, most of them Yiddish; now it boasted restaurants, bodegas, and copy shops. We took the service elevator to the second floor and entered through a giant metal door marked "The Center." The rooms were tiny and laid out at eccentric angles, connected by ramps, ladders, and narrow hallways. There were cubbyholes and concealed closets. The Computer Room was tucked above the kitchen. The Enrollment Office was tucked beneath a stairwell. Cameron had wanted it this way, Christopher told me. A futuristic spaceship was his vision, and his Helpers had built it for him with their own bare hands—not for pay, either, or job experience, or any of the other things that motivate people on the outside, but simply because they loved him and were aligned with his purpose.

Christopher

Before I could laugh, I was besieged by well-dressed Helpers wearing name tags. It would be a mistake to assume that all of the volunteers at these places are half-wits and cripples. Of the eighteen who surrounded me now, one was a cardiologist, another a junior associate at a prestigious law firm, another a tenured professor at Bard College (of bicycle repair, I believe), and two were soap actors; only the other thirteen were crippled half-wits. They were all extremely friendly, though, eager to know all about me. Unwilling to entrust them with the truth, I dished out an elaborate chronicle of my life, which began with my surviving, against all odds, a late-term abortion on a Cuban beach in 1936, and ended with my winning, for my study of gastric imagery in the love letters of Mr. James Joyce, the Pulitzer Prize for nonfiction—an honor I turned down on ethical grounds when I learned the size of the check.

As they moved in closer, licking their chops, I noticed the Enrollment Board, which stretched the length of the office. On it, written in a full spectrum of inks, were the month's registration and deposit totals. It said that fifty-seven guests were expected for tonight's event—my name was among them, misspelled, "B. K. Snoop."

Suddenly, a bell clanged and Christopher rescued me from my assailants. We were funneled into single file, handed name tags, and herded into the Course Room. A heavily-rouged virago instructed us to sit wherever we liked. Another Helper, of Pakistani origin, announced that gum chewing and smoking were strictly forbidden, and that, once seated, no one would be allowed to urinate until the event was over. Christopher and I plopped into folding chairs in the back row. On the small wooden stage, two Helpers, one a fat man, the other a scrawny woman (both sporting unfashionable sideburns), fixed the room with gooey grins, high beams on, making eye contact with each guest, as though it were love at first sight each time. Christopher watched them with an easy smile. Did he find them endearing or amusing? I could not tell.

Craving some attention (I was, after all, his date), I leaned over and whispered, "Can I hold your hand during the scary parts?"

Before he had time to wince, there was a thunder of applause. Helpers and Graduates, including Christopher, sprang to their feet and cheered. The guests looked at each other, then we stood up, too. Cameron appeared, striding straight-backed through the noise, grinning, and looking all around like a barker in the center ring of a thriving circus. He jumped onto the stage and pivoted, his arms swinging. He faced us, his expression supremely calm. The din lasted for a full minute, rising and falling in waves.

Finally, he lifted a hand.

"Focus!" he shouted.

Everything stopped.

He let the silence resound for a moment, then cleared his throat, but did not speak. He began a slow survey of the faces. Helpers reacted to his azure gaze as though it were the barrel of a rifle. They blinked, twitched, opened their eyes wide. After he had taken us in, he smiled broadly, showing his teeth. They were sparkly white, but with an unusually large space between the front two, which gave him a comical aspect. He bobbed his eyebrows. Everyone laughed.

"This is an important night," he said quietly. "As you know, this is the biggest Guest Night we've ever had. Very few of you can understand what this means. It takes a geometric perspective to see where The Weekend is heading. It takes a mind that can see through walls. It takes *me*." A smattering of uneasy laughter was dispatched by Cameron's sharp glance. "Someday, there'll be three or four Weekends going on all at once and a

Christopher

thousand people in each one. One day, they'll be held in stadiums, like rock concerts. I'll be a speck with a microphone, but every person in every seat will get the message. They'll experience that they're unlimited." He lowered his voice to a near-whisper. "And tonight will have sourced it."

Silence, then more applause.

Cameron dashed away, pointing to the Goal Board. "There it is, guys! A course with seventy-six students by the summer of '84. And we've done it! And that doesn't even count everyone who's gonna sign up tonight!" He let out a mighty whoop. Just about everyone else did, too. He strode back to where he had been standing.

The room settled.

"There's something *else* about today. And it's more important than anything else. It's something I decided not to prepare you for."

"Thanks a lot," a Helper muttered.

Cameron coughed a laugh, then his face turned serious again. "It looks like Pammy and me're gonna be takin' us a little vacation."

Looks of amazement everywhere.

I was confused. "Who's Pammy?" I asked Christopher.

"His wife," he whispered back, with a touch of annoyance, as though I should have known. "They founded The Course together. He's not monogamous."

"Surprise, surprise."

"We leave tonight," Cameron explained. "Pammy gets back from work, then off we go. The limo's downstairs. Our bags're packed. And guess what? This means you guys'll be running the show for a while. What do you say? Are you ready?"

Everyone talked at once.

Finally, a weedy pansy with spiked red hair and thick glasses popped up. Cameron pointed, permitting him to speak.

"I think it's great, Cameron," he said. "Really great that you and Pammy are giving this to yourselves. And it's coming at the right time, 'cause the Lifers are ready to own the organization a hundred percent. We're gonna move to the next level. I can feel it."

"What's a 'Lifer'?" I whispered, annoying Christopher again.

"Someone committed to full-time Helping for the rest of his life. They don't get paid. They live here."

I nodded as though I were impressed, as though this were a canny career move.

"Good, Rick. You're seeing it," Cameron said. "Anyway, Pammy and I are goin' to Florida."

A few people laughed. He shook his head at them, smiling indulgently. "You think we're just like you, don't you? You think Pammy and me're just gonna go unconscious on some goddamn beach. Take the same kinda vacations *you* take." Cameron strode back and forth along the lip of the stage. "No, the truth is, I've decided to take Pammy to meet my mother."

Stunned silence.

"You *talked* to her?" someone asked.

"*Why?*" another asked, sounding a bit crushed.

No one looked more aghast than Christopher.

Cameron stopped and shrugged his shoulders. "No reason. I don't need a reason. You guys need reasons. I just picked up the phone. We talked for an hour and, lemme tell you, Mom is one powerful lady. Problem is—" He began to laugh in gulps. "Problem is, she puts her power into destroying herself. Her life's a mess!" He laughed in bursts and threw a hand to his forehead. "Oi, what a mess!" He began to pace again. "First of all, she's fat. Real fat. She has *elephantiasis*. Can you believe it? I mean, I thought you had to live in Africa to catch that and she doesn't even leave her trailer!"

No one found any of this as funny as he did, but then, de-

Christopher

spite his august calling, he really was quite a lighthearted little chap. An admirable quality, which called to mind the great Gautama Buddha, who, sitting in the shade of a ficus tree and being told of the world's latest tragedies and misfortunes, used to laugh his big, fat ass off.

When Cameron's laughter had stopped and the redness left his cheeks, he went on. "Maybe you're starting to see why I wanna go down there. My mom's sick. So, what I'm gonna do is bring her something even better than chicken soup. I'm gonna bring her my relationship with Pammy." He stopped and beamed endearingly. "We'll cook for her, teach her about diet, natural healing, exercise. And guess what? I'm not even gonna mention The Weekend. I mean, she said no, right? A million times. Why struggle with it? Instead, I'm just gonna *give* her The Weekend. For free. And she won't even know it. I'm gonna give it to her in the way I am with Pammy. In the man I've become."

I glanced over at Christopher. His eyes were astir. He was thinking, "If only *I* could heal *my* mother in *my* way of being, in the man *I've* become."

"Get real," I whispered.

As that delicious, self-confessed genius, Gore Vidal, once said, three topics inspire immediate interest in any audience: sex, death, and money. As though to prove the first third of this maxim, Cameron abruptly switched gears and applied himself to Interactive Sexuality. Sure enough, not a minute into his talk, every nerve in the room tingled with fascination.

"All sexuality is interactive," Cameron said. "When sex isn't interactive, it's dead. All interaction is sexual. When interaction isn't sexual—isn't based on an *exchange of energy*—it's dead, too. Most sex and most interactions are dead. But once you create interactive sex in your life, and tons *of* it, you're gonna discover something. You'll realize it's unimportant. I know that's hard for most of you to believe, but it's like all Attachments.

Like Approval or God or Survival, all the things that convince you you're limited, that make you suffer, it's just something you gotta let go of. See, that's why I'm always on your back about achieving your goals." His hands were churning the air now. "Not because these things are important, but because once you finally get all the cash and sex and fame you want, you'll see that it's all bullshit. Then you'll get down to the only thing that *really* matters. Which is the creation of meaning in a universe where none exists."

He closed his eyes. Was there more to say?

Yes.

"The Weekend is the most meaningful thing you will ever encounter. It creates a context for you to give the gift of unlimitedness to yourself and to all your loved ones, which is really the only thing in the world that's worth your precious time."

Cameron broke the spell by glancing at his watch. He looked confused suddenly. He turned to an unshapely galoot whose tag read "Hyacinth."

"Where's Pammy?"

"She's late."

"Yeah, I know," he snapped. "Call her at work."

Distracted by the thought of her tardiness, Cameron dropped the subject of sex and returned to his mother. His childhood in Florida was happy, he told us. There was no man in the house. He and his mom were best friends. They took vacations together. Car trips. To Memphis, D.C., Monticello, even out West once, to witness the boom in the desert. And then there were shorter trips. Jaunts, she called them. To the opening of a mall or supermarket, or to a Chinese restaurant she'd heard was inexpensive and good. Once—he wasn't sure when—she came into his bedroom while it was still dark out and drove him up the coast to a path by the beach. They lay on blankets and watched the sun rise over the gray ocean—just the two of them—and the whole time she talked about other sunrises she had seen in other corners of the world and how one day they would take a trip together and watch the sun rise over all of the world's most beautiful cities.

The way Cameron sighed, he might as well have been talking about a dead lover. Dead, because his mother was different now. She was crazy, dirty, untalkative. Her body was grotesque. In a few short hours, she would meet him and Pammy on the broken-down front steps of her trailer and greet them in the humid darkness. Would she be able to see what they had come to offer? Would she be able to experience The Weekend?

I confess I enjoyed this part of the show. Clearly, the man could be captivating when he wanted to be. I imagined having sex with him. Interactive sex. It was not wholly unappealing. He was lithe, and handsome when he refrained from laughing. I snapped out of my reverie when the great man, having reached to a small table and found it empty, shouted, *Where the fuck is my mineral water?!*

A Helper named Jackie ran up breathlessly. She had bobbed, curly hair, white at the edges. Her pitted skin was muddy with foundation.

"I'm sorry!" she cried. "I'll get it! I got busy!"

"You got *busy?*" Cameron moved to her quickly. "God damn it! Something comes up, *delegate!* Cover your ass! *Don't screw me!*"

She nodded, her eyes barely open. "I . . . I got it, Cameron."

"Yeah, I bet! Lamebrain! I wonder if you're capable of getting *anything!*" He slapped the air and turned away.

Perhaps I overestimated his Helpers, but I got the feeling that all of them, even the most blindly obsequious, sensed, along with me, that Cameron's outburst had nothing to do with mineral water. It was the fact that this was a momentous night and Pammy was late. Aware, no doubt, that his tantrum was not inspiring us to dig for our credit cards, Cameron steadied himself.

"Okay," he said, exhaling heavily, "let's try a Process. Everyone stand." There was a muffled scraping of chairs on carpet. "Walk around the room and find someone, anyone. Look into their eyes and the first one of you who feels like talking, talk. Say what attracts you about the other person. Anything. Their eyes, their lips, their hair, their tits. When the speaker's done, the listener says, 'Thank you,' then you move on to someone else. All right? Begin!"

He jumped off the platform and dashed toward the back of the room. I suddenly found myself holding hands with a sparkly-eyed Filipino named Gabriel, who was struggling to name my most appealing feature. I might have ended his suffering by speaking first and telling him how much I liked his nutmeg skin, but I was distracted by Cameron's voice, right behind me.

"Hey, Paul," he said, "is she here yet?"

"Nope."

"Well, well, looks like Pammy's got herself lost. Looks like she's gonna miss out on Florida."

"You'd go *without her?*"

"Damn right. And I was almost getting mad about it, too. Can you believe it? *I* was getting mad because *she's* gonna miss *her* vacation!"

I snapped to attention when Gabriel muttered queasily, "I like your tie."

I wasn't wearing one. It was an ascot. But I thanked him, anyway, and skipped off.

In the next ten minutes, I was told that I had a fun hat, a

Christopher

powerful aura, unique jewelry, big hands, blue eyes, and sym-metrical ears.

Now, it was time for *me* to dole out some applesauce. I spot-ted Christopher, hurdled a chair, grabbed him by the shoulders, and spun him around. He was shocked. I took both his hands in mine. A first. They were moist and soft. An electrical current ran through me. Through us?

"I love your——" I began. But then his face changed. He was filled with dread. "E-e-everything," I stammered. I had no idea why I said it. I had intended to say "smile." My face was prickling and my hands were shaky. He thanked me and sprinted away. I took a step, then stopped. Cameron banged violently through a swinging door.

"Okay, shares!" he said as he retook the stage.

For a moment there was hesitation, then a small girl with eyes like pinwheels stood up. Her name tag read "Beck."

"I just wanna say that Roy said he liked my mouth, which is so cool, because I've always had this habit of chewing on the in-side of it. Here." She pulled open her bottom lip and pointed to a ragged spot. "Anyway, last week I met this guy and I haven't bitten my cheek ever since, because I really like giving blow jobs, but I never really do it much because my mouth is always bleeding, but I like this guy so much I want to be able to do it, so I stopped biting my cheek, and I'm never gonna do it again."

A burst of applause.

Cameron distractedly adjusted the cuff of his plaid blazer. "Great, thanks. Next!"

Six young men popped up. He paused and studied them, then pointed to a fish-faced boy, no doubt a chemistry grad stu-dent, who looked unused to living on the planet.

"I just want to say," the boy began, "that the process helped me see that I shouldn't be here. I'm here for the wrong reason.

I'm just here to get laid!" He laughed in spasms, spittle flying from his lips like steamed milk. All around him, hoots and laughter.

"You're right," Cameron said. "You are here for the wrong reason. But that doesn't mean you won't get laid."

More laughter.

"Next!"

A dozen more disciples stood, including Christopher.

He looked at them, glanced at me, frowned for some reason, then pointed at Christopher. "Look, guys, it's one of our recent Graduates! He was the star of the last Weekend, but he still hasn't signed up to be a Helper yet. Can you believe it?"

While everyone shook their heads, Christopher nervously rolled up a white shirt sleeve. He looked at the floor. When the room was quiet, he spoke. "I had trouble, Cameron. Not telling people why I was attracted to them—that was easy. I had trouble listening to what people had to say about *me*. I didn't want to hear it. I didn't want to be desired."

"Hmmm," I thought.

"Let me tell you something," Cameron said. "You're a fuckin' mess."

Silence.

Christopher swallowed hard. "I know."

Cameron stole an impatient glance at his watch, then said casually, almost as an afterthought, "See, you've gotten creamed a whole buncha times. Ever since you were a kid. So now you don't risk anything. You don't really interact, so you don't really know what sex is. Or love."

Christopher, spooked, sat slowly. I slung out a comforting arm, not around his shoulder (I was afraid), but around his chair.

Cameron continued with the shares. Every few minutes, he

Christopher

would ask us to discuss among ourselves what he had just said and, while we did, he would escape to the back of the room. I could hear him asking Helpers if Pammy had arrived yet. Each time, when he learned that she had not, he would return to the stage with his gestures more frantic and his speech more aggressive. I was fascinated, anthropologically speaking. I had never seen an avatar come unglued before. Finally, he ordered a Helper to put his suitcase in the limo, but to leave Pammy's in her bedroom. When the Helper balked, he shooed him away with impatient scorn.

"One more!" he snapped, "I've got a plane to catch!"

There was confusion until a Samoan-looking woman with a face like a medicine ball rose to her feet.

"Well, I've gotten involved with a very nice man." Her smile was timid but smug. "Our relationship has become *very* serious. A heavy involvement. We've spent the last—"

"*Enough!*" Cameron tore at the air like an insane conductor. The woman gasped and started to sit. "No! Don't sit, Wallawi! I'm *talking* to you!"

The woman rose, bewildered, turning in every direction, trying to find in the equally bewildered faces around her some explanation for his fury.

"Now, you said two things." He started to pace, struggling to remain calm. "First, you said you were involved. Well, I'm here to tell you not to involve yourself! Know what *involved* means? It means there's something in the world that's bigger than you are that you've rolled yourself into!"

"Aren't you involved with Pam?" someone called out.

"Don't you want us to be involved with The Center?"

"A person is at least partially involved if—"

"A person, but *not me!*" Cameron said fiercely. He reached up and wrestled with his tie. "I'm *not* involved with Pam! I'm not involved with *anyone!* That's why I can lead you!" He stopped in the center of the stage. "Because I interact! I play! I flow!"

I heard a scrape. I turned around in my seat. A door had opened. A woman entered. It was Pammy, I knew it. Her hair was short and brown like Cameron's. She was handsome in a gray-eyed-Athena way. Her upper torso was shapely, but her lower half was thick and wide. She wore drawstring pants, a yellow T-shirt, black woolen socks, and Indian sandals.

Cameron noticed her presence.

Then, one by one, so did everyone else.

She opened her mouth to speak, but Cameron pointed at her. "*Shut up!* I'm in the middle of something! Sit!"

A chair slid up behind her.

"Now, let's look at what else Wallawi said. She didn't just say she was involved. She said *heavily* involved."

He looked around the room. Every eye was on him. No one moved or spoke.

"How many of you are fat? Raise your hands! Come on, tell the truth!"

Slowly, there appeared in the air a thicket of hands. Mine was not among them. First, he would have to define his terms.

"Great!" he said. "Over half." Cameron looked over and saw Pam sitting with her hands, boneless, on her lap. "Look, folks, Pammy isn't raising her hand. And if she ain't fat, I don't know *who is!*" He laughed, alone, and resumed his pacing. "Now all of you fatties understand something of the nature of heaviness. Because, just like Wallawi here, you can't imagine involvement *without* heaviness. You're heavily involved with everything you touch! Food, sex, love, hate. And your heaviest involvement of all, of course, is with your own stupid selves! Now, let's take Pammy here." He pointed at her, but no one looked. "She's your Co-founder and, like most of you, she's selfish. But you think

Christopher

that bothers me? Never! 'Cause I don't get involved. I don't get *near* her crummy problems! When I plan a trip and my bags're packed, I don't care if she shows up. Yeah, that's right, babe." He turned his eyes to his wife. "Forget Florida. Forget showing my mother anything. I'm goin' without you."

He barked out a string of laughs. "Want to know why my mother has elephantiasis, folks? Because she's heavily involved with herself, just like Pammy here. I mean, elephants oughta be king of the jungle. But they're not!" He lifted a fist and hit his chest. "Lions are!" His voice was torn and pleading as he turned back to her. "You're a lioness, God damn it! So act like one! You're not an elephant, you idiot! *You're not my mother!*"

Her face was motionless, her eyes calm and inscrutable.

He jumped off the stage, landed, and shouted, "Are you aware that you're late?"

She nodded mutely.

"Are you aware that you broke an agreement with me?"

She nodded again.

"Are you willing to keep your agreements with me in the future?"

Another nod.

"Good." He walked closer, planted his feet, and grinned sweetly, showing the gap in his teeth. "So . . . you ready to go on vacation? Ready to make a difference for someone else? Whaddaya say?"

"Cameron——" She rose tiredly and landed a heavy step. "She's dead."

Cameron's face hardened.

Christopher sat forward in his chair. His eyes were filled with keen and painful interest.

Pammy said in a flat voice, "Before I left work, I called your mom to see if we could bring her anything and her neighbor answered. Last night he noticed her newspaper was still lying on the front lawn. He looked in her window and saw her on the floor. She was okay. She was just lying there. She had a pillow. He took her to the hospital, but they couldn't find anything wrong with her. So they didn't call you. They were gonna release her tonight. But then about two hours ago she died. They don't know why. She just did."

A queer smile wiggled across Cameron's face.

"I guess she didn't wanna see me," he said, trying to make light.

Pam lumbered over to him. As soon as she touched his face, his head dropped and he moaned. His hands fumbled to her stomach. He mashed his loose-lipped mouth into her shoulder. Dry sobs rose through his body like vomit. The Helpers watched as Pammy lifted a heavy arm and curled it around his head to comfort him.

In between stomach cramps, Mr. Friedrich Nietzsche managed to scrawl the following in his notebook: "I must bear the fate of all idealists, who see the object of their adoration tumbling from its pedestal." Even though he had written these words a hundred and eight years before about the superb Mr. Richard Wagner, they might just as well have been written that night by Christopher about Cameron.

Riding the subway home, he was silent. His posture was stooped, his face tortured and gaunt. His eyes, devoid of light, were haunted by their old anxiety. And no wonder. What could be a greater shock to the system of a young believer than to see his savior, upon the death of his mommy, bawling like a baby? Especially when said believer had held up said savior as the perfect embodiment of enlightened detachment toward Mother?

As much as I was secretly pleased that Cameron had tumbled from his perch, I was also touched by the boy's pain. Sitting

Christopher

at his side, as our missile flew through the bowels of the City, I reflected on similar moments from my own life—moments when my golden calves had been slaughtered, my imagined routes of escape violently closed, my most cherished ideals turned to dross. For what is existence, but a systematic assault on our illusions, a continuous excruciating reminder of the vanity of human wishes?

Christopher was growing up right before my eyes.

Walking home, he marked the end of his flirtation with unlimitedness by asking for a fag. I might have refused him, supporting his decision to quit, but I had learned, sometime between my birth and the death-by-overdose of my adoptive mother seventeen years later, that no one can prevent anyone from doing harm to himself. It is best to stay out of the way. The sooner the addict reaches bottom, the sooner he decides whether to live or die. I gave him the rest of my pack.

We turned and trudged down the sloping sidewalk to our dwelling. At Arabia, Patty was visible in the storefront window, readjusting a tangled vine. Christopher did not invest so much as a glance in her direction. We climbed our stairs in silence and stopped on the landing. I proposed a drink. He refused. As he stepped into the shadows of his cell, I decided to offer him a bit of unsolicited counsel.

"Take care of yourself," I said.

He nodded glumly, then shut the door in my face.

June

Not unexpectedly, Christopher sank into an even darker depression than the one that had preceded The Weekend. He stopped showering and shaving, and he rarely left his cell. His mind soured until the future, which had lain before him like a land of dreams, now seemed a gray, profitless promontory. His disgust at the Fates expressed itself in rancor. One evening, apropos of absolutely nothing, he told me that my cologne was "fruity and awful," my blazer "hideous," and my Jean Genet sailor-top "embarrassing." Then, a half hour later, just as I had begun to see straight, he referred to me as a "trust fund baby." My feelings might have been hurt even worse had he not been even more uncharitable toward everyone else. Mary, whom he had always referred to as "Mary," was now "what's-her-face," or, sometimes, most cruelly, "that actress." His mother was now simply "the cannibal." One day, when Arabia was closed for extermination, we shared a platter of Alaskan crab legs at the Parnassus, where he met the divine Cassandra for the first time. The next day, he referred to her as "that weird old hag." Even my

Christopher

beloved Mr. Algernon Charles Swinburne was not safe. Late one night, after I had treated him to a particularly stirring recital of "Hermaphroditus," he snickered and called him a "convoluted, little queer."

Not only did he return with a vengeance to smoking and drinking, but he also began to eat, for the first time in his adult life, flesh. No more falafel; now it was chicken, lamb, and beef, served clucking, baaing, and mooing. While I tend to pity and despise vegetarians, I must say, the way he tore barehanded at these undercooked animals was positively australopithecine. He also took up a more alarming habit. He began to flirt with Patty in a way that can only be described as suicidal. He greeted her with a long, double-breasted hug and wet smooch on the cheek, parted with a few more kisses, and in between tipped her in a way which I found profligate to the extreme.

For some reason, Tarek did not seem to mind. He certainly noticed what was happening (Homer would have seen it), but he never let it interrupt his coarse banter with his dusky pals. Stupidly, the only person jealous of the dalliance was I. Stupid, because I knew perfectly well that his crush had nothing to do with her mind (none), her body (squishy), or even her spirit (demolished goods); it was merely another expression of the boy's desperate need for comfort. Of course, I resented her. I had been there for the lad through thick and thin. I deserved to be his anodyne.

It was time to make my move. I had spent five months oiling the spring, testing the bar, and trimming the bait. Now I would set the trap. The timing seemed good. Not only was he sinking fast, surely nearing bottom, but we had never spent so many nights together and enjoyed such easy intimacy. Recently, he had lighted a fag for me between his own two lips. A few nights before, after I had beaten him at chess for the very first time (while he was in the loo, I had flicked one of his rooks to the floor), he slapped me on the shoulder and called me a "stud."

On Wednesday night, June 13 (the moon full of mischief), I knocked on his door and invited him over for cold pizza. He said no thanks. I suggested we read some poetry together. He said no thanks. I dangled the lure of a nightcap. Fortunately, half his genes were alcoholic. He fell into my sofa and watched eagerly as I poured him a jelly jar of my best Cabernet Reserve (accents of cheddar; dastardly snap of horseradish).

As he grew increasingly woozy, I set the stage by telling him all about the Carlyles' harrowing marriage, the not-so-buried moral of which is the utter implausibility of heterosexual couplings. He changed the subject to Mr. Henry Miller, in whose oeuvre he was now thigh-deep. I told him that his time would be better spent reading a map of the Paris sewer system. He did not reply.

As midnight neared (his speech slurry, eyes heavy), I moved my chair close and plunged into the fray. Flags flying, I began my offensive with a quotation from the brilliant, batty Mr. Aldous Huxley who once said, "Hell is the incapacity to be other than the creature one finds oneself ordinarily behaving as." I boldly suggested that perhaps the only way out of his current hell was to broaden his horizons, explore fresh terrain, push the envelope, experiment with the forbidden, think outside the box, et cetera. As he was no dummy, I fully expected him to read between the lines of these dreary bromides and laugh in my face. But he did not. I was reaching him. His eyes had grown alert and a thousand possibilities seemed to be storming his drunken brain all at once.

I moved closer and continued my assault. As banal words of encouragement poured from me in torrents, his legs eased apart. I eyed the amber stitching of his denimed crotch. My colon grew restless. I hastily shed my tweed (Atlantic Blue),

Christopher

tossed it, and inched my mouth toward the Cupid's-bow of his lips. I explained that all great changes begin with a single step off a precipice; it is only then that one finds one's wings and soars toward the sun.

"You are an artist!" I pleaded. "Your failure thus far will tell you that you are not. So will every indignity foisted on you by our vile, materialistic culture. So will your vengeful mother, but the truth is the truth! It can only be denied at the peril of your soul! You're an *artist*, Christopher! Your only enemy is your fear, your hunger to be ordinary and lead a small, safe life. Since the moment of your birth you've been well behaved, struggling to live up to impossible ideals, but at what cost, my boy? You're blocked as an artist and as a man! It's time to strike out wildly, declare your independence, assert your freedom, *bellow a Promethean No!*"

He grinned.

I lunged.

I slipped and cracked my knee on the floor, splashing my hundred-year-old kilim.

I was in the grip of the grape.

"I hope you have some seltzer," Christopher said, jumping up.

I crawled to my feet, rubbing my smarting cap.

While he worked on removing the stain, I limped in tight panicked circles, my hands in my pockets, struggling to wrangle down my bucking manhood.

"God, relax," he laughed, looking up at me. "It's no big deal. You should probably throw it out, anyway."

Minutes later, we were settled back in our seats. Sadly, the moment was lost. Perhaps because there had never been one. I had reached the boy, yes, but only with my text. My subtext had utterly eluded him, for he began to vamp now on the literal meaning of my hollow words.

"You're right, he conceded. "I'm so fucking sick of being

good! I'm always worrying about everyone else's feelings, but what has it gotten me? Nothing!"

"What would you do, Christopher," I thrummed seductively, desperate to get things back on track. "What would you do tonight if you were bad? *Real bad?*"

A light flickered in his dark eyes.

He smiled mischievously.

A few minutes later, he was gone.

He did not return until sunrise.

I know because I was still awake.

The next afternoon at Arabia, he told me how he had passed his evening.

Rather than return to his lonely cell, Christopher had, encouraged by me and emboldened by Dionysus (born of fire, nursed by rain), ventured out for an evening of "real bad" behavior. He stopped first at a Smiler's convenience store, where he bought a peach wine-cooler (yuck) and a pack of brand-name cigarettes (waste of money), then began his long journey westward. As he walked, he remembered my words. Yes, I was right. No doubt about it. His life was a fucking joke. But tonight he would change that. Every great poet sang of the joy of enriching the soul, but so few ever praised the equal thrill of wrecking it.

He entered Times Square. In those days, it was no theme park ruled by a rodent. It was a sordid quarter, lighted like a gangster film and smelling of the pissoir, home to packs of entreprenoirs who prowled every dismal corner and craven passage, muttering offers of affordable sin. But Christopher was not afraid. His resolve was firm. Beneath his civilized veneer, he told himself, he was actually brave and foul. A man. Tonight, he would plumb the depths of his animal nature.

Christopher

He found the place he sought, an establishment he had passed in countless taxi rides. He finished his cocktail with a hearty gulp, then dropped it along with its paper bag into a trash can. He lifted his arms and pushed through the turnstile as though it were a high, cold wave. A red neon arrow pointed up a mirrored staircase. As he mounted the steps, head spinning, he eyed himself in the glass. His cheeks were blanched and damp, his eyes a bit mad.

The enormous room upstairs was red. Loud music swirled. Flashing colored lights danced along mirrors. He moved to a line of booths. An Asian girl sat in one, a Caucasian girl in the next, then a Black, then a Latina. The Asian blew him a wee kiss. He dropped his eyes and forced himself to walk slowly past each booth. He must choose wisely. But cowardice sized in his chest. He did not dare look at their faces, so he merely eyed their spangly shoes.

Finally, he stopped at a pair of rhinestone pumps and, fighting a facial twitch, defiantly looked up. Innocent eyes stared back at him from beneath an arc of sky-blue shadow and furry brow. The Latina. She was young, dressed in a pink, frilly slip which barely concealed pert breasts that looked sore from recent growth. He did not care for her makeup. He pictured her in his bed in the morning, squeaky clean after a hot shower, greeting him as he came in with her breakfast. Then he remembered with a jolt that the point was to degrade her, not to make her pancakes. He lifted a hand and blew her a nasty kiss.

"Hey, honey," she said, enticing him forward with a long blood-red fingernail. "Only cost you a dollar."

Christopher wheeled around, arms swinging, nearly knocking over a timid senior citizen, and staggered to a counter where he proudly slapped down a crisp bill. The cashier, grim and mustachioed, slid back a silver dollar. Christopher thanked the lady, then returned to the booth and got in. He unfastened his belt and inserted a coin. A plastic divider opened, humming, to reveal a filmy plastic window. The girl sat behind it holding a black receiver to her ear.

"Hi," he said into his phone.

"Hey, there. What's your name?"

"Henry Miller." He sounded confident, but he was growing more frightened by the second.

"I'm Mercedes."

He cleared his throat.

"I'm Henry Miller," he repeated.

She smiled, waiting for him to go on.

After an interminable silence, Christopher blurted impatiently, "Well, show me your tits."

She laughed and pointed a fingernail. "You gotta show me your *thing* first."

Christopher, impatient, dropped the phone, yanked his pants down, and looked at her in a gutsy way.

"Ta-da!" he sang.

A motor hummed and the plastic divider began to fall.

"Hey! Hey! What's going on?! That was only like a minute!" Mercedes waved good-bye, receding to the other side of the earth. More time would cost another dollar. He slammed the divider with a fist, then zipped up, and burst out of the booth. He wanted to debase himself, not get ripped off.

A few minutes later, he dropped another silver dollar into another slot and, again, a divider lifted, but this time it revealed a long, oval chamber. In the center, a naked woman danced wildly to pounding drums. She was emaciated; her body moved like a rope. All around the chamber there were other open windows, each framing a fervid male face. The girl made a slow circuit, then stopped just inches from Christopher's window, snapping her pelvis. She had a short, thin, purple scar on her lower abdomen. She grinned extravagantly and moved in closer, shuffling her feet, shaking her groin in his face like a dust mop.

Christopher reeled out of the booth and thought he might be sick. He staggered toward another bank of booths, marked "Video." He fell in, gasping. When he had sufficiently recovered, he deposited a quarter. The camera whirred. Two French women made oral love in a painter's garret. Nothing stirred in his trousers. In the next film, a Swedish bombshell raised and lowered herself onto the meaty lipstick of a helpless collie. In the last, a buff black buck with luscious breasts plundered the posterior of an All-American surfer boy. (A trenchant cinematic commentary on American race and gender relations in Orwell's year.) As the vignette built to its inevitable climax, our young hero was well aware of what he was supposed to do—the linoleum was sticky beneath his sneakers—but he was entirely unexcited and his bladder ached.

He unzipped his pants and urinated instead.

Midnight found him continuing his toot, traipsing cobble-stoned streets past empty lots and slumbering warehouses. Rather than surrender to the emerging fiasco, he was more de-termined than ever to get it right. He turned a corner. On the other side of the avenue stood a pack of Paphian girls. He saw one that suited his fancy. Leaning against a streetlight, she was generous of thigh and bosom. Her shorts were sparkly red and her high-heels silver. Her big, blond wig was a tumble of waxy curls. Perfect, he thought. If he was going to hire a whore, at least she ought to look like one. And, best of all, she was *black*. He thought of Kenneth Gill, the gentle cabby whose life pur-pose was to honor black heroes with his lens. What would he think of Christopher now? He was about to defile a Nubian princess. Would Kenneth still consider him *very much a human being*? Still suggest he read himself to sleep with something beautiful?

"Ha!" Christopher thought.

He walked to her in as straight a line as he could manage. Boom-boom in the chest, wet hands, shoulders rigid. It was always like this, he lamented, whenever he faced something new and forbidden. It didn't matter if it was a first kiss or a first feel or a first line of cocaine at some awful frat party—he was always afraid. When he got closer, he saw that the woman was half a foot taller than he was. When she noticed him, she grinned and a hand fell to her towering hip.

"Well, well," she said, looking him up and down. "What *have* we here?"

"How much is it?"

"How much you got?" He flashed a bill. "What you think you gonna get for *that?*"

"Everything."

"Not for no *twenty dollars.*"

His lip curled and he shrugged. "Take it or leave it."

He couldn't believe how *male* he sounded.

Much to his surprise, she angrily snatched the bill, then grabbed him by the arm and led him around the corner into a parking lot.

"Don't you have a room or something?" he asked.

"Not for no twenty dollars." She dragged him over to a shadowy bend in the fence and shoved him into it. Within seconds, his jeans and briefs were around his knees.

(Allow me to catch my breath.)

Through his drunkenness, he realized the enormity of what he was about to do. He would never be the same. He was driving a stake, once and for all, through the heart of his idealism. She grabbed the fence with one hand, lifted her skirt, and went up on tiptoe. He jumped back, startled, yelping like a prescient collie.

Christopher

"I'm . . . I'm not ready!" he whined.

She looked down and saw that he was right. She wearily knelt on the rough tar and set to work. He leaned back and laced his fingers into the mesh of the fence. He shut his eyes, longing to escape. That *is* what he was paying for, wasn't it? To lose himself? The pleasure was just the means to that end. He yanked a deep breath and tried to disappear. Soon, he would be free, leaving behind his failed marriage, his spoiled students, his unstarted novel, his utter inability to live. He heard a swish of passing traffic and it incited in his mind a spinning collage of cruising police cars, bright lights, and a mug shot of himself in the *Post*. Then he heard smacking noises and thought of this poor harlot, this hapless victim of Reaganomics, bobbing and gobbling simply to survive another day. He could tell she was growing impatient. Of course she was; twenty bucks and here he was taking his sweet time. Shit, now he had *her* feelings to worry about, something *else* to distract him. He wanted to get it over with as badly as she did, but he was numb and drunk and there were all those cars driving past and those darned smacks and pops. Where were they coming from, anyway? Her sinuses? He opened his eyes and what he saw on her stomach sent a shiver of alarm through him——tiny stretch marks.

"Oh, my God," he whispered. "You have kids!"

She eased back and frowned up at him. "Now how is that any of *your* damn business?"

"Does he know? Your son? Does he know what you do?"

Her eyes flared indignantly. "What's the matter with you? I don't have time to be wastin' with this shit!"

"All right, I'm sorry, but——"

"You some kinda faggot? You gonna bust a nut or not?"

"Hey, you know what?" he cried. "Forget it! Just . . . just keep the money! Please! I insist!"

Surprised, she laughed and stood, then jerked down her skirt and walked away, bidding him farewell with a twitch of her lush derriere.

Across the avenue, a scrawny white colleague of hers walked to the curb as a Checker cab drove up. She said something to the passenger inside and lifted her halter top. The taxi roared away. She screamed an obscenity. The black woman reached her and said something. The white girl smiled and handed her a cigarette. They stood together, smoking and laughing, easy in the summer night. Christopher, watching, doubted they were talking about him. His noble act had already been forgotten. If the full moon had been visible, he would have cried out his anguish to it, but it would not have been much of a cry. He had smoked too many cigarettes and was short of wind.

He trudged away, whimpering. Never in his short life had he felt so defeated. Somehow, his idealism had turned the tables and driven a stake through the heart of his virility. So what if the woman had a kid? She was an adult, for Christ's sake. She *chose* to walk the streets. And, yet, he could not banish the image of her little boy (or was it a little girl?) waiting for Mommy to get back from work. Did Mommy at least gargle before she tucked him in?

"What are you?!" Christopher cried out suddenly, shrill and histrionic. "A man or a *fucking saint?!*"

A homeless man turned and gawped at him, wondering if he was supposed to answer. He could not find a reply, so he went back to foraging in his garbage can.

Dionysus waved his ivy-wreathed wand once more, and the lad stopped for another wine-cooler. Staggering home through Midtown, Christopher wondered if he had been in any way improved by his journey to the center of the night. Had he at least *learned* something? Maybe he really was a saint. Was *that* what he had learned? And was it okay to be a saint instead of a man?

Christopher

And if not, *why* not? Suddenly, he stopped, face-to-face with a curious, little fellow.

" 'Scuse me, s-s-sir—" the stranger stuttered pitifully, his eyes fluttering. "C-c-could you h-h-help me?"

"Shit, I must have Good Samaritan written all over me," Christopher inwardly groused, then he dug clumsily for a quarter.

"N-n-n-o!" the man insisted. "I j-j-just wanna go h-h-home. My wife's waiting for me! G-g-gotta get that last bus! To Ho-Ho-Hoboken!"

Christopher took a closer look. The man wore tawny work boots, jeans, a hooded sweatshirt, and a corduroy jacket—he wasn't homeless at all. He was a laborer.

"What's stopping you?" he asked.

"The t-t-telephone!"

The man took a piece of paper from his pocket and handed it over with a rough hand. It was a bank envelope, folded in two. Christopher unfolded it and on the front in perfect blue script it read: *Mr. and Mrs. Joseph Peters, 360 West End Avenue. For Deposit Box Only.* Then a local phone number.

"I c-c-called the lady, but she h-h-hung up, because I st-st-st—"

Christopher had known a stutterer in college who hated to have his sentences finished for him, but he was too drunk to be thoughtful.

"Stutter?" he suggested.

The man nodded emphatically. "And I wanna return it!" With fumbling dry fingers, the man took back the envelope and opened it. "See? F-f-found it on F-f-fifth Avenue."

Christopher peeked inside and saw two coins framed in cardboard sheaths. The man shook them nervously onto his own palm. Christopher reached for them, but he jumped back.

"Relax," Christopher said, "I'm not a thief, I just wanna take a look."

"I w-w-wanna go home. Last bus to Hoboken. My w-w-wife, she——"

"Yeah, yeah, yeah. Just hold 'em up. Let me see."

The man displayed the coins on his palm a foot away. With his other hand, he pulled tight the hood of his sweatshirt. The first was a Liberty Nickel. The case read: *Good condition, $900*. The second was tiny. On it was written: *French gold piece. XF condition, $1,350*.

"You don't need to take a bus," Christopher said. "Take a cab. You're rich."

"What? No, I'm not! I gotta——"

"Look." Christopher spoke slowly and suggestively into the man's little eyes (as though to a retard or a policeman). "A lot of people wouldn't return these. You understand that, right?" The man looked crushed. "Come on, knock it off. What are you, a saint? Don't you need the money?" The man nodded pitifully. "Well, you could sell these to a dealer for lots of money. Five hundred bucks. Maybe more."

"Help m-m-me call! I-I-I gotta get home! I've g-g-gotta job in the morning!"

Christopher surrendered. "Fine, fuck it, let's go."

Incredible, he thought, as they walked away together, that of all the people to find the treasure, it was one of only a few dozen New Yorkers who would actually return it. And who does he turn to for help, but another saint! Life was wondrous sometimes. His black mood began to lift.

"So what do you do for a living?" Christopher asked, as they reached the pay phone.

"A g-g-glazier."

"Doughnuts or windows?"

Christopher

"T-t-twenty years," he sputtered, then he reached into his pocket.

Christopher waved it away. "It's on me."

"N-n-no!" The man shook his head, dropped in a quarter, and punched out the number, reading it from the envelope.

He handed the receiver to Christopher.

It rang once, twice, three times. Christopher scratched his thumbnail against the command, "Love God," etched into the coinbox.

A breathless woman answered on the fourth ring.

"Mrs. Peters?"

"This is her daughter."

"Did your parents lose some coins?"

"What? You found them?! They're my father's! Oh, thank God!"

"Not me. *Another* Good Samaritan."

"Oh, thank you!"

"The guy who found them—" He turned to the little man. "What's your name, sir?"

"J-J-J—"

"John?"

He shook his head.

"Jacob?"

In one difficult burst, he spit out, "George!"

"George found them. He's a glazier. He stutters. He called you before, but you hung up on him."

"I thought it was an obscene phone call!"

"That's what I figured."

"I'm so sorry! I thought someone had seen me on TV and gotten a hold of my number. I'm on a soap, and, you know, we get these creepy letters all the time. And since I'm here alone . . . my parents're out of town . . . when I got the call, I just—"

"Well, look, don't worry. There's nothing to be afraid of. He's just an honest glazier and I'm a helpful novelist."

Her tone suddenly turned soft and personal. "Oh, you are? That's nice. My *father's* a writer. He writes poetry."

"My name's Chris Ireland."

"I'm Martha Peters. Thank you *so much* for calling."

"A soap, huh?"

"I'm so embarrassed! It's so egocentric of me to think——"

"Who do you play?"

"Twins. Is the man upset with me? I mean, he *will* return the coins?"

"Definitely. He's as honest as they come."

"Thank God! You know, there's a reward."

"What?"

"Oh, yeah, my father placed an ad in the *Times*. Seven hundred dollars. So you tell George to stay right where he is. It'll take me a little while to get there. I just got out of the shower. Where are you?"

Christopher looked up and read her the street signs. He had walked farther than he thought. He told her where he was.

"All right. Let's see . . . I've got the check right here. My dad left it. All I've gotta do is get dressed and jump in a cab. I'll be there in twenty minutes, okay? Don't let him go anywhere."

"Twenty minutes," Christopher repeated.

George grabbed Christopher's sleeve and began to choke: wife, bus to Hoboken, work in the morning. . . .

"Relax!" Christopher pulled his arm free. "Martha, can you get here sooner than that? He has a bus to catch."

"But I have to get dressed. Will he leave the coins with *you*? Does he want money?"

"Hold on." Christopher turned and grinned at the absurd question. "Hey, George, want some money?"

George looked puzzled.

Christopher

Christopher whispered coaxingly. "Go on, take some."

George thought for a moment, then he looked up, his eyes rounding. "Two h-h-hundred?"

"He wants two hundred," he told Martha.

"But he's entitled to seven. My father's more than happy to pay it. All he has to do is wait."

In the silence that followed, Christopher felt his thoughts connect with the woman's; they clicked neatly like billiard balls.

"You know——" she began, "if *you* could . . ."

"No problem."

"Will you? Give him the two hundred and when I arrive, I'll give *you* the check. Why not? You're entitled."

Christopher smiled at the perfect beauty of it. Just when he had thought his idealism had won, the universe was giving him another chance to kill it. The swindling of a common laborer. What would Del Ramsay think of *that*? So much for *this* New Democrat. Then it occurred to him that he might be able to come away with more than cash. This might be a chance for sex. Not just any sex—*actress* sex—the type that Mary had so often refused him. Then he remembered that his crotch was still tacky with slattern-spit. If he didn't shower and then made love to Martha, anyway, that was about as vile an act as he could imagine. It sent a diabolical thrill through him. At long last, the death of St. Christopher!

"I'll give him the money," he said softly, "but instead of waiting here, why don't I just bring the coins to you?"

He waited breathlessly for her answer. He imagined her standing now in her bedroom, naked, her towel pressed against her bare breasts. Her wet hair sent droplets snaking between her slender shoulders. Her long, graceful arms and legs were dotted with goosebumps.

"Would you really do that?" she asked sweetly, touched by his generosity.

"My pleasure."

"Really?"

"Absolutely."

"You're *so nice!*"

"That's me."

"Okay, look, the address is on the envelope. It's on the corner of West End and Ninety-second." She seemed genuinely excited. "And to pay you back—I experimented today with apple pie. Do you like apple pie? The first slice is yours. Would you like that?"

Christopher couldn't believe his luck. He hung up and ran toward a bank machine. He tripped and fell, palms first, off the curb. He had forgotten he was drunk. He crawled up, wiped his stinging, bloody hands on his jeans, then resumed walking, but much more slowly now.

On the way, George grew talkative, saying how happy his wife would be when he came home with the money, what bills she would pay with it. Christopher felt only contempt. How could anyone be so stupid? He saw himself, his *old* self, in the trusting, little nitwit.

"S-s-slow down!" George begged.

"Careful," Christopher thought. Impatience might give him away. He began to walk, one step at a time, like a groom down the aisle.

At the automatic teller, the man asked, "W-w-what about you? Don't you get a r-r-rr—?"

"Nope," Christopher snapped proudly, punching in his secret code. "Don't need it. I'm rich in spirit."

The machine spit out the cash and Christopher handed it over. The man took it with a look of delight, as though it were a clutch of new eggs. Then he reached into his pocket and gave Christopher the envelope.

"We're pretty honest guys, aren't we?" Christopher said,

Christopher

blowing into the envelope and looking inside. The coins were still there. He glanced up with a smile. "We must have had pretty good mothers, huh? Listen, you'd better hurry if you're gonna make that bus."

"Th-th-th——"

"Don't mention it."

They shook hands and parted.

In the taxi, Christopher sat back, head spinning, palms burning, and planned his strategy. It was almost three; he would have to work fast. She would still be in her robe. One look at him and she would immediately relax. She couldn't possibly expect him to be as good looking as he was. He would pocket his reward, then he would gobble the pie, sip the tea. The lights would be low. In a moment of spontaneous emotion, he would recite a poem. From memory. One of the Millay sonnets that had worked so well with the girls in college. Something about death——its length and breadth——how it beckons in the rain and rips the sleep in two. Lyrical shit like that. And then, when he was finished, he would lean across, and, feigning shyness, brush a kiss across her All-American lips. She would ease back, her robe opening.

Christopher looked up into the rearview mirror, into the rheumy eyes of a young Liberian cabby. "Guess what?"

"What?"

"I'm about to make six hundred dollars for a half hour's work."

The hack cracked a grim smile.

"I'm serious. And I'm gonna get laid, too. Is this a great country or what?"

Christopher handed the cabby his last eight dollars and jumped out on the corner of West End and Ninety-second Street. He removed the envelope, read the address, then looked up at the number on the nearest building. Not even close. His face twisted. He dug into the envelope and removed the coins. He studied the Liberty Nickel. It was worn with age, as smooth as a cathedral step. His mouth fell open and he grabbed the other coin. It was French, all right. A ten-centimes piece minted in 1979. Mind reeling, he dashed to a pay phone and punched out the telephone number. Again, "Love God" was etched into the coinbox.

After twelve rings, a man answered.

"Is Martha there?" he asked.

"Who?"

"Martha Peters."

"This is a public phone. At the Port Authority."

Christopher hung up slowly. He glanced over his shoulder, as though he expected someone to be there, watching. But the avenue was empty. He looked up. The sky was empty, too.

When Christopher finished his story, he dropped his head into his hands, clutched his hair, and groaned. Patty, a trained food-service professional, ever alert to behavioral nuances, called out from across the restaurant, asking if he needed more iced tea. Scowling, I waved her away. This was no time for her bovine ministrations; the boy was in ruins. (No surprise. It is often the case, after a debauch, that one feels more lost and alone than before.) But I was not well either, because something frightful was happening inside my chest. A sharp, unfamiliar ache. I thought it might be a heart attack. Or perhaps Tarek had served me, among the raisins in my House Special Rice, a sprinkling of mouse dung. And then the truth hit me.

I nearly fell out of my chair.

I was in love.

While such an event, for you, Sentimental Reader, might be

commonplace, for me it was nothing short of a cataclysmic second.

"My God, is this how it happens?" I thought. "An arrow from out of the blue?" Then it occurred to me that Cupid's shaft might have been flung months before, even, perhaps, on the morning I first met the boy, and I had been too arrogant to feel it. But Cassandra had felt it. Of course she had. It explained her enigmatic smile and her cockamamie suggestion that the boy and I were destined to be wed. And then it occurred to me that perhaps I *had* felt love winging toward me, but only in my blood, not in my conscious mind. Was this why I had once longed to give the boy a tender mother's hug? Was this why my fancy could not banish the image of Christopher from its nightly roving? Was this why I had been willing to sacrifice myself body and soul for the boy? I wanted to sing. Or, at the very least, reach across, take my beloved's bitten hands, and kiss them tenderly.

It might surprise you to learn that I had only fallen in love once before, but it was true. It happened in college and ended tragically a few years later. I had been, ever since, a hopeless Invalid of Eros. The underlying reason for my unwillingness (or incapacity) to love again I had long ago narrowed down to the following: my birth mother's abandonment of me when I was six hours old; my adoptive father's repeated molestation of me until I was nine, my adoptive mother's successful suicide attempt when I was seventeen, and the fiasco that had ensued the *first* time I had fallen in love. Regardless of which was the cause (perhaps all four), "hornier than a three-balled tom cat" was how Cassandra had once described me, and she was right. With my heart so well defended, every yearning for union I had harbored since that first rejection had started and ended with my glands. Yet, here I was, at the outmost verge of my forty-eighth year, longing not to "make the beast with two backs" with the boy (only those who have actually viewed me making love can really understand what Shakespeare was getting at), but to comfort him, wrap him in my flabby, freckly arms and rock him gently, late into the night.

I could feel in every fiber of my being the very inscape of our future together. I would slow him down, mend his tattered spirit, hold him safely until everything dire in him settled and his pain found its true voice in tears. And for me he would do the opposite. His energy would stir me, lift me from my melancholic moods. There were days when I traveled the streets of this filthy maze like a piece of barely animated matter—every word, every gesture, numb and automatic. What a divine rescue it would be, I thought, to lie with my head on his lap and listen to him talk a blue streak. With such a bright and voluble companion, I would rediscover hope. And, by way of thanks, I would love him as he had never been loved before.

Sitting there, head down, picking at my salad, doing my level best to conceal from Christopher the revolution going on inside me, I groped for something to say. I understood for the first time the notion that love makes one inarticulate and pathetic.

Finally, I sat back and yanked off my bib.

"I think you should see a therapist," I blurted.

He lifted his eyes from his bloody lamb. "*What?*"

I opened my coin purse and flipped through my vast collection of business cards. Of all the experts in the field of whom I had firsthand knowledge, none seemed a better fit for Christopher than Dr. Gaby Geitman. A no-nonsense Jungian from Long Island (of the Great Neck Geitmans), she had saved my life just a few years before. I had consulted with her after a bad week, which began with my discarding my medication, reached its climax with my staggering in my bathrobe and slippers in search of an affordable backyard barbecue, and ended with my slapping a Puerto Rican cop. Because the judge believed that I had provoked the incident (in fact, it had been the cop's tone of voice), I was sentenced to six months of psychological counseling and ordered to return at once to my twice-daily snack of lithium. I cannot say that I remembered a great deal about Dr. Geitman, except that she provided free tissue and did, in the end, *reach* me—no small feat. Her bottom-line counsel was for me to stick to my medication and never correct a cop's grammar.

I handed him Dr. Geitman's card. The gesture was generous, yes, born of second love, but, truth be told, it was also a tad selfish. When one writhes for the first time on a shrink's leather, there is absolutely no telling what one might discover. He might discover that Cupid had flung *twin* arrows on that fateful day in January. He pocketed the card, but I feared from his sickly expression that he intended to throw it away.

The fortnight that followed was the worst in Christopher's young life. Heat. Rain every weekend. His divorce made final. Calls from friends left unreturned, calls from Grace returned. (Each was a hammer blow to his failing spirit. She gave him updates: Grammy was, miraculously, much improved, fully conscious now, but still incoherent and unable to stand. A bedsore the size of a baseball had opened on her rump. Then Grace would talk about herself. Endlessly. Once, Christopher dropped the phone, splashed water on his face, opened a bag of corn chips, then ran out for a pack of cigarettes, only to return and find her still working her fatuous way through the same Jamesian sentence.) Yes, June had been unspeakable. His flow of students was drying up, he had yet to commence *Love's Sad Archery*, and twice there was blood in his stool. (It was not rectal cancer, which would have at least been *something*, a distraction; it was hemorrhoids, old ones, aggravated by poor diet and buried rage.) Some nights he slept not at all, tossing and turning, wracked by sweats, or else staggering through seedy quarters, broken-hearted, drinking, muttering dismal clichés. His days were spent in bed, hungover, his large head propped up by pillows, reading biographies, dreaming of the works he might have written and the life he might have led if only he had been born whole.

Soon it would be July.

Another month.

Another month beginning with *J*.

He still had not rung Dr. Geitman.

As for me, I was forced to stand by and watch my beloved suffer. Of course, I yearned to save him, but, as I've said, I know the folly of jumping in after a drowning person. You dream of hauling him to shore for a life-saving mouth-to-mouth, but all too often you end up locked in his arms on the ocean's floor. Some days, I cried with frustration. Some days, I wanted to slap him silly, but, as I knew that clinical depression knows no discipline, just as it knows no succor, I did not. Instead, I waited for the day when he said, "Enough!" and reached for Dr. Geitman's card.

Which is not to say that during this period I did not have demons of my own to combat. One night, frightened by my newly discovered love and the pain it was causing me, I rebelled, burrowing deep into my cookie jar. Just like Christopher in Times Square, I, too, sought to drive a wooden stake through my idealism (even though mine was still in diapers). My destination was a club lying near the Fifty-ninth Street Bridge. Within moments of my hopping a stool, a half-dozen slim Asiatics converged on me as though I were a tourist in a Third-World bazaar wearing a suit made of cash. They grinned, preened, and flounced, pretending they actually liked me, and all they asked in return was that I buy them and myself a ten-buck bottle of beer. Later, when my six ounces were drained, I took the lad of my choice by the hand (tinier than the rain's), and hauled him into the shadows of the bridge and had my way with him——which was for him to have his way with me.

Historically, such a divertissement would have cured whatever ailed me, but history did not apply. No mere words, even in Newspeak, can describe the despair I felt after that little lichee pocketed his hefty fee and wobbled off on his tiny pumps. My remorse was out of all compass. I felt as though I had committed some unpardonable crime not only against Christopher and against myself, but against some pure, incorporeal thing that hovered over both of us. I might as well have squashed a nightingale or wronged a skylark.

As I was as much a stranger to shame as I was to romantic love, I sought to banish it with excessive cocktails and bracing immersions into cold baths of Mr. John Milton, but the soul-stain remained. A day or two later, I decided, in a fit of self-delusion, that the reason for my troubles was obvious: *I had chosen the wrong lad.* I grabbed my blazer and cap and returned to the bar, like a monkey to his vomit. There, surrounded by gaudy mirrors and whirling disco lights, I plucked out a lad even more nimble, even more delectable, only to be left, at passion's end, with my despair redoubled. Yet, the very next night, I set out again.

July

On Wednesday morning, Christopher and I were awakened by an explosion. Our eyes flew open simultaneously. I wrote it off as a car bomb and flung myself back to sleep. Next door, Christopher correctly identified the noise as that of a large firecracker, but he did not sleep. The air was as stagnant and hot as mutt's breath. His temples pounded from last night's mistakes. He pressed his chest into the mattress and tried to resubmerge into Lethe. What surprised Christopher was that he could not. Although he might have *appeared* to be sleeping, and at times let out sounds that resembled snores, behind his lids he was alert, even, much to his own confusion, giving serious thought to what he would do with his day.

Ten minutes later, when he swung his feet to the floor, his skin bore the crisscross markings of the mattress and his eyes were puffy. He ran a hand through his hair—it was crusted with salt. He pulled open the venetian blind by his bed. The room reverberated. He lifted an arm as though to block a blow and fell back on the bed, squinting into Helios's fiery eye. He had not opened the blind since Mary's departure. Why now? The whole

Christopher

thing was like a dream. Why was he getting up so early? Why was he torturing himself like this?

He walked into the living room and looked around. It was overrun with newspapers, dirty dishes, take-out cartons, and wine glasses. Is it possible he had actually lived here with a fussy wife? He crossed the room, slowly, carefully, watching his shapely feet as they stepped over empty cans, half a banana, his father's wristwatch, cassette tapes, the crematorium of a toppled ashtray. It was not until he was already in the shower, embracing himself in a shiver against the chilly blast, that it occurred to him that he had not showered first thing in the morning for the past three weeks.

"I'm definitely dreaming," he thought.

But he was not. He was being mysteriously stirred to action. The hot water kicked in, thick steam rose, and his hand lifted a razor to his stubbly chin. Why was he shaving? He had no reason to.

Leaving the loo, naked, he noticed an odd sprightliness in his step, and, before he had time to consider, he was reaching for the phone and punching out a number. After two rings, my machine picked up. My voice was authoritative and perhaps sexy. " 'As poetry was created and invented for the delight of our souls, if it comes short, ever so little, from the summit, it sinks to the bottom.' Horace said that. So there."

He listened to the beep, then to the sound of the tape running. He wanted to say something, but he did not know what. Another beep and the machine clicked dead. He hung up, his brow pulled tight. Who else could he call? No one. Since his divorce, all his friends had fallen away. Or had they been pushed? He looked at the television, dazed, then crawled forward and grabbed the remote control. He watched as a contestant spun a large wheel. He flipped to a soap opera and saw the earth spinning on its axis. A news magazine lay next to him on the floor.

The cover showed a teenage black boy spinning on his head. Why was everything spinning today? Christopher reached for a pack of generic cigarettes, squeezed, and found it empty.

He flipped to the news. A young Peace Corps volunteer had been beaten to death by a villager in Togo. They flashed a picture of the young woman and spoke of her idealism and generosity. Watching, he felt tears pool in his eyes. He did not know what to make of them. He had not cried in any way large or small since Mary left. Why now? He didn't even know the girl. Did he see *himself* in her?

He turned the channel. A Fourth of July parade was starting soon on Wall Street. He imagined himself moving along with the mass of red, white, and blue. He was vastly happy, waving a flag. The image would ordinarily have made him sick, but now it was good. He was tired of being miserable.

Christopher awoke two hours later to the sound of whispers in the hall, followed by a fiery fizzing. A snake of explosions crackled. A child laughed and ran away. Then Christopher heard the barbarous shouts of Muscat Xuereb, our Maltese super. He crawled over and listened with his ear to the door. Whimpered pleas. The crack of a slapped face.

He rose to his feet and snapped off the television. It was a holiday and no one was slapping *his* face, no one was pulling *him* indoors—he was living in a free country and he ought to take advantage of it. He would visit Grammy. But, no, if he did, Grampy would tell his mother, and, by the time he got back, his answering machine would be full of her voice. There had to be a better way to celebrate. For inspiration, he opened the window. He blinked into the sun and saw an old thermometer attached to the sill just a few inches away. He had never noticed it before. It read seventeen degrees. It was broken. Four stories below, the street was its usual furnace-clot of cars. Directly beneath him, a spavined old man emptied a urine bag from around his ankle into the gutter. A young black girl stood nearby, watching in horror. Her friend was ten feet away, shielding her eyes, calling the man nasty. Christopher thought of himself in Times Square. She was right, the old man *was* nasty; all men were. Or was it only white men?

The phone rang.

He grabbed it.

"I heard a pained silence on my machine," I croaked. "It sounded like one of yours."

He chuckled. "Yeah, it was. How *are* you?"

"Asleep. What's the matter? Now you sound like you've won the lottery."

"Do I? Yeah . . . I just . . . I dunno . . . feel *happy*, I guess."

"How wonderful for you. As a person."

"Seriously. You wanna do something?"

"Come again?"

"Go out. Have some fun."

"Why?"

"It's a holiday."

"Oh, *please*. Where was your patriotism on Flag Day?"

"When's Flag Day?"

"Three weeks ago tomorrow, you pinko. Open up, I'm catching my death."

Christopher threw on jeans and a T-shirt and opened his door. There I stood, barefoot, wrapped in white chenille, my wet hair loosely turbaned. I held a yellow princess phone connected to a thirty-foot cord.

"Let me *see* this happiness of yours," I said.

My eyes narrowed and I scrutinized. Yes, no doubt about it. His eyes were gleaming again—just as they had been when he first met Blandina, when he first signed up to work for Hart, when he first told me about The Weekend. It struck me suddenly, with a shock, that the boy might very well be suffering

129

from manic-depressive illness. How else to explain these sudden shifts in mood? I happened to know quite a bit about the disease. Not only had I been falsely diagnosed with it myself on more than a half-dozen occasions (in fact, I am cyclothymic), but my adoptive mother had suffered from an acute case—until she was cured overnight by a bottle of sleeping pills.

"And *why* do you feel so good?" I probed suspiciously, as I stepped inside and hung up the telephone.

"I don't know," he said, following suit. "But it wasn't something I ate, that's for sure. I haven't eaten in a day and a half."

"Something you drank?" I asked, with a "don't you dare lie to me" stare.

"Nope. And I doubt last night's wine would have made me feel any better."

"I beg your pardon?" I had served him a fast-flowering seven-dollar Capriccio, with a bouquet no bride in her right mind would waste on a pack of spinsters.

He laughed sweetly. "Come on, it was the worst ever. Where did you buy it, a filling station in the Bowery?"

"As a matter of fact—"

"Well, I don't care why I feel good. All I know is, my will to live is back. It was inevitable, I guess. I mean, there's no way I could have felt that rotten forever."

He was twenty-five, for heaven's sake, what did he know about the human heart and how long it can feel rotten? But before I could tell him as much, it struck me that maybe it wasn't a mood disorder at all: *Maybe the lad was in love with me!* It would explain everything: the restored gleam, the reborn will to live, and why I was the first person he called to share the news. As though reading my mind and wanting to disabuse me of my delusion, he laughed and whacked me on the shoulder.

"Come on, let's go! Throw on one of your kooky getups!"

Christopher

His words were hurtful.

By way of rebuttal, I chose my best Hebridean three-button and a traditional Kerry walking cap.

When we arrived, the highway was already swarming with pedestrians, joined in an exodus south. On foot, on bike, on skates, in strollers, thousands of Manhattanites, desperate for any distraction from their dreary, untenable lives, hurried to get as close to the launch site as possible. Fifty yards ahead lay a tunnel. When we reached its dark mouth, I stopped nervously.

"That's far enough," I said.

"But if we—"

"Sorry, kiddo. I don't *do* tunnels."

"Why not?"

"They appear in my dreams, baring teeth." I turned on my heel and walked to a concrete wall. He hurried up behind me, pointing to the Fifty-ninth Street Bridge which jutted out just below us.

"Isn't that going to block our view?"

I reached into a crumpled paper bag and unscrewed a flask of bianco. "If it doesn't, that might." I flicked a wrist at a heliport just a few hundred feet away. "But who cares?"

"I do. I don't want to miss a single firework."

"Well, tough titty."

Now that I knew my beloved's high spirits had absolutely nothing to do with me, they were beginning to cloy. It was the height of bad taste, this sort of boyish rah-rah coming from a lad who just weeks before had signed his name on the floor of a peep booth with a jet of urine.

Were we on the verge of our first quarrel? I wondered.

My answer came quickly.

Grinning, Christopher suddenly ejaculated, "I love this stupid holiday! I love this ugly town! I even like you, you freak!"

My knees went weak. I did not know which word hurt worse, "like" or "freak." I turned and looked at the basin where the river gathers and purls before slinking its slimy way to Randall's Island. I could barely see through the scrim on my own tears. It was hard to breathe, but I had to say something. If I did not, he would look over and notice what he had done and I would die of embarrassment.

"In the words of Mr. Charles Baudelaire," I gasped, cramming my agony into a tiny box at the base of my spine, 'The masses are born fire worshippers.' " I held up an imperial but quivering hand. "But as I am not of the masses, I dislike fireworks. In fact, I detest them. Good night!"

I started to walk away, but he grabbed hold of my tweed and jerked me back. He pointed to a group of children who had settled nearby. I wiped my eyes and looked. A burly Sapphist wearing overalls and a painter's cap knelt in front of a deformed retard, slapping his limp hand, telling him, not, not, not to eat pebbles! I then noticed that *all* of her charges were either retarded, deformed, or handicapped, or a unique combination of the three. Nearby, a blind boy sat propped on the curb. He stared up, his useless eyes scanning the sky like arbitrary spotlights. Next to him, a little girl sat flat, legs agog, saliva dripping like egg white from her fat lips. Every few seconds she sneezed convulsively and her head snapped down, nearly hitting her knees. My stomach fluttered. I gulped grape.

Christopher gawked at the children: their huge, distended faces, their oversized joints, their scrawny limbs as white as marble. The one that really caught his eye was the most pitiful, the pebble-muncher, who sat slumped against the cement wall like a stringless marionette. His attenuated torso was a jumble of flippers. Now that his handler had upbraided him, she was making all nicey-nice, offering him a drink from a wineskin. The tot nodded excitedly and emitted a barking squawk. She laughed and let fly a squirt of orange liquid. His eyes shut and his long tongue unfurled. The ade flowed copiously from the corners of his mouth and down his Cyndi Lauper T-shirt. I suppose it should have made me grateful for my own gifts, but it did not. It only made me sad.

Christopher turned back to me and, again, I saw that awful gleam. I looked away, down at the dark water that danced with the beaded lights of the bridge. "Good Lord," I thought, "no wonder I've fallen in love with him. He's as insane as my adoptive mother." After severe depressions, she, too, had exhibited sudden shifts toward vivacity. In fact, she sometimes grew so adorable that she forgot to feed me. This is why the "freak" remark had cut me so deeply; my mother, too, when giddy, had always known exactly where to insert the needle. Christopher sighed, clearly disappointed that I had yet to utter a single sympathetic word about the children.

"You know," he reflected softly, "sometimes you think you've got it all figured out, then you see something like that. . . ."

"I *never* think I've got it all figured out," I said, a bit more snippily than I would have wished. I was afraid to let him know that the children had moved me.

Soon, the wall was crowded. All around us, goons unfolded lawn chairs and jerked smelly babies out of strollers. A couple unstrapped their little girl and settled her next to us. Her eyes were as round as coins and sparkling brown. (She looked a bit as I imagined Christopher might have looked at that age.) She eyed him sidelong, sneaky. He smiled at her, then clenched his teeth and crossed his eyes. She giggled, covering up. Suddenly, cheers, shouts, and everyone waved. A police boat motored past. The mayor, fat-waisted, mugging absurdly, stood inside, arms uplifted. He gave closeted homosexualists an even worse name. Christopher was not watching him, however. His eyes were fixed across the river, to where a bloody dusk stained the east. I watched as a deep, inexplicable exhilaration took hold of his spirit. (Another symptom of mania.) He inhaled the night air with a force like lust. A cry lodged in his throat. He wanted to howl, expel his joy into the sky like a rocket for us all to see.

"Let me tell you," he muttered, finally. "I wouldn't trade my life for anyone's!"

"Who's offering?" I tarted.

"Jesus Christ, will you knock it off?! What's wrong with you?! Why won't you let me feel good?!"

Shocked by his attack, all I could do was whimper, "Are you aware that periods of bottomless despair followed by periods of baseless elation are symptomatic of something known as *manic-depressive illness?*"

He burst out laughing. He thought I was joking. His anger at me was gone. He slapped me affectionately on the back and sighed. "God, what a beautiful evening. I love everything just the way it is. It's even okay that we have people like that." He gestured toward the hopeless tots. "I accept it all. All that exists is holy."

He turned around in search of something else to praise and was stopped by the sight of a young homosexualist. When the wind blew, his clothes snapped around his wasted body like a flag. His hollow eyes stared back at Christopher unamenably, almost defiantly. He was clearly dying.

"I like *him*, too," Christopher said softly, his face suddenly square and serious.

The dying boy then met my eyes and grimaced, as though I were unsightly. He turned and whispered something to an old tea hound at his side, who looked at me and began to nod. Then the young man looked back at Christopher. He and my beloved stared at each other without moving. Christopher wanted the boy to know that he understood, knew that this was his last summer on earth, and that he felt his pain. The young man's eyes slowly changed. They began to shine warmly. Christopher was about to smile when suddenly the boy looked up. His eyes filled with a wonder that was almost like terror. Christopher spun around, just in time to see the first missile burst at the top of its flight, then arc into a shower of slowly falling fire.

Back on the avenue, we walked in silence. Between us and utter darkness there was only the lurid guide of streetlights. With each block we traveled, our silence gained volume. We turned west and walked up our street.

"Let's get something to eat," he said. "I'm starving."

"No, thanks."

"Why not?"

"Any more excitement and I run the risk of a coronary thrombosis."

He laughed. "Oh, come on."

I stopped at our stoop. "No, really, I'm not interested. I have some reading to do. Tonight, the saddest of all English poets, Alfred, Lord Tennyson. Good night."

"Are you serious?"

"Look, you're ecstatic," I snapped, no longer able to conceal my hurt. "While I am merely *me*. Just a sad, old—What was the word you used? Oh, yes—*freak!*"

He burst out laughing. "Is that why you're being so nasty? Come on, I didn't mean it. I was just kidding."

"Clearly not."

"It was a joke! I swear!" He patted my shoulder.

Instead of feeling better, I felt patronized. Humiliated. I wished I had kept my mouth shut. My blouse was soaking wet. I longed to be alone with my wounds.

"Come on, big guy, don't bail on me," he urged. "You can be in a good mood, too, you know."

"Really? Do you have some cocaine?"

"You don't need drugs. Come on, let's go some place fun. It's New York! It's summer!"

His face was flushed and his eyes were glimmering again.

"No celebrating for me," I said softly, turning away. "I'm poor, ugly, and unlovable."

How and when had I turned into a Hebrew mother?

"No, you're not. You're just like me. You're just scared of life."

That was the last straw. I narrowed my eyes and spit haughty venom, "Why, thank you, Grace, for the free diagnosis!" With that, I skipped up the steps to the front door. I flung it open, and then, just to make myself feel even worse, I turned around and looked. Christopher, head down, was walking away. No wonder it had been thirty years since I had allowed myself to fall in love. It was excruciating. I would have stopped loving him at once if only I had known how. I climbed the steps to my apartment, and, grieving that I did not enjoy fireworks, hurled myself face-down on my queen. My sheets smelled of ganja. I had not changed them since my night with Claude.

Meanwhile, Christopher reached First Avenue where the sign flashed at him in orange. Without thinking, he dashed across. By the time he stopped running, clutching his side, he had traveled ten blocks.

Then he glanced over and saw her.

His favorite student.

At one time or another, I had seen or met all of Christopher's tutees, but had never considered them to be a threat. They were, as a rule, spoiled, wealthy jail bait. I had not, however, seen or met *this* child, due to the fact that even Christopher had met her only once. But I had certainly heard all about

Christopher

her. Just weeks before at Arabia, during his enlightenment period, he had told me every detail of their meeting. At the time, I
thought nothing of it. So what if he was smitten? She was a
chicken dinner.

Even though, after so many years, it still pains me to discuss
her (the green-eyed monster mounts me even now as I write),
you deserve, Brave Reader, the whole truth and nothing but.

One afternoon Christopher received a panicked call from
his employer, asking him to do what he dreaded most: teach a
class. He threw on his clothes, ran to a nearby private school,
found the room, burst in, and strode to the lectern, asking politely for everyone to shut up. The class was the usual intellectual mess.

He began with an eye-opener. "Turn to test four. These first
questions are in the form of analogies. Analogies are relationships. You all know something about relationships. You have
them, crave them, demand them, destroy them, right?"

Only a couple of students smiled.

He found an example in his workbook. "Okay, look at answer C: 'Narrate' is to 'Climax.' Is there a relationship here? Are
the words linked? Can you make a sentence between them that
defines their relationship?" A few of the smarter students shook
their heads. "Of course, there's a relationship! Never narrate
your climax!"

A handful of students laughed and a dozen more sat up as
though yanked. Within minutes, he had them in the palm of his
hand. Each of his naughty jokes inspired a domino wall of laughter tumbling to the back of the room.

He began a vocabulary drill. "Inveterate, chronic, egregious,
flagrant, pathological, remorseless, consummate, glib! All
words to describe liars. It's good to learn words in groups."
Then he turned to a boy and asked him what "egregious" meant.
The boy's answer was egregiously wrong.

The door opened. There she was. Doing her best to enter silently, she slithered between desks, but it only made her entrance all the more noticeable. Christopher smiled. He was ready to address her tardiness, nail her to the wall with a playful pin. But when she looked back at him, he could not. His jaw eased open and his arms fell to his sides. The class noticed his dreamy focus and turned to its source. What they saw was a small, round girl with pale skin under a thick carpet of black hair. Her small black eyes were suffused with, but not encumbered by, a deep, delicate sadness. Her nose was a button.

The drill went on, but for Christopher it was over. Unable to control himself, he delivered almost everything he said directly to this new arrival. Finally, he pointed to her and a tingle ran up his arm.

"What's your name?" he asked.

A smile appeared and disappeared across her face like a zipper opening and closing. "Daniella."

"Antediluvian!" he said loudly, using a brisk polysyllable to conceal the fact that he was altered.

"Antediluvian . . . antediluvian . . . antediluvian . . ." She smiled into space and wriggled in her seat. Her hands swam as she conjured.

"If you can't put it in words," Christopher said, "why don't you act it out for us? Do an interpretive dance."

The class laughed, but instead of retreating into shyness or hurt, Daniella sat up higher than before and looked at him with glee. Suddenly, Christopher felt like a Fifth Avenue store window dusted with snow on Christmas eve. He used vocabulary to give voice to his feelings. He told her he would give her words until she got one wrong, then he would move on to the next student.

"Reverie," he said.

"A dream," she replied, wearing a sleepy expression.

"Pulchritude."

"Physical beauty."

"Angst," he gasped.

"Uhmmm . . . worried. Upset, anxious."

"Antediluvian."

She burst out laughing. A hand flew to her mouth.

"What?" he asked. "You haven't learned it yet?"

"Adam and Eve?" she asked.

"Yes," he said, "absolutely."

As the lesson progressed, the rest of the room grew sluggish. Their chins in their hands, they battled sleep, their faces dripping down their arms like candle wax. But Daniella was upright. Her eyes never left him. When he dared to stare back, they gently flared, as though asking, "What? Am I doing something wrong? All I'm doing is looking at you. I like looking at you, but if you think it's wrong, I'll stop." He suddenly found himself, for the first time since his separation, yearning to hold a woman in his arms. But, of course, it could not be she. She was just a child.

The class ended.

As the kids shuffled out, Daniella sidled up to him, flashing a guileless smile. She asked if it would be possible to receive private instruction from him—she liked his teaching style. He smiled politely and told her no, it was impossible, absolutely impossible, he was booked, then he grabbed his workbook and sprinted away.

The night he shared with me this tale of self-restraint, he was proud of himself and deeply relieved. He had done the right thing, the only thing, and the best part was, it was a test he had to pass just once. As he was rarely asked to teach a class, there was no reason he should ever see her again as long as he lived.

He was wrong, of course, because on that holiday night, at the precise moment that I contemplated suicide, the Fates served her up again, this time on a silver platter. (If I had imagined such a thing were possible, I would never have let him venture out alone.) She sat, companionless, framed by a café window, reading a paperback. He stepped closer. She was everything he remembered. Pale skin, shocking against the ebony of her hair, perfect teeth, sweet, sad eyes. His heart surged. She was a ball of flowers. The complete opposite of Mary.

During sex, Mary had held him in a muscled grip. He would lie on her heavily and kiss, grab her hair and pull it back ever so slightly, not to hurt, but to remind her and himself that she was in a man's hands. And she would respond as heroines did in the romances she loved—rolling her eyes and murmuring amorous nonsense. But then, all too often, fear would get the best of him. Like an actor bungling his business, he would wrestle with his zipper, struggle to kick off his shoes, and she would laugh. In a flash, the soft focus was gone, the candles were blown out. Don Juan was dead. There was nothing left but the deed.

He knew it would be different with this girl.

Clearly, Sirius was on the ascent that night, because, before he knew it, Christopher found himself standing inside the café. She wore a man's white shirt that reached to the thighs of her striped pants, covering all that was abundant. He understood why. None of her peers could possibly appreciate her body. In more civilized times, she would have been carried naked on a chaise longue, from painter to painter, an Impressionist's luscious ideal. She stopped and checked her plastic wristwatch, then she turned and looked off into the middle distance with a serious expression, like a chary shepherdess. He couldn't stop himself. He walked confidently to her table and said, "Serendipity."

She looked up, startled.

"Remember me?" he asked with a smile.

She slowly smiled back. "Of course. You're that substitute."

Christopher

"That's right."

"What're *you* doing here?"

"Just walking by. I saw you. How did you do on your test?"

"Great. Double 710s. My counselor doesn't even think I have to take 'em again."

"Hey, good for you. Do you mind?" he asked pointing to the chair across from her.

"Please," she said, "but only if you promise to use a lot of big words. You know, in case I decide to take the test again. I'm a total sponge."

He sat and touched back the cover of the book she was reading.

It was *1984*.

For the next hour, he interrogated her. She lived on Fifth Avenue, with her mother, an opera singer. Her father was a Cuban painter and he was dead. She attended one of the best private schools in the city and hated it. She had no real friends there. She hated the parties, the drugs, the drinking, the loud music. Her best friends were her cousins, but they lived in Florida. She couldn't wait to go to Yale, as her father had, to be free, to actually learn something. But that was still a ways off.

He asked her how old she was and she said, "I'll be seventeen in three months."

As she spoke, her hands ducked, darted, swooped, and spun, carving the air like swallows at dusk. She talked of her early childhood abroad, her lonely summers in Newport, her odious stepfathers. Finally, he interrupted and asked what she intended to study at Yale. She dropped her hands into her lap and told him to guess, because she had absolutely no idea.

"An actress?" he floated.

"No way!" she said, nearly spilling her cappuccino. "I'm not *totally* insane. Besides, I'm way too fat."

Leaving the diner, walking through elephants of shadow,

they were accosted by three short-legged classmates of hers. They had a happy story to tell about Ashley Tanner and her botched nose job (bobbed into a ski slope, double black diamond). As the girls walked, they blindly bunched around Daniella, forcing him back a step, but he did not mind. It gave him a chance to admire. She strode in plunging strides, her lower back curved up, so that her rump was raised—not on display for men, nothing so crass, just a gentle reminder that she was a mammal.

At Madison Avenue, the girls scuttled off to a penthouse weenie roast and Daniella turned to face him.

"You wanna go somewhere?" she asked shyly.

"Really?"

"Yeah, it's a holiday."

"Where?"

"You decide."

He took her to Arabia. (He had said it was his favorite place, but he knew the real reason he had chosen it: It was next door to his apartment.) They sat, bathed in red light. As Patty had yet to surprise Tarek with his new air conditioner, the place was uncomfortably hot, but neither minded. They had each other.

As she spoke, Daniella poked nervously at the candle on the table. "It was just before Christmas three years ago. My mom was really worried about my dad because he was in the hospital trying to get off tranquilizers. But Barlow . . . my mom's husband at the time . . . he was an old guy who drooled a lot . . . he wanted to go to England to some antique furniture show. So we went, even though my mom was worried about my dad."

She pulled in a steadying breath.

"Anyway, my dad called on Christmas Eve and said he was out of the hospital. My mom couldn't believe the stupid psychiatrists would let him out right before the holidays, because everybody he knew thought he was gonna be in for a long time, so they went off on vacation, like we did. Which meant he was all alone. My mom didn't want me to talk to him because he sounded really, really bad. She called my aunt who lived right across the park from him and told her to check up on him and we'd get back as soon as we could. So, the first thing my mom did when we got back, like three days later, was go over to his place. He didn't answer his bell. The super let her in. They found him in bed, on top of it, naked, with an empty bottle of pills next to him. He was still alive, though. The ambulance people tried really hard for a long time. But it was too late."

Christopher studied her. All of her attention was fixed on her own tiny fingers as they rolled a piece of wax into a ball. Just as he was about to murmur something sympathetic, she added, "It's weird, but, like, two weeks ago I was in my room doing homework, and I was thinking about my dad. How weird it was he didn't leave a note. I just thought he would have. And then, all of a sudden, I just knew he did. *I knew it.* So I went in and asked my mom. She got this shocked look on her face and said he *did* leave one, but she didn't want me to see it before, back when he died, because I was too young, and she thought that when I was older maybe I'd ask and then she'd show it to me. So she called the police and got them to send her a copy. They have to keep the original because it's still considered evidence."

She stopped and looked at him, smiling shyly.

He asked her what it said.

She heaved a deep breath, then went on, reciting from memory. "Darling, I can't see the end of the tunnel. Not this time. What's kept me going this long is you, only you. And now you are a woman. Well, almost. Just a few more years, and . . .

and you're lucky. You have a good mother and so many loyal friends who care about you. Please never forget how much I love you. And try to forgive me. All my love, Dad."

Daniella's eyes, shiny with tears, lifted and entered his. If she had moved an inch, the tears would have slid down her cheeks.

Later, back in his apartment, without warning, he began to talk about the two of them, not as individuals, anymore, but as a couple. He told her that any romance between them was out of the question. She grinned and said that she had not even realized the notion was under consideration.

"But how come?" she asked curiously.

He tried to explain, but he found himself abandoning his arguments before he had even begun them.

Finally he blurted, "Isn't this uncomfortable for you?"

"No," she said softly, but with emphasis, "It's not, not at all."

Maybe not, he told her, but it was still wrong—illegal, in fact—and even though lately he had been trying to loosen up and take more chances, to be suddenly face-to-face with something so clearly immoral, yet feeling so much temptation toward it, was absolutely excruciating for him.

"You don't *look* unhappy," she said.

"Well, what do *you* think we should do?" he asked with a hint of exasperation.

"I don't know. I guess, it's up to you."

It was.

He swallowed. Suddenly, he was eight years old, standing on a diving board of a public pool. He wanted to jump, but he knew how badly he swam and how deep the merry, blue water really was. Yet, the thought of *not* jumping was even worse than the thought of jumping, because he knew that to turn back was to stay the same person he had always been. He would never have another chance like this again. The next time it would take less courage. So, he took a deep breath and hopped into space. As the water closed over his head, he screamed. It took two lifeguards to haul him out.

Heart pounding, Christopher moved to Daniella, fell to his knees by her chair, and kissed her once on the mouth.

"I'm so glad you did that," she whispered.

Then she moved closer, touching his neck and hair, pressing her mouth into his, first from one angle, then another, then another, as though she wanted to kiss him in a hundred ways all at once. His arms trembled. It was not holding and kissing her that frightened him. It was *being* held, *being* kissed.

Finally, he guided her to the sofa.

Before he could stop himself, he whispered, "I love you."

Although he knew it was an insane thing to say, it struck his ear like a line of stark, primitive poetry.

And she whispered, "I love you, too."

He held her tighter and wanted to cry until no two people on earth were ever left alone like this, to grope in darkness, without fathers.

Hours later, lying in his arms, cocooned in shadow, she murmured, "It didn't hurt this time. Not at all."

"You're a woman," he said.

"And you're a man."

He chuckled skeptically.

"Come on," she insisted. "Don't lie. Admit it."

He could not.

An hour later, they stood in front of her Park Avenue apartment building.

"So you don't think we'll ever do this again?" she asked with a hint of disappointment.

"Probably not."

"Not soon, anyway."

"That's right."

"How come again?"

"I'm a mess."

"Oh, yeah, right." Then she playfully pointed at his face. "Listen, I'll make you a deal. I won't press charges, but only on one condition."

"What?"

"Don't feel bad about what happened. Ever. Only think good things about us."

He smiled. "Okay."

She kissed him. "I don't believe you."

When, later that night, under fierce interrogation, Christopher confessed to me all that he had done, sparing me not a single gory detail, I experienced an inward violence I had not felt since boyhood. I wanted to strangle her. Him, too. Even more galling than his treachery was that he felt not an ounce of remorse. In fact, he was *proud of himself*. He called it the bravest thing he had ever done. Also, he claimed that as no one had been lied to and they had both been healed by it, how could it possibly have been a mistake?

I concealed my wrath, but I began to pace, my mind entertaining, like Ms. Medea's, images of butchery. Here the lad had endured six months of chastity (rarely even masturbating, he claimed), building up unimaginable testicular pressure, and he had thrown it all away on whom, on what?! A child! While, I, an *adult* who loved him, lived right next door! Suddenly, my rage was drowned by a mighty wave of the most abject self-pity. My chin trembled. For six long months, I had listened, nurtured, comforted, wined, dined, and coddled the boy, ad nauseam. I had endured his temper's lash, his ego's hurtful gibes. I had subjected myself to vicious attacks by his rooks and queen. I had given all I had to give. And how had I been repaid? With glib betrayal.

This inner torture, I was also forced to conceal.

Finally, I managed, "Healing for both of you? Excuse me for a moment while I reach for my barf bag."

"Don't be bitchy."

"Bitchy?" I chuckled gaily. "What have you healed? Do you think this actually solves anything?! You'll be twice as unhappy tomorrow!"

His smile was condescending. "We'll see."

Of course, I was right. He woke up the next day positively paralyzed with self-loathing. I nearly wept with joy. But this was no time to be petty, if for no other reason than that I was convinced now more than ever that my beloved was seriously ill. What he had done with Daniella was classic manic behavior, marked as it was by impaired judgment, wild impulsivity, and goat-like sensuality. I insisted, once again, that he call Dr. Gaby Geitman. And, hallelujah, this time, having finally touched bottom, he agreed.

Much to my surprise, Dr. Geitman did not agree with my diagnosis. She did, however, think there was plenty of work to be done and, after his first visit, requested that he commit to three sessions a week, which he did. Thankfully, Christopher entrusted me with every detail. This was most flattering, as Dr. Geitman had told him not to talk with anyone about what took place on her leather—she believed it queered the process. Their work centered largely around his relationship with Grace. That was not unexpected, for as Cameron Jaspar liked to say, "Even when you're sure it's your father, it's always your mother."

What I learned about Grace over the next few weeks disturbed my sleep. Of course, I had known the woman was wicked, but I had no idea that she was actually the embodiment of all human evil.

Here is the sad tale in the shell of a bitter nut:

On December 13, 1958, Christopher tumbled, bleeding and wailing, straight into the heart of a moribund marriage. Grace was unhappy because her husband drank and her husband drank because his wife was Grace.

Grace's only comfort was her bright-eyed baby boy.

They were inseparable.

Until they separated.

A week after Christopher's third birthday, Grace decided she and her boozy husband needed a vacation. As they had no friends with whom she dared entrust her precious toddler, she dumped him off at the home of a complete stranger. A nursery, Grace called it. Christopher called it a kennel. When they picked him up two weeks later, little Christopher had changed. He was no longer bright-eyed. In fact he was anxious, weepy, clutchy. Before meeting Dr. Geitman, Christopher had always believed that the trauma of his abandonment had been the most obvious one: He missed his mommy. But now, twisting on the leather, he began to have memories of what really happened. After Grace left him, yes, of course, he had panicked. In fact, he even had dim memories of lying in a dark, strange room, crying out (preverbally), "What did I do, Mommy? What did I do?" But he also remembered something else now: He had gradually fallen in love with his caretaker. He could not see her face, but he knew that her hair was long and soft, her smell fragrant. He melted into her gentle care, so palpably different from the desperate attentions of his mother.

Then Grace returned.

Christopher could actually remember now the horror of the moment, and horror it was, *for he had forgotten that she ever existed*.

Christopher

He now believed that it was *this* trauma, not the trauma of separation, that had, in fact, done the deepest damage—for not only did he live in constant fear of abandonment (so much so, that he had handed off his wife to Phillip before she had even had a chance to reject him), but once a woman *did* leave, he held on to her memory for dear life, in case she should ever return. This explained why, since his separation, he had been such a monk. Though, at the conscious level, the last thing on earth he wanted was a reconciliation with the miserable Mary, the shattered infant inside him was loath to move on.

Back to the past:

As he grew up, Christopher sought to atone for his betrayal of his mother by cleaving to her like a terrified marsupial—which is just the way Grace liked it. It gave her dominion. She reared Christopher to be as strong and competent as any man, but also as nurturing and emotional as Grammy had *not* been. In short, she programmed her son to fulfill her every narcissistic need. By way of reward, she called him "my little everything." It was an unsavory romance, to say the least.

To this day, he still remembered the morning when his sister, Anna, scared, all whispers, had knelt on the shag, opened a dresser drawer, and from beneath pulled their father's underwear, socks, dickey, and peace symbol, and then pulled a *secret*.

"Look," she said. "It's Mommy!"

The photos were black and white and Grace was naked in each one, her back arched, her hair tousled, her unspoiled breasts offered to the lens. Behind her there were dim lamps and a shapely vase. No children. The world contained no color then and was endowed with weight. Christopher, eight at the time, studied the photos for a long time, then Anna gasped. Someone was coming. He jammed them back and they dashed away. That night, they promised each other that they would never, ever, look at them again. Christopher did, however, the very next morning, and again and again for weeks afterward.

Grace was not pleased when her son began to sprout hair in his armpits. Uncomfortable with the feelings it engendered in her, she sought to find a gentle way to distance herself from his advancing pubescence. She couldn't find it, so she settled for the violent. One night, when he was eleven, Christopher had a dream that a dog had lost its tail. The next morning, he asked Grace, the expert, what it meant. She sat him down and patiently explained, "It means you're what's called an Oedipal child. You want to have sex with me and you think when Daddy finds out, he's gonna cut your penis off."

When Christopher told me this, a spurt of something Greek splashed my epiglottis. I crossed quickly to the kitchen and pulled out my best Bordeaux.

I filled two flutes.

"Are you okay?" he asked curiously.

"The woman should be flayed!" I roared.

"Tell me about it," he said. "I was a kid. I didn't want to have sex with her or anyone else. I barely knew what sex was. But she was my best friend, for Christ's sake. It scared the shit out of me. Gradually, over the years, I sorta forgot about it. That is, until——"

I had feared there would be an "until." I handed him his glass, then flung myself into my morris chair and waved for him to continue.

Christopher was thirteen. An autumn morning found him sitting at his mother's vanity. His hippie hair was as long as a girl's and Grace owned the only brush in the house. Sun poured through white lace curtains. Birds sang. He brushed without a care, his mind dallying in far-off corners. Then, suddenly, a flash in the mirror: bare flesh, wet skin, open towel, snakes of wet hair. Grace, fresh from the shower. His body bent, eyes collapsed. He stared down at the vanity. He dared not move or breathe. She'll see me soon, he thought, see me and cover up, ask me to go.

Christopher waited.

He heard her drying off.

She still hadn't noticed him.

He had to do something, so he coughed.

She saw him and screamed, "Get out! Out!"

Christopher jumped up, eyes still averted, and pleaded, "I just needed to use your brush! I'm sorry!"

She screamed again, pointing at the door as though he didn't know where it was. "Get out, *you pig!*"

On the landing, she slammed the door behind him. He ran to his bedroom and threw himself down on the floor. As he cried, something closed deep inside him like a fist: *his heart*. He never trusted her again. He was civil to her certainly, even friendly sometimes, but in his marrow, where it mattered, she was now and forever the enemy. Noticing the change in his behavior, Grace retaliated in various ways. As he grew older and taller, she would smile, shake her head, and say, "I can't believe it, my beautiful boy is turning into a hairy, disgusting man." Or she would say, "I'm very open-minded, you know, if you're gay, just tell me." If, during an argument, he said, "Oh, screw you." She would reply, often in front of his friends, "You wish."

When it was time for him to leave for college, unlike most teenagers, who pack a few bags, planning to return in summer, he packed everything he owned. He was finished with her. There was a soft knock at the door. Before he could ask who it was, she entered, directly from the bath, and asked, idiotically, if he was still awake.

He did not bother to answer.

"So you're really leaving, huh?" she asked.

Her nightgown was completely transparent. He looked away, planted a knee in the center of a box, and taped it shut.

She laughed, enjoying her own cutesiness. "So you're *really, really leaving*."

"That's right." He glanced over and, despite himself, noticed the decline of her breasts, the heap of her stomach, and the nightmare patch of her crotch.

He looked away angrily. "Please put some clothes on."

She chuckled. "What do you mean? I *have* clothes on."

He shook his head and told her that it was indecent what she was wearing, such a turn-off.

Immediately, he regretted his choice of words.

"Well, it isn't meant to be a turn-*on*," she said, lying with a smug little smile.

He wanted to scream, "Get out, you pig!" But he did not, *could* not, because every cell inside him was shutting down, drowning in an awful wave of numbness.

When Christopher had concluded with his tale, he sat back and mustered a smile, but his eyes were ineffably sad.

"With a mother like that," I whispered, finally, "it's a wonder you're ambulatory, continent, and orgasmic."

"Tell me about it," he chuckled. Then he absentmindedly tore at a cuticle.

"And what have you *learned* from all this?" I asked gently. "What have you and Dr. Gaby come up with?"

His answer came fast. That his relationship with his mother had inspired in him not a fear of women, not at all, but a fear of Woman (there was a huge difference, he claimed, but he never told me what it was), and that this fear drew him only toward impossible love objects. Dr. Geitman's goal for him, and his goal for himself, was that the next person with whom he made love would be someone whom he both cherished and respected as much as they did him. In short, the person would be his equal in

Christopher

every way and he would see them as they really were, not merely as a projection of his own tattered psyche.

The next afternoon at the Parnassus over a Monte Cristo and a corn on the cob I shared my good fortune. "He said *person*. Not *woman*. Next *person* I sleep with."

Cassandra grinned in a spunky way that belied her sixty-two years. "You're shittin' me."

"No! And he says he wants someone whom he can cherish and respect and see as *they* really are."

"That's you!"

"Someone who is *not distant*."

"You live right next door."

"Indeed, I do."

"You're in, Troopie."

"We shall see." I calmly sipped my Manhattan, but inwardly I boogied like a schoolgirl.

Cassandra stepped closer and, in the furtive tones of the coven, suggested I eat all but twenty kernels off my cob, then nail it over the door to my lair. If I did this, I would marry the next young man to walk beneath it. I told her that that would not be necessary. She shrugged at my cockiness and then, ever a lady, insisted that I do something nice for Dr. Geitman, by way of thanks. That night I took a stroll in Central Park and the next morning delivered her a half-dozen tulips.

August

Zeus himself set the stage for the heartbreaking melodrama about to unfold. It began with a blast of wind at the precise moment I entered Christopher's cell. He jumped off the couch and rushed over to the front window. I joined him. Outside, everything was turning dark, as though an enormous hand were being lowered over the block. A bolt of lightning shocked the air and, moments later, Olympian thunder shook our very blood. Below there was panic—cars honked, pedestrians scattered. A handful of rain splashed the glass, then another, and another, and soon the pane was alive with a million rivulets. When, a moment later, the sky split open and dropped its mighty burden to the ground, it came almost as a relief.

Smoking under Arabia's awning, Tarek jumped to his feet just as Christopher and I ran over from next door, our heads ducked under pages of last month's *New York Review of Books*. Tarek jerked open the door and we entered on his heels. The room was hot and redolent of lamb and B.O. It was empty but for three of his friends. Yahia, the most cultured and articulate, sat with his hands elegantly folded, a clove cigarette poking out

Christopher

between two impossibly long fingers. Next to him was the bus-boy and cook, Tarek's little nephew, Aziz, a hopeless gink. Next, was a stranger—a gorgeous houri of perhaps twenty-five years with a beauty mark on his cheek and eyebrows like black velvet. I suspected that were he an American, he would long ago have surrendered to his true nature and done whatever was necessary to become a woman.

As we commandeered our usual corner, Tarek strode to the center of the room, his big arms lifted, stirring the humid air. "Is good!" he reassured us. "We be okay, I think." He lunged toward the front door and opened it. The room was immediately fresh-ened by the storm. He grabbed a standing ashtray and set it against the door. "Air condition!" he sang. "Homemade air con-dition!"

His friends chuckled. Christopher and I did, too, but not sincerely. We were famished. We opened our menus. (For no good reason; we had memorized them months ago.)

"I wonder where Patty is," Christopher said, with a hint of worry.

Right on cue, we heard the squeak of sneakers on iron steps. A black curtain parted in the corner and Patty entered, her big blue eyes round and scared, like a child's during a ghost story. She wore a black robe flecked with cheap sequins, and, between her big bosoms, a string of well-worn worry beads.

Tarek walked over with a smirk. "Wife! Pretty wife! What you do down there? You hide?"

She laid a protective hand on her tummy. "I was just bein' alone. Sometimes a person needs that."

"I *never* alone!"

"I'm talkin' about *people*, not crazy Arabs."

"Crazy Arab?" Tarek boomed. "You crazy *wife!* It's hundred ten degrees and you sit in W.C. all day. You think it's Turkish bath!" He laughed, nodding at his friends until they laughed, too. Then he looked at us, but, as our stomachs were in the process of digesting themselves, the best we could offer were polite smiles.

"Aw, you're all nuts," Patty said. "It only gets that hot when you got the grill on, but since we don't have any *customers*—"

"We're customers," Christopher suggested sweetly.

She noticed us for the first time and was embarrassed. Before she could apologize, Tarek cut her off.

"Know what I think, my friends?" He laid a hefty paw on her shoulder, then turned his plump cheeks to the room. "I got pretty wife!" He stroked her lank hair which hung in sweaty strands. "Like Miss America!" She snarled and swatted his hand away. He doubled over in laughter, clapping, and stumbled back to his friends who laughed just as hard and patted him on the back.

"You're not so pretty either, ya know!" she shouted. "You leave a lot to be desired!" She walked over to us, throwing her head back. "He talks like a big man, but he's lazier'n anyone. What can I getcha?"

She opened her pad. We ordered chicken souvlaki sandwiches with sides of humus.

"I *lazy?*" Tarek cried, incredulous.

She wheeled around, her breasts nearly knocking off my hat. "Shut up! We got customers!" Then she turned back and smiled at Christopher. "You want somethin' to drink?"

We ordered beers. She walked back to Tarek's friends, ripped off the check, and handed it to Aziz, who grabbed it and skittered behind the counter. It was only then that Tarek noticed that Yahia and the pretty one were still chuckling at the way Patty had spoken to him. His face reddened and expanded. He walked to Patty and spun her around.

"You say I lazy?!"

"Let go! Come on, Terry! Ow!"

Christopher

A flash of lightning. She broke his grip and backed up to the counter. In the refrigerated shelves, behind her stove-pipe calves, lay rows of meat and seafood, pale under fluorescents. A rumble of distant thunder.

"We're different, that's all! I like somethin' to do. I'm more hyper."

"Bullshit!" Tarek snatched at her dress, grabbing a fistful of sequins. "What you say? You say you like work?" He shook her. "*You like work?!*"

"Yeah!" she cried helplessly.

Christopher's eyes filled with alarm. He was raised to be a hero—his instinct was to come to her rescue—but I reminded him with an even more alarmed look that it might prove suicidal.

"We've got to do *something!*" he whispered.

"No, we don't. Remember the words of the Bard: 'Sudden storms are short.' "

"What are you talking about?"

Of course, Shakespeare was right, because Tarek laughed and abruptly released her. "Okay! I got job for you! Very fun. Do it all day, all night, okay?"

"What is it?" she asked suspiciously.

He took one of her hands, lifted it to his mouth, and kissed it, then bent it back with a snap. Her knees buckled and she began to sink. When her mouth reached the level of his zipper, Christopher started to rise from his chair, but I grabbed his shoulder, holding him firm.

"Trust the Bard," I whispered. "This, too, shall pass."

"Oh, come on!" Patty mewled, beginning to cry. "Don't be gross!"

Tarek relished her agony.

His friends did, too.

Suddenly, Christopher shouted, *"God damn it! Leave her alone!"*

Tarek looked over at him, his eyes deadening. Then he smiled and let her go. Patty fell to a carpet. A gust tickled the leaves of the dusty plants in the window. Tarek reached down and helped her up.

"I want you tell this boy," he whispered, stepping close, his mustache almost touching her mouth, "why you no love me."

Her eyes opened beseechingly. "But I *do!*"

"Then no complain. Be quiet. Make me happy."

"But I don't know what you want!"

"I tell you."

"Okay, but don't be gross, okay?"

"Go to deli." He reached into his pocket and presented a fold of bills. With a fat thumb, he slid forward a ten. "Get ice cream for me and friends. We have party."

She looked down at the bill, then watched herself carefully take it, as though it were a card from a magician's deck. Tarek handed her a cheap umbrella. At the door, she smiled back at Christopher, then yanked open the door and knocked the ashtray to the floor. Butts and ashes scattered. Rain splashed against her leg. She looked back, frightened, but Tarek was not angry.

"Go, go," he said, waving her away like a bad smell.

With the bumbershoot opened in front of her, she stepped outside. Through the window we watched her disappear into the storm. Muttering oaths to himself, Tarek righted the ashtray, then pulled up a chair and sat at our table. Aziz laid down our humus and a basket of pita. Physically, Tarek was as handsome as he was repellent. His hazel eyes and white teeth glistened like gems against his smooth beige skin. He wore black linen pants (badly wrinkled), white leather shoes, and a silky black shirt unbuttoned to reveal a thin strand of gold lying in the valley of his hard, hairless pectorals. The chain bore a dainty, little cruci-

Christopher

fix. I wasn't surprised. Muslims don't drink alcohol and abuse their spouses like this. Certainly not in public.

"You like my wife," Tarek declared to Christopher.

A triangle of pita poised just inches from his mouth, Christopher stopped and glanced at me, hoping for some support. I smiled and shrugged. I had begged him to stay out of it; now he was on his own. He cast his gaze toward the behemoth.

"Yeah, I do," he said. "She's a nice person. She has a good heart."

"She stupid!" Tarek countered.

Excellent point, I thought.

"I don't think so," Christopher said. "Not at all."

Tarek nodded, taking this in. "You no like me," he continued. "Why not?"

There was no threat in his voice, only curiosity.

"It's not that I don't like you," Christopher replied, reaching for his water glass. "I just hate the way you treat her. She loves you."

Tarek nodded blankly, then rose. He walked over to the door and gazed out at the deluge.

"It rain very hard," he said softly.

"It will rain all night, I think!" the pretty one called out.

"Yes, Ahmed, all goddamn night."

So the angel's name was Ahmed.

Aziz whisked the last of the ashes into a dust pan. "Rain, rain, go away, come back again but not today!" he giggled, then he hopped to his feet.

Yahia smiled affectionately at the little dolt as he scurried back to the kitchen.

"No, no," Tarek said, "rain is good. Too hot. Need rain. Maybe tomorrow we have customer."

Ahmed shook his gorgeous head. "Radio say hot, hot all week."

"Shit," Yahia muttered, stamping his clove into the ashtray. "I'm tired of this. Too much summer. It's worse than fucking Cairo."

Aziz returned with our beers.

"Let's go to beach!" he piped, setting them down.

Tarek lighted a cigarette inside cupped hands, then exhaled a plume of smoke. "Maybe, yes. If tomorrow very hot, maybe we close. Go to beach."

Ahmed flashed a flirtatious smile at me.

The plot thickened.

"Harry, my friend!" Tarek shouted suddenly. "Where you been?" He turned back excitedly to the room. "It's fat man!" He held open the front door. Tablecloths swung like bells. Outside, a thump of boots and Harry, a white American, entered, pumping his umbrella, flapping raindrops. He was, indeed, fat. A Hawaiian tent barely covered his gargantuan belly. He dragged a chrome chain attached to the collar of a German shepherd who could also have stood to lose a few pounds. The dog, seeing everyone already seated, moved to a space in the middle of the room and shook wildly. His leash and license jangled. Droplets flew.

"Here, dog, here," Harry said, plopping into a chair. His voice was strained, his accent Queensian. "*Here!*" He snapped his chubby fingers. The dog turned and stared at the sound for a moment, considered ignoring it, but finally walked over and collapsed in a heap at his master's feet.

"Where you been, my friend?" Tarek asked, twisting a can of beer from a six-pack he had plucked from a cooler. "We no see you."

Harry jammed a menthol between his blubbery lips. "Aw, I been workin'! What else is new?" He reached into a pocket bulging over the fold of his thigh, pulled out a silver lighter, and, crossing one short leg over the other, lighted a fag, pulling hard.

Christopher

"I been managin' this new girl. A real talent, this one. Gonna make me rich. Great tits, good set of pipes, plentya chrimsa. I told you 'bout her, remember? Phyllis Schmidt? Well, her name's Dolly Cage now. Sings mostly show tunes. Took her to a club a frienda mine runs out on the Jersey shore. Schmancy joint. She did terrific. Broke a leg."

Tarek handed him a beer.

Aziz laid our sandwiches on the table.

Ahmed was visibly excited, moving in his seat. "I tell you, *I* like to be singer! I *very* good singer!"

As I bit into my sandwich, I imagined him belting out "On the Street Where You Live" as he ravaged me.

"Yeah?" Harry said. "Well, here's some advice. Save your singin' for the shower. 'Cause, talent ain't enough. Most important thing is chrimsa and you ain't got enough to light a match." He lifted his beer can. "Here's to amateurs, Terry, may God have mercy on their souls."

Yahia made a confused face. "What's this word you use? 'Chrimsa'?"

The fat man leaned back with authority and patted his shirt over his gut, like a dignitary straightening his napkin. "Chrimsa is what Reagan has. It's what you need to get ahead in this country. It means charm. Pizzazz. Nothing else gets you success over here. 'Cept maybe a gun."

Tarek smiled. "Tell me, friend, what about my wife? She got chrimsa?"

The fat man screwed up his face as though he had a mouth of something rotten. "You kiddin' me?" He pointed to the floor with his menthol. "Dog here's got more."

Laughter all around. Confused by the commotion, wanting to understand, the dog began to bark.

"I guess he don't like the comparison," the fat man noted wryly.

"Dog *bite?*" Aziz asked, leaning down to pet it.

"No, not you," the fat man said. "Only niggers."

Christopher almost choked. His liberal heart skipped three consecutive beats. He began to eat more quickly, clearly eager to escape.

"Oh, my wife, my wife!" Tarek shook his head wearily. "Not happy. Complain all night, all day."

"No wife for me, thanks," the fat man said, whipping out a handkerchief. "I'd go nuts in a week." He brought the handkerchief down and wiped his damp, hairy neck. "Women—not all of 'em, mind you—I'm talkin' about *American* broads—all they want is love. That's their number one biggest thing. They're always tryin' to make you love 'em more. But, then, see, if you love 'em *too* much, they fuck your best friend." He wiped all the way down to his fist-sized navel. "I remember when I was married, my wife usedta say—"

The front door opened. Patty returned, hugging a soggy paper bag.

"You look wet," the fat man noted sagely, subduing his animal.

"Screw you, Harry!"

"Where is umbrella?" Tarek asked.

"It broke!" She walked over and dropped the bag on the counter. It split open and four pints of ice cream tumbled out.

"What kind?" Tarek asked.

"Vanilla."

Shocked, he checked each pint. "Vanilla? Vanilla? Vanilla?"

"Yeah? So what? You like it."

"But we got *party!*"

"Well, I don't know what they want!" She crossed to a drawer and sifted through silverware. Her teeth chattered. "Everybody likes vanilla. If you were from here, you'd know that. It's everybody's favorite."

Christopher

"No offense," Harry said, "but I'm a hundred-percent American and I ain't too fonda vanilla. I always figured it was for girls."

"Aw, go to hell, fatso!"

"God damn!" Tarek cried. "You see?" He pushed her away from the drawer.

Again, Christopher's eyes flared angrily. Again, his reflex was to come to her rescue. I held him hard by the wrist.

"Merely observe!" I whispered.

In fact, more than anything now, I was afraid that if he caused a scene, we might get kicked to the curb, and I had not yet had my fill of Ahmed—not by a long shot.

Patty pressed her face between her hands. "Don't start, Terry! Please! You know I'm not feelin' good!"

"You *drunk!*" Tarek reached among the pints and found a small, separate bag. He ripped it open and a premixed screwdriver rolled out. "Shit! You see?"

"I'm real unhappy!" she cried.

The fat man leaned over to Christopher. "Just when *is* happy hour around this joint?"

Ignoring him, Christopher pushed away his food and glared at Tarek, his hands balling into fists.

"I unhappy, too!" Tarek shouted. "Ahmed unhappy! Aziz unhappy! Yahia unhappy!"

"I ain't been happy since JFK got shot," the fat man said, grinning at me.

"Me, neither," I mouthed silently, just so that he would feel included.

Tarek threw up his arms. "But we don't drink like goddamn pig! We dress nice, take bath!"

He turned away, furious, and grabbed a fork. Seeing what it was, he threw it down, grabbed a teaspoon, and set to work on the ice cream, but he managed to lift only frozen shavings. He swore to himself as they curled around his huge knuckles. Patty watched, sniffling. He caught her out of the corner of his eye.

"Go to sleep!" he roared. *"Party not for you!"*

She choked back a sob, picked up her cocktail, swept aside the black curtain, and disappeared. Christopher gestured for the check, then, determined to escape, he tore into the last of his souvlaki with appalling voraciousness. No sooner had he taken the last bite and wiped his mouth free of tahini than Tarek plunked down two bowls of ice cream and two spoons.

"You eat, my friends," he said.

"Yes, *sir!*" I said with Shirley Temple glee, grabbing my bowl and digging in. The look Christopher threw me was flagrantly hostile. He felt betrayed, and I cannot say that I blamed him, but for the past seven months I had devoted every waking moment to our union. I deserved a night off, a little me-time. While Ahmed was no substitute for true love, he was certainly a charming diversion.

After he had distributed the bowls, Tarek realized there was one extra. He walked to the curtain and shouted, *"Stupid, you want ice cream? Come up now! Fast!"*

When silence replied, he turned and snarled in my direction. "She drunk again."

"John Barleycorn," I sighed sympathetically. "The bane of the working class."

Tarek walked over and offered his wife's dessert to the dog, who had been whining and squirming since the first bowl was served. He watched as the beast's pink tongue lapped at the snowy mound.

"He like," Tarek said.

"I like, too," I said, gesturing flamboyantly with my spoon at Ahmed. This display of blatant effeminacy was meant to send a message, and it did. Ahmed bobbed his velvets and moved his chair three feet closer.

Christopher

"Oh, yeah," Harry said, smacking his lips. "Everybody loves ice cream. We all scream for it."

Tarek grinned when he noticed that Aziz was already licking his bowl clean. He grabbed him by the neck and ground his giant fist into his little head. "Bad boy! Eat too fast! Man eat slow! Woman eat fast!"

Ahmed, agreeing, laughed and flicked his rosy tongue at me. I twinkled back, and I fancy showed some crimson in my cheeks. He picked up his chair and moved closer. It was a veritable mating dance. Christopher did not like it. Had it been a nature show, he would have changed the channel. Could he be jealous? I wondered. If he was, then bedding Ahmed would serve a dual purpose. One immediate and glandular, the other long-term and romantic.

"This is gettin' filthy," Harry said. "I'm startin' to enjoy it. Me, I don't care how broads eat, just so long as they suck. Now my girlfriend, Dolly, she sucks like a lady. Sticks her pinky out and everything."

This news lifted Tarek's spirits. He glanced at the curtain behind him, then lowered his voice. "Oh, shit, I tell you friends. My goddamn wife, she don't suck. Every night I get in bed and I very good." The room fell quiet. "Touch hair, say how beautiful, how much I love her! Then I take off whatever piece of shit she wearing and I ready and she say, 'No, Terry.' I say, 'What is this bullshit?!' 'I don't want to make love,' she say, 'I want to *talk*.' I say to her, 'You shut up!' " Everyone roared. Tarek looked around, pleasantly surprised. He had not intended this to be funny.

Up until now, Christopher's eyes had been throwing daggers at me. Now they lobbed grenades. But I refused to capitulate. Ahmed was a stranger to Arabia. If I left now, I might never see him again. Besides, what was stopping Christopher from leaving without me? This question, which began as a rhetorical one, soon resuggested the obvious: he was jealous!

"If you ain't gettin' laid by your wife," Harry said to Tarek, "then what's the point? Defeats the whole purpose."

Tarek leaned close and muttered to the fat man. "She my fiff wife."

"No shit!" Harry said, eyes bugging.

"Yes, fiff."

"What, are you stupid?"

Tarek glanced at the curtain, then whispered even more softly, "She think she only one. First love." He patted his fist against his heart. "Each wife, different country. Egypt, Lebanon, Italy, England, now United States."

"He has had five restaurants, too," Yahia added.

"No!" Harry exclaimed.

"Yeah, five, too!" Tarek insisted. "But Patty think this first one."

Unnoticed by the group, Ahmed moved his chair even closer to mine. Our legs were almost touching now. I smiled at Christopher, as though I found the discussion absolutely enthralling.

"Will you hurry up!" the lad growled at me.

I showed him the contents of my bowl. As I had been eating at a tortoise pace, I still had quite a bit left.

"Yes, five restaurant, five wife," Tarek continued. "And I thirty-seven years old. When I fifty, I have fifty restaurant in fifty country, but no more wifes. Shit, I got green card now. Go home, I say to Patty! Go!"

The fat man smiled and reached for another fag. "Yeah, in my book, marriage ain't even worth considerin' unless you got somethin' goin' on the side. My problem is, when I was married, I never cheated, so my wife lost all respect for me."

"Patty no cheat," Tarek said, throwing a hard look at Christopher, making sure that nothing in the boy's expression belied his assertion.

Christopher

Christopher stared back, his face utterly impassive.

Ahmed was so close to me now that I picked up his scent: an olfactory triptych of baby oil, chick peas, and damp camel.

Tarek stole another look at the curtain. Certain that his wife was sound asleep, he began his tale. "I swear to God, my friends, last week, Friday, ten o'clock, slow, no customer, wife sleep, a car drive up in front. Mercedes. Girl get out. Beauty! Have wine like this." He tucked an imaginary bottle under his arm like a riding crop. "She say to me, 'Tarek, for long time I want to drink with you, but I think it's no good 'cause you have wife. Now I no care you have wife.' "

The fat man's eyes lighted up.

The dog whimpered for more sugar.

Christopher looked as though he might overturn the table. His suffering was profound. I might have given in, but Ahmed was so close to me now that I could have kissed his nose without leaving my chair.

Tarek lifted a palm. "I swear to God, I tell Aziz go home and I put sign in window say closed and I drink whole bottle of wine with her."

"What'd she look like?" Harry asked. "A real hog?"

"No! Beautiful! Eyes. Oh, eyes. Like Persia girl. Nineteen, twenty years old! Jesus Christ!"

"It's true," Ahmed whispered to me. "I know her."

"Eyes like Persia girl?" I inquired.

He nodded, then glanced down at my blossoming groin.

"A whore, I bet," the fat man said.

"No, no!" Tarek insisted. The half-whisper had turned into a half-roar. "Park Avenue!"

"They got all kindsa whores over there."

"I swear to God, we drink, laugh like hell! She tell me, oh, you very strong and handsome! We must go to my house!"

As a man of vast worldly experience, I am rarely, if ever, surprised by human behavior. There is very little under the sun that I have not heard about, witnessed, or attempted, but what happened next almost knocked me, quite literally, out of my chair. Without warning, Ahmed dropped his hand onto my aching lap. Tarek's tale had evidently gotten to him. Or was it simply me? Either way, I was happy. I had made a new pal. I greeted his delicate paw with a surge of blood flow.

Tarek lowered his voice again. "We get in cab and go to Park Avenue. Apartment big. Painting. Flower curtain. Silver. She walk me down hall and say, very quiet, this is mother-father room. They sleep. This is my sister. Twelve. She sleep. This is sister. Fourteen. She sleep, too. And this one, this is my room. And she take me inside and pull me on floor. Jesus Christ! I have her on floor! Shit, I don't believe! When I finish, I so happy, I want to fuck mother and sister and sister—whole family!"

"Not the *father*, I hope?" Harry asked.

"No, not father," Tarek said.

"Good. Otherwise I'da had to excuse myself."

"And then she take me to kitchen and she fall down on knees!" He set his feet wide apart like a sultan. "I stand there, I swear to God, she suck my dick." He laughed joyously. "I king of America!" He walked back to his seat. "Then I come home. Sun is up. I have beer. I go to sleep and Patty not know nothing!"

"He is very *bad*," Ahmed murmured to me.

An odd bit of righteousness, I thought, considering he was in the process of kneading my manhood. Still, to be polite, I would have agreed with him, but I could not. I was breathless. And, to make matters worse, not three feet away sat my true love, staring at me in a savage way that suggested he might be aware of what was transpiring. Stricken by a qualm, I glanced into the corner and noticed something terrible: *the curtain was moving.*

Christopher

Christopher must have seen the alarm in my eyes, because he looked, too.

It moved again.

Then we both heard sneakers squeak down the steps.

Christopher erupted. He rose from his chair, made a strange snorting sound, threw down some cash, stormed to the front door, yanked it open, knocked over the ashtray again, and burst into the night, slamming the door behind him with a crash. Everyone was shocked. Tarek looked around the room for some explanation.

Casually, Ahmed removed his hand from my crotch, shrugged his shoulders, then rose and sauntered over to the six-pack. In one swift move, he yanked off a can and popped it open—a macho gesture designed to mislead. I quickly zipped my fly, but I made it look as though I were straightening my napkin. Inwardly, I was all aflutter. This was a moment of supreme existential import. I had to make a choice that would forever define my character. My options were two: stay where I was and, at night's end, surreptitiously slip Ahmed my business card, or rush away this instant and give immediate succor to Christopher, but risk never seeing my swarthy fondler again.

Of all the courageous choices I had made in my life, it was the easiest. I rose stoically and tossed down a puddle of change. I felt something brush against my leg. I looked down and saw that I had accidentally fed my napkin into the jaws of my zipper. I yanked it away, tearing something, and flung it into the corner.

"What is wrong with boy?" Tarek asked me.

"*You,*" I said haughtily. "Your tale of adultery was despicable to the extreme. Neither I nor my idealistic young friend will ever darken your doorstep again."

I marched to the door, then froze dramatically. I whipped around for a parting shot. "Lucky for you, my young friend is savvy enough not to let his distaste for you diminish in any way his passionate advocacy for the cause of Arab independence everywhere!"

With that, I stepped into the storm, leaving behind five shamed men, one wrecked woman, and a dozing dog. While others have experienced moments of valor as meaningful and substantial, few were ever as proud of themselves afterward. I walked through the purifying rain with my head held high.

When I entered Christopher's cell (strangely, the door was ajar), he was beside himself. Before I could utter a word, he leapt up and carried on for a full twenty minutes about the tragedy of this beautiful, kind woman being driven to the brink of insanity by this bully.

I let him run himself down for a while, like a gerbil on a wheel, then I gently suggested that his time might be better spent looking at *why* the plight of one ugly, unhappy woman was inspiring such distress and rancor in him. Could it be, I said, that the scene had triggered some early memory of his mother's plight back in the days when she was trapped in her own miserable marriage? Was he perhaps transferring onto Patty his longings to rescue Mommy? Might this not, in fact, lie at the heart of *all* his messianic quests?

He was not open to this line of inquiry. Somehow he mistook my earnest desire to enlighten him for a lack of concern for Patty. He wheeled on me, eyes blazing, telling me he was tired of my "superior shit," my "Oscar Wilde bullshit," my "constant negativity." And as far as my analysis of his motives went, he had Dr. Geitman for that, thank you very much.

When I started to object, he cut me off.

"I don't wanna hear it!" he shouted. "I wanted to stay . . . tell that asshole what I thought of him . . . and you sat there shaking your head at me . . . grabbing me . . . slurping your ice cream like it was a goddamn day in the park! Why didn't you back me up?"

Christopher

"Well—"

"I'll tell you why! Because you were too busy flirting with that pockmarked creep!"

"*Jealous?*" I said, lifting an eyebrow.

"What?" he fairly shrieked. "What the fuck do I have to be jealous about?!"

"Don't be coy."

His voice cracked with incredulity. "You let him put his hand *on your dick!* Don't you have any self-respect?! You walk around like a fucking aristocrat, but you're completely insane! With your silly clothes and . . . your jewelry . . . and your ridiculous walk! Look at the way you live! Don't you know how crazy you are? You're just a pathetic alcoholic who doesn't have a good word to say about anyone! Or anything! You despise women, you despise yourself! You don't *love anything!*"

He grabbed his jacket, stormed to the door, and slammed it behind him. For a few long minutes, I simply stared at the door, waiting for him to come back and apologize. The emotion that overcame me was wholly unfamiliar. I had never been insulted so effectively. Finally, I fell to my knees and began to cry.

Two hours later, when it became clear that Christopher was not coming back, I rose and slouched back to my lair. In my bedroom, I stood before the full-length mirror that hung on my closet door. I stared deep into my own anima and whispered, "Bryce, what is the truth?"

Slowly, reality came into focus. My outfit *was* vaguely flamboyant. I did drink too much and wear many rings. And, yes, I *was* a bit hard on the fair sex. But he was wrong about love. I did love something.

When Christopher returned five hours later, bloated with beer from closing down a neighborhood barrelhouse, he spotted

Patty. (This, I only learned later. Alas, much later). She was ghostly in the cast of the streetlight, cautiously descending the front steps of Arabia with a big white suitcase.

"Hey, kid," she said when she saw him. Her tone was cheery, as though they were meeting on a sunny afternoon in the middle of errands.

"Where're you going?" Christopher asked, walking closer.

"Seattle."

"Now?"

"Yup. I've had enough," she replied. "I'm outta here."

"Forever?"

She fought away tears with a big smile. "You bet. You know, I've just—" She searched for the right words. "Had enough, you know?"

He was only a few feet away now and he saw that her bottom lip was swollen and cut and that there was a trail of sticky blood along the part in her hair. He felt a surge of fury.

"What did he do to you?" Christopher asked.

"He wanted the money I saved."

"He *hit* you?"

"Yeah. No big deal."

Christopher stepped closer and smoothed back her hair to see where the blood began. "Does it hurt?"

A cool wind blew her formless dress so that it clung to her low, round figure.

"Yeah, but, you know, when it's all over, it's just so good, it barely even hurts."

"I think you need stitches."

It was as though she had not heard him. "You know, I've been diggin' and diggin' to find out what it's all about with me. I think I finally know. I found that little golden nugget I always heard about. I guess I'm just someone who always thinks everybody is real, and I finally figured out that Terry's not. None of

Christopher

his friends are either. And I never knew it. You know, it's like the forty Arabian nights. Or thieves or whatever. A guy's supposed to ride in and take you away and make everything good. And then . . . well, life's not like that. It's much harder, you know? Then one day, you don't wanna get up in the morning. You start to cry. You cry till you think you're goin' crazy. And then . . . then you find that little golden nugget. And you say, hey, this is me. I'm real. And this guy, *he's* the one who's crazy, not me. But when you're young, you dream. You get married thinkin' it's gonna make everything perfect."

"I know what you mean," he said softly.

"But then you're on your own again. And nothing gets better till you stop believin' in fairy tales."

He studied her face and she seemed, suddenly, formidable, a person to be admired.

"You sure you're gonna be okay?" he asked.

She seemed soothed by his warm tone, but uneasy at the same time. She cast her eyes to the ground.

"I'll just get a taxi."

"You want some help with your bag?"

"Naw, you get some sleep."

She stumbled as she lifted the suitcase, then she staggered a few steps and looked back. "I'm gonna miss ya, kid. You been a real good customer."

"Thanks. I'll miss you, too."

Her next steps were more steady.

"Are you sure you don't want to shower before you leave?" he called out. "Or rest? You could sleep on my couch."

She did not look back. "Naw. My mom's waitin'. I called her. She's real glad I'm comin' home."

He watched her diminish down the hill. When she reached the avenue, a taxi appeared from out of nowhere and stopped at her feet. The driver must have leaned back and opened the door for her, because, as soon as she stepped from the curb, it opened as if by magic. She hauled her bag in with both hands, then the door slammed and she vanished with a roar. Christopher turned to go and flinched when he saw Tarek sitting on the patio of Arabia, his face slashed by shadows.

Christopher approached warily.

The big man lifted a hand and gestured him to a chair.

Christopher didn't take it. "Well, *you* must be happy. You can move on to wife number six now."

"No, no more. Only girlfriend now. Too many beautiful girl in America. Too much money."

He opened a fist and showed a wad of twenties, crushed and sweaty. He beamed down at them with pride, as though they were the product of long and satisfying labor.

"She try to steal from me," he said. "But I no let her. Tomorrow I buy air conditioner."

To return to the wisdom of that brainy four-eyes, Mr. Aldous Huxley: "If loving without being loved in return may be ranked as one of the most painful of experiences, being loved without loving is certainly one of the most boring." This quotation sums up only too well the weeks that followed my tiff with Christopher. Whenever we passed each other on the street or stairs, I suffered shooting pains through my alimentary canal, while he was overcome by an instantaneous need to yawn. A vicious cycle ensued in which his yawns merely intensified my pains and my intensified pains merely widened his yawns. At one point, determined to put an end to it, I stepped in front of him and smiled as sweetly as I knew how, but he threw me a go-thither glance and walked around me as though I were a smear of dog-dirt.

That he could freeze me out like this I found absolutely incomprehensible. I was, after all, his mother, father, mentor, biggest fan, best friend, Big Brother, and biographer. Also, I loved him with all my heart. I was indispensable to his happiness. How could he not know it? Did he think neighbors like me grew on trees? One might ask why I did not simply take charge, apply my knuckles to his door, and demand that he count his blessings. The answer is foolish pride. "Why should *I* do the apologizing?" I thought. All I had done was accept a few sneaky caresses from a Levantine chanteuse. In what civilized country is that a crime? And it was not as though Christopher had any claim on my freedom. *He wasn't my boyfriend*. Besides, even if what I had done *was* in some way a betrayal, was *his* behavior not far worse? He had, after all, since the day we met, repaid my generosity by ignoring me, rejecting me, stepping out on me, mocking me, and, most recently, excoriating me without mercy. The fact that all but one of his criticisms were spot on only made it the more unpardonable—at least in my book. My one consolation was that Christopher's selfishness was not going unpunished. He had never looked worse.

September

My beloved and I did not speak a single word to each other between that gruesome August night and the second week of October. The following late-summer idyll is, therefore, based solely on my own fertile imagination, vague conversations that took place between Christopher and me at a much later date, and on text I obtained from his diary.

Now, Righteous Reader, before you gasp that the pinching of a friend's diary, even for a single afternoon of hasty photocopying, is the height of perfidy, allow me to submit the following in my defense: First, I agree with you, and, second, it was not strictly a diary, deeply personal and endowed with a pet name, like, say, that of Miss Anne Frank. It was not even equipped with a cute little lock. It was simply a spiral notebook, a casual repository for anecdotes, observations, and insights, meant to provide him with raw material should he ever break out his typewriter and get to work on *Love's Sad Archery*. Since, at the point that I stole it, I doubted that he ever would, and I already suspected that I might one day want to pen a memoir of my own, I could not let an entire month of my beloved's life go unchronicled, could I? Even if it was a month in which I played no significant role.

This next movement of our tale begins on the afternoon of Friday, August 31, when Christopher found himself stowed in the backseat of a little red sports car belonging to Ted Palmer (an old college chum), and Ted's wife, Julie. Since the backseat of a sports car is in no sense a seat at all, Christopher was forced to lie sideways, sprawled atop matching suitcases, his duffel on his lap, his legs bent uselessly in front of him like a paralytic's. He was profoundly uncomfortable, but took solace in the fact that they were already four hours into their drive.

Their destination was Provincetown, Massachusetts, which between the wars had been home to Portuguese fishermen and their families, and haven to scores of Greenwich Village artists and assorted bohemians, but today, was summer-Mecca to pot-bellied tourists, their husbands, and a vast multitude of sun-starved homosexualists. For those of you lucky enough never to have visited, P-town lies at the very tip of Cape Cod— a curling tendril of sand winding forty-five miles into the cold Atlantic.

For months, Ted and Julie had been planning to spend their Labor Day by the sea. At the last minute, after their reservations on Prince Edward Island had gone mysteriously missing, they chose Provincetown because they had once spent a snowy weekend in nearby Truro, attending Christopher and Mary's wedding. Although neither had ever visited Provincetown itself, it was the only place on the Cape where they could, at so late a date, secure a decent room for the holiday weekend.

Coincidentally, Christopher had also decided to venture to Provincetown that day. First, because he had not escaped the City since the fiasco of Washington and, second, because he knew that several key scenes of *Love's Sad Archery* were to take place in Truro and to bring them alive he would need plenty of fresh detail. When Julie learned of the harmonic convergence of their plans, she immediately offered him a lift, but failed to mention that he would be tossed in the backseat like a sack of soiled linen.

They streaked northward now beneath a blinding blue sky. Ted, eager to reach their destination and relax, drove far too quickly, his mirrored glasses fixed to the road, his little body hunched forward in a decidedly unattractive way. Julie sat back, her bare feet crossed on the open window. Squinting into the sun, her long brown hair whipping in the wind, she munched a daring peach.

"What a perfect day!" she cried, "I can't believe it!"

"It gets even better," Christopher said, his head behind Ted's. He wriggled, trying to take some of the pressure off his shoulder. He could barely feel his left hand now. "Some afternoons there isn't a single cloud and the air is gold."

"Gold?" she asked, closing her eyes into the wind and showing all her lovely teeth.

"Yup, that's why so many great painters worked here."

"Wow. You know, I used to paint."

"I know," Christopher said.

"When was that?" her husband asked, snapping his head. "High school?"

"College," Christopher said.

Julie smiled at him, then tossed her pit out the window.

They flew onto a bridge, a graceful arch over a cleanly cut canal. Once they had crossed it, they were on sand. Quite soon, everything turned tasteless. Every sign on every little shoppe was fashioned to look antiquated. Ye Olde this and Ye Olde that, burned crudely into shiny plastic and wood as though by the hands of Puritan craftsmen.

"See," Christopher said, "the Cape is just a giant sand bar."

Christopher

Julie looked and saw fat tongues of sand extending from the median onto the gray asphalt.

Christopher pointed his dirty sneaker. "Those weird pines grow everywhere."

The little pines were cramped and awkward, twisted on their heads in top-heavy configurations, like freeze-frame photos of a middle-aged man (abandoned; feelings hurt) tumbling down, limbs flailing, from a high window to a bloody crack on the pavement.

They flew past town after town, but, as they neared their destination, the traffic abruptly thickened. Ahead, there was a bottleneck where three lanes merged to two. As they came to a near-stop, Ted whipped off his shades and hit the horn. Then again. And again.

"I'm sure that'll help," Christopher noted dryly.

Ted shook his head. "You know, buddy, I feel bad you don't have a room."

They were the first words Ted had spoken to him in two hours. Christopher sensed that he had not really wanted him to come along. They had been close once, but that was years ago. Now they were in touch only because Julie made the effort.

"Don't worry about it," Christopher replied. "I'll find something. If I don't, I'll sleep on the beach."

"Saint Christopher," Julie said, turning back with an amused but admiring smile.

Her choice of words shocked him. He had thought his bid for canonization was a secret. Anyway, it no longer applied. He had slept with an underage girl. (The Vatican considers this a deal-breaker. An underage boy is another matter altogether.)

"Yeah, what do you want, a *medal?*" Ted belched a laugh. When no one else appreciated his joke, he frowned and turned serious. "I mean, it's nuts. There's no reason for you to be broke.

I know you're going through a hard time—what with your divorce and all—but why not at least make some money?"

This was an old argument between them.

"Look—" Christopher began patiently.

"No, *you* look. What the hell *else* do you have to do? It's not like you're writing or anything. My firm'll sponsor you. You'll pass your Series 7 and be making fifty thousand to start. That's a helluva lot better than teaching similes and subjunctive whatever to a buncha spoiled brats, isn't it?"

"Sure, if I cared about money," Christopher said, slithering onto his back. "But I don't. I just need enough to survive."

Ted let his frustration with Christopher blend with his disgust at the traffic. He leaned hard on the horn. Julie plugged her ears, annoyed. Christopher couldn't believe he was having this conversation again. Why did he even bother? In college, he and Ted had had the pursuit of girls in common, then they both got married. Now what was there? He turned his head and stared up blankly at the roof, as though it were the lid of a coffin. He brought his bag up to his chest and closed his eyes. He thought of his poor, sick Grammy, lying semiconscious on an air mattress, her breasts slumped sideways, her tiny legs splayed, her face heaped into a flabby scowl. The last time he had visited, he studied her chart, which told him, among other things, that often in her sleep she cried out that she wanted to die. All day, Christopher sat at her window, staring out at the landscape, tinged gold and red by the first approach of autumn, and listened to Grampy whispering in his wife's ear, begging her to forgive him for putting her there. Hour upon hour, he squeezed her hand, tears rolling down his cheeks, whimpering out songs from their courtship, the ones they had danced to at the Roma Club. Before going home, Grampy announced his prognosis. "You're my miracle girl, Rosa! You're gonna be home in no time!" Christopher opened his eyes and spoke to the back of Ted's head.

Christopher

"There are more important things than making a living."

"Yeah, like what?" Ted asked.

"Making a *life*."

"Oh, please!"

"I agree with him," Julie said.

"Oh, really?"

"Yeah, really."

Ted smirked and inched the car forward. "We're driving in *my* new car to the fancy hotel room *my* hard work paid for, and you're saying making a living isn't important? A little bit hypocritical, wouldn't you say?"

"I didn't say it wasn't important." Each of Julie's words was painstakingly pronounced. "I just agree with Chris that there are *more* important things."

"This'll be faster. Hold on." With a yank of the wheel, Ted veered off the highway and raced onto a two-lane winding road, thick on both sides with towering trees and hidden houses. They passed hills of sand and valleys of dense brush. When they broke into the open, the sea was visible on their left. It was the gentler half of the Cape, the bay side.

Christopher was grateful the talk of money had ended. Now, he could concentrate on feelings beginning to stir inside him; namely, his anxious melancholy at returning to the Cape for the first time since his wedding. The beauty of the bay only made him feel worse. His future, too, had once seemed as beautiful, and now it lay strewn before his lonely imagination like so much smoldering wreckage, while the bay's beauty, by way of ridicule, had not changed at all. He closed his eyes and reminded himself that it was not his despair that had brought him here, but his will. Tomorrow he would set pen to paper, taking his first decisive step toward the creation of *new* beauty.

They sped along the bay's smooth swing, passing bungalows

not much bigger than garages with names like Seabreeze, Salty Cabins, and Duneway.

"Maybe we should have gotten one of those!" Ted shouted above the wind. "What do you think they run?"

The sky began to darken. As they approached the town, raindrops splashed the windshield. Ted closed the windows and sent the wipers slapping. Boats rocked in the harbor. American flags whipped like skirts.

"How do you expect to find a room in this?" Ted asked.

"Wet," our young hero muttered.

"Now, see, if you earned a decent living, you could stay at our hotel. They still have a few vacancies."

"Hey!" Julie exclaimed, turning quickly and touching Christopher's leg, "why don't you just sleep in *our* room?"

Christopher smiled and snorted. "Great idea, huh, Ted?"

"That's why I married her," Ted smirked. "Big heart, no brain."

Julie, unamused, thought for a few seconds. "Okay, then, how about we get you a room. Our treat." Christopher knew that this idea would go over no better than the first, but she was insistent. "It's no big deal. Really."

"Sure, not for *you*," Ted muttered. "It's my credit card."

Christopher glanced up at his friend's worried little eyes in the rearview mirror.

"No, thanks," Christopher said. "I want to be alone. I have work to do."

Ted's brow slowly relaxed.

Although it was raining, Commercial Street was jammed. On both sides stood the same quaint-looking shops with the same faux storefronts. Pedestrians, many of them carrying umbrellas, crisscrossed the road as though it were a parking lot, grazing Ted's fender with their shopping bags.

"Assholes," Ted groused.

Christopher

"It's like a movie set," Julie said, her mouth ajar. "It's so ugly."

"Don't worry," Christopher chuckled. "You saw how incredible it was lower down. Just spend your days back there. That's what *I'm* gonna do."

When they reached the hotel, Ted pulled over and Christopher crawled out. The small of his back ached. Holding his duffel to his chest, he kissed Julie's cheek, waved at Ted, then dashed away. He flew down the street, vaulting puddles, dodging pedestrians, and ducking beneath awnings. He sprinted past a line of benches near Town Hall where a clutch of old queens smoked brown cigarettes beneath lavender umbrellas. (Mild exaggeration.) Nearby, a well-endowed horse, rump twitching, chomped at a bucket of hay. In the carriage behind it, comfortably protected, sat a burly lesbian in a motorcycle jacket reading a magazine about motorcycles.

By the time he had passed the business district, the rain had stopped. The air was quiet, the sky low and dove gray. On both sides stood charming little wooden guest houses, their picket fences guarding tidy, bright gardens. Whenever he saw a vacancy sign, he went inside to inquire, but the rooms were far too expensive. It was a busy weekend; they could name their price. The rain came and went a half-dozen times as he walked. Soon, his clothes and duffel were drenched dark. When he passed the last house, he stopped dead. In front of him, an empty vestige of sand curved out for a mile before it disappeared into the quickening sea. He stood for a long time, staring out as though a room might suddenly appear there, then, with a weary sigh, he turned and retraced his steps. He walked now with his head down, his shoulders stooped, his bag banging against his knee. He knew what Cameron Jaspar would say. That he *wanted* it this way. If hardship was what he had, it was because hardship was all he thought he deserved.

Ted lay in his underwear, stretched out on the plush queen, manning the remote control. He studied the violently flashing pictures with a benign smile. Across the room, Julie tucked well-folded clothes into a dresser drawer.

"Let's have lobster tonight," she said.

"Very funny," Ted chuckled.

"I thought this was a vacation."

"Of course it is."

"So, why are we already economizing?"

"I don't believe you." He smiled and rolled onto his side. "You're such a *woman*, you know that? We spend a fortune on the room, and you figure, hey, we've already started spending, so let's spend some more. Bring on the lobster! Champagne! Caviar! Let's buy a room for our friend!"

"I hate caviar."

"Now a *man* says—" He lowered his voice to show his rationality. "We've started spending, yes, fine, we've been extravagant, but now's the time to be smart." Grunting, he hoisted himself up. "Anyway, money's got nothing to do with it. I just thought it would be fun to act like a coupla dumb tourists tonight. You know, walk around town, eat hot dogs, taffy, cotton candy, shit like that."

She grimaced.

Ted walked to a wide mirror that ran from the floor to the ceiling near their bed. "Huh," he noted, "it's a skinny mirror." He stripped off his underwear. His legs and arms were spindly, but his chest showed a faint residue of muscle. He studied the thickening at the waist. He poked at it cautiously, as though it were a dangerous animal that might or might not be dead.

"Do you plan to shower before dinner?" she asked.

"Naw, you go ahead."

She lifted her sweatshirt over her head, then, leaning against the closet door, pushed down her jeans and underwear. Her bare legs were long and strong, her breasts round and ripe.

"What are you looking at?" she asked.

"Your body," he said, eyes bright. "It's like a goddamn ad for sex."

Shaking her head, she walked into the bathroom.

A few minutes later, she emerged, toweling herself. Ted was watching footage of President Reagan addressing the Republican National Convention. Cameras panned the bouncing, cheering crowd. They wore paper hats, waved signs.

"Man," Ted muttered, "he *is* a great communicator."

On the small front porch, a line of old fairies sat under an awning, between glowing lanterns. Most wore jeans and cowboy boots; all nursed cocktails or beers; some held cigarettes. One blew a lugubrious air on the harmonica. Christopher opened the rickety gate. When he reached the porch, he asked if there was a vacancy. The baldest of the group turned and shouted indoors, "Oh, Saa-aam!"

"What is it, Ralph?"

"You have a cusss-tomer!"

A few seconds later, a silver-haired codger with a limp appeared, dressed in crispy denim.

"What can I do for you?" he asked in a low, sour voice.

"I need a room."

"I'll say he does," one of the men purred with a slight Southern accent. "Poor kid's soaked half to death."

"How long for?"

"The whole weekend. But I don't have much money. I need the cheapest thing you have."

"That'd be me," a plump man said, pointing languidly to his own nose.

"Hush!" said Sam, limping to the door, beckoning Christopher to follow.

Inside, everything was knotty pine. A fire crackled behind a grate, lighting the room in eerie, dancing stripes. Sam grabbed a ledger with a tattered leather cover and opened it on the counter. He ran a crooked finger down the page.

"Well, friend, I can give you the Rustler's Room for one night and the Bronco Room for another. After that, well, we'll just have to see."

"How much?"

"Thirty bucks *per*, pay when you leave."

"I'll take it," he said.

A voice came behind Christopher. "You got friends in town?"

He turned and looked. The man was fifty, nearly albino, and wore yellow clam-diggers. His eyes were red and runny.

Christopher smiled anxiously. "I don't think so. I'm really just here for work."

"On Labor Day weekend? Hope the tax people believe that."

"Just research," Christopher said, looking away.

"What kind?"

"Timmy, stop it," Sam commanded. "Business first." He turned the ledger around and pointed to the only empty line. Christopher squinted to see it.

"Welcome to The Corral," Sam said, as Christopher signed. "It's a friendly place. Most of the boys've been summerin' here for twenty years or more. Come and go as you please, but pipe down after midnight. If you need anything, just holler. Water's pretty scare, though, so flush only when necessary. You're free to have guests."

He limped around the counter, gesturing with an open hand toward the porch. "Come meet the boys."

Christopher

When Julie awoke the next morning, she knew by the amber glow of the blinds that the sky had cleared. She hurried her husband out of bed. As they were about to leave, he dropped a *Playboy* into their bag. She considered objecting, but then she remembered what he had been telling her for days: that this was his vacation not hers, that he was actually vacationing *from* something, because he worked hard all day, and not for himself either, but for *them*, as a couple, as a family; whereas the word vacation didn't really apply to her, did it, seeing as how she didn't have a job?

The water was busy with waders and swimmers. While Ted ran down to test the water, Julie unpacked. Standing with her back to the bay, she let the wind billow their towels to the sand. Ted ran up making a scrunched face and told her it was freezing. He fell onto his towel and slathered white goo on his body and face, then slipped on his mirrored shades and a white golfing visor.

"How do I look?" he asked, grinning.

"Like an idiot," she said.

After ten minutes, Julie turned and touched his face with the back of her hand. "Hey, big boy, wanna go for a swim?" He did not answer. She looked closer and saw that he was sound asleep behind his mirrors. She thought for a few seconds, then jumped up and ran for the shore. Her suit slashed high into her hip, making her legs look even longer than they were. Higher up, it clung tightly to her tiny waist and full breasts. "I've done nothing productive this year," she thought, "but at least I've kept in shape." But then as she turned and began to jog up the beach, it occurred to her: Why? What for? For her health, her husband? Not really. The only reason she kept in shape was to please other men. But why do that, what was the point, when she was married and would be till the day she died? She lost her breath and stopped. On the horizon, clouds sailed by like toy ships. She turned around and saw that the only people on the beach now were men, tanned and lean, lying back on their elbows, studying her with an unsettling disinterest. They approved, but so what? She wanted to be desired. She ran back even faster than she had come.

Breathless and glistening, Julie stopped at her towel and found Ted gone. She spotted him thirty feet away, sitting with a pair of college girls who looked like sisters. They were gymnast-tiny with chestnut tans and pert little tits. Ted smiled boyishly, sifting sand through his fists, his eyes darting from their overeager smiles to their taut legs. Although she couldn't hear what he was saying, she knew he was regaling them with tales of his work on Wall Street. She dashed over and skidded to a stop, spraying sand onto his chest and face. "Wanna fight?" she said, grinning and putting up her dukes. The girls were frozen, aghast. Ted, spitting sand, crawled to his feet, doing his best to hide his humiliation. "Excuse me, but we're on our honeymoon!" Julie grabbed him by the arm and hauled him away. When they reached their towels, she expected him to laugh, but instead he pinched her arm. She yelped, threw him a glare, then reached down for her bag. Ted kicked sand straight into her face.

"You *like* that?" he hissed. "You think it's *funny?*"

"*Fuck you!*"

"I'm your *husband!* Maybe you wish I weren't! Do you? Because it can be arranged!" He kicked more sand. "Tell me the truth, God damn it! Right now!"

The intensity of his anger surprised her. She twisted off her wedding ring and threw it at him. It hit him in the hand and bounced away. He lunged for it. Julie ran to the shore, galloped through the water, and ducked under a cold wave. She stroked and stroked, pretending she did not hear him when he called her name from the shore.

Christopher walked the unspoiled lanes of Truro, feeling the stirrings of an unfamiliar contentment. He had decided hours before, when he set out on the day's adventure, to go easy on himself. He would write only when the mood struck, and even then he would attempt only simple descriptions. So far, he had stopped five times and filled six whole pages with all that he had experienced on the drive up and three more with his search for a room. The words had flowed effortlessly. It's funny about writing, he mused, like most things it was either easy or impossible.

On the bus back to The Corral, the mood struck again. Now that he had exhausted the subject of yesterday, he would set to work on today. His goal was humble and defined: tell the truth of his senses without self-criticism or fear. He wrote for the next four minutes. Despite my urge to redact, even rewrite, the meager entries he scrawled, I will, in the name of narrator-reliability, offer them to you now exactly as they met my eye when I, weeks later, read them over for the first time:

A cool wind plays with my hair, first from the front, then the back, then the side, then the front.

A painter applies layer after layer on canvas, colored wash after colored wash. The last hue applied, the one that meets the eye, will be informed, almost beyond detection, by these buried washes. So it is with the green of the pines. Buried black alters it, lends the trees a nearly invisible link to death.

The song of crickets everywhere. Like a million squeaky wheels on tiny machines, pulsing in rhythm to secret work. A cricket jumps

*to my chest, then to my hand. Twitching antennae, a tiny tail, an
ass of armor. A grasshopper appears, too, looking for a friend. He
pauses, then clicks himself into the nearest camouflage.*

The air is sweet for napping.

*Stepping barefoot onto hot sand, digging in deep at the heels and
rolling the arches, provides an aching thrill. The sensation rises
to my crotch and stays there even after a dozen steps.*

*The bay is a blinding reflection, hard and flat as glass. Sinking
clouds run through with lances of purple, violet, and red.*

In the tower a bell is cocked, the clapper lolling before it strikes.

Here, we have a portrait of the artist, striving at long last, à
la the singularly untalented Mr. Henry David Thoreau, to give
utterance to the subtlest shades of his solitary perception. I confess that beholding these words for the first time as they slid out
of the photocopier, I could not help but feel hurt. I had done
everything in my power to deliver the boy to mental health, and
now, at long last, he had broken through, found his creativity
again, and where had I been? Not sitting at his side, holding his
quills (metaphorically) as the young Dora Copperfield does
(quite literally) for her beloved David, but stuck back in my
lonely lair, my ear pressed to the wall, wondering how on earth
he could remain silent for so long.

At six o'clock, when Julie returned to the hotel, there was a
note at the desk from Christopher, telling her where he was
staying and nothing else. She opened the door to their room,
certain that she would find Ted napping. He rarely missed his
preprandial snooze. But he was lying on the bed, wide awake,
still wearing his sandy swimsuit, gazing forlornly at the ceiling.

Christopher

The television was on. She dropped the note on the dresser a few inches from her wedding ring.

"Do you hate me?" she asked, twisting on the ring.

"A little," he said, lowering the volume.

An hour later, Ted cracked the tail of a two-pound lobster. Juice squirted his bib. Although he chattered amiably, on a wide array of subjects, ranging from money to cash, Julie saw that he was still hurt. His tiny eyes had become even smaller, as black and shiny as beetles, and his sunburned brow was etched with worry. His personality was gone, too. In its place were lifeless humor, hollow observations, and intense concentration on the mechanics of a sloppy meal. When they left the restaurant, Julie hooked her elbow in his and turned him toward the ocean. She was filled with sudden optimism. She would undo the damage.

"Come on," she said, "we're going for a moonlight walk."

He walked a few steps, then stopped dead, jerking her back. "I'm too tired."

Back in the room, Ted watched as she threw a big T-shirt, bearing the logo of his brokerage firm, over her naked body.

"Unbelievable," he murmured.

Ignoring the compliment, she slipped under the covers and opened a book. He opened *Playboy* and flipped to the back of the centerfold, where he learned what Kimberly liked and did not like. Then, restless, he found the remote control and watched a bad movie.

"Its badness is half its charm," he said.

"What's the other half?" she asked.

He smiled and tilted back the cover of her book. "*Jane Eyre*. Why're you reading that?"

"It's good."

"How do you know?"

"Chris said so when he gave it to me."

"He gave it to you? Why?"

"We're friends. Friends give each other gifts."

Ted looked away, considering the outlandish assertion, then he shrugged it away and turned off his lamp. He cuddled up close, wedging a hand between the mattress and the small of his wife's back. A minute later, she sighed, laid down her book, and shut off her lamp. She punched her pillows, then settled into darkness. Out of nowhere, Ted grabbed her face and gave her three quick kisses on the mouth. She kissed him back, but so hard that she pushed his face away.

"What's wrong?" he asked.

"Nothing. I'm all right."

"You like when I kiss you?"

"Uh-huh."

"So, how 'bout putting in your thing?"

"Don't call it that!"

"I'm sorry." He brushed her hair away from her face, then nibbled her cheek. "Come on. Put it in."

"It's not spontaneous."

"Well, if you put it in ahead of time, it would be."

"Oh, honey," she exhaled, "it's been such a hard day. Let's just be close."

"We're close right now."

"You wouldn't even take a walk with me."

"*God damn it!*" The room exploded with light. He was up, eyes aflame. "We're in bed! I'm hard! How close can we get?"

She shielded her eyes from the light. "Don't yell at me! I don't feel like making love, okay! What do you want me to do, fake it?"

"Yes!" He threw back the covers. "At least it would show you cared!" He threw himself naked into an armchair and snapped the remote like a gun at the screen. "You're so damned cold!"

Christopher

Julie considered for a few seconds, then stretched over and turned off his light. The room flickered with the light of the television.

Within minutes, she was sound asleep.

When she awoke, heart leaping, it was to the sound of Ted screaming in the dark. She lunged for the light.

"What is it?"

"Nothing, I just— Oh, Jesus, God! The mirror!"

He staggered away, squeezing his wrist.

"What did you do?"

"I punched it!"

"Did you break it?"

"I think so!"

"Where?"

"Not the mirror! My hand!"

He fell back into the armchair. There were tears in his eyes. "I can't stand it!" he cried. "My wife doesn't love me!"

In stark juxtaposition to the connubial joys of the Palmers stands the creative junket of our young hero, which continued the next day, unabated. His journal entries, lengthier now, begin with evocative descriptions of the previous night's solitary dinner, of the long shoreline walk that followed it, and of a second restless night spent at The Corral. Then he returns to his pastoral meditations. As you will see, after a few observations, pithy and mundane, he stumbles at long last on the crux of his odyssey, its buried purpose:

The morning sea is an emerald corrugation.

The woody clap of a screen door.

A car with a sticker: I Love Field Hockey.

A woman with a dog whose belly touches the road tells her friend: "I've basically just been hiding, adjusting to life without him."

I can either see or think, not both at once.

The climb to the church is steep amidst a litter of fallen leaves and needles. I crunch a pile of twigs as I climb over a low fence. I am reminded of snakes. Sure enough, one wriggles into the brush.

A field of gravestones. The song of crickets rises from the drained grass. A tune older than the first Paine or Ebenezer or Hatch or Stranger or Given or Dyer or Snow.

I lie on my back. I crack an eye into the sun. I turn my head and see the church where I was married. How certain the future seemed. Planned to have children by now. Instead, I am a child.

I look away to an ornate stone. There with the Givenses, facing me, it bears a willow whose branches pour like tears into a fountain. It reads: "Katherine Smith beloved wife of John Dos Passos. 1894–1947. My sweet, my lost love."

I remember how she died. A wink of sunlight across her windshield, a screech of tires, and she was gone forever.

I start to cry. First time since my wedding day. I still love Mary, never stopped. I cry for a long time.

A dying tree drops an apple.

The restaurant looked like the home of a fallen New England family. The paint, gnawed by salt air, was badly cracked. The chimney had lost a few bricks. Inside, Christopher worked his way through a plate of fried clams, while Julie, unable to eat, shared with him all that had transpired since their parting— every sorry detail. It culminated in her telling him of the long hours she had spent that day tending to Ted and his broken hand. They had not left the room once. She rubbed his back and fed him brownies and orange soda. She read to him, from *Playboy*, a short story by John Gardner, which she enjoyed very much, but he did not. The whole time, she was absolutely desperate to escape. The moment he fell asleep, she stole his car and sped to The Corral.

Christopher listened patiently, reserving comment, but his writer's ear was recording everthing. Tonight, before going to bed, he would set it all down, plus everything that followed. Why? Why was Christopher so concerned with Julie's romantic travails? After all, it was his and Mary's demise he intended to depict in *Love's Sad Archery*, not the Palmers'. The reason was simple and auspicious. For the first time in his young life, he was thinking like an artist, and an artist knows literary pay dirt when he sees it. And pay dirt, it was. Consider: Christopher's terrible year had begun with the escape of his unhappy wife, and now, approaching year's end, here was *another* unhappy wife ready to flee her marriage, but, even better, this second wife seemed to be suddenly smitten with *him*. He suspected that she was on the verge of offering herself to him if not body and soul, then certainly body. And where was all this taking place? In a restaurant not five miles from the church where he and Mary were wed. The irony was almost too wonderful to be believed. As was the symmetry. If he slept with Julie, it would make an ideal last chapter for his novel. Elegant. Everything would have come full circle. (*La Ronde*.)

But then, *truly* thinking like an artist, he patiently worked the meaning through to its conclusion. If he did sleep with her, what would be the emotional effect on his autobiographical hero? Would it ease his suffering? Would it offer redemption? And what of the reader? How would the reader view him? Was such an act in any poetic or Karmic sense, *just*? Might his protagonist's betrayal of his friend (foot soldier of Plutus, worshipper of Mammon) serve as a metaphor for art's ultimate victory over commerce? In short, Christopher was wondering not how the drama that he was living would end, but how it *should* end. The thought that he, and only he, would be its author filled him with excitement.

Julie emerged from the restaurant first, sniffling back tears, sagging under the weight of all that she had confessed. Christopher, a few yards back, stopped and looked up at the empty sky.

"Where did the moon go?" he asked, and, as he said it, he felt it to be not only an honest question, but a fine line of dialogue, as well.

"I'll bet you wanna call it a night," she sighed.

His brow rippled with confusion. "I thought we were going for a walk."

She smiled happily and her cheeks flushed. "Sorry, for a second I mistook you for Ted."

"Well, don't make that mistake again." He took her firmly by the elbow, and there was something in the way he did it that reminded him of Phillip taking Mary's arm at the poker game. "Good stuff," he thought. He led her up a long, dark slope. At the top there was a thrift store, a barber, an apothecary, a news dealer. The shop windows were covered with tatters of paper, announcing concerts, films, flea markets, housing for the winter. They passed a soda machine, then he led her down a steep, winding lane.

"Let's go there," he said, when they had reached the bottom. He pointed to a dessert parlor. The tiny patio was entirely taken over by teenagers bathed in a blue light. As Christopher and Julie approached, they heard their voices:

"It is not!"

"Yeah, there's one more day of summer."

"Not till the twenty-sixth. Three more weeks."

Christopher

"But not schoolwise. Schoolwise summer's almost over."

"So what?"

"So everything."

"Yeah, summer's too fast."

Their elegiac and fatuous banter was punctuated by the electrocution of a mosquito.

"I've changed my mind," Christopher said.

They walked instead onto a spit of land that extended a hundred feet into a marsh. They passed a hand-painted sign: "Take only photos. Leave only footprints." When they reached the end, there were two tree stumps with a pine board lying across them. They sat, then saw for the first time, out of nowhere, the reappearance of the moon. It was at the half, curved low and orange over the town like the smile of a jack-o'-lantern.

"Your marriage is a mess," Christopher murmured simply, echoing the word that Cameron Jaspar had used to describe him at the Guest Night. But it wasn't true anymore. He wasn't a mess. He would be all right. How had he saved himself? He thought it had something to do with his months of suffering and with what Patty had said about fairy tales and maybe with his crying that afternoon in the churchyard, but he knew it was futile to look for causes. Better simply to thank his lucky stars.

Because the harsh words he had spoken to Julie were his first in response to what she had told him at dinner, they shocked her pain into the open. She bit her lip and her face crumpled, as though the small bite hurt. She cried out, grabbed her hair in two fists, and fell against him. The board shook with her sobs. He stroked her back and looked out at the silly moon.

"I feel so trapped!" she wailed, finally. "I feel like his mother! All he ever wants is to be *alone* with me!"

"What do *you* want."

"To be free!"

"To do what?"

"Read! Paint again!"

"Ted says you have nothing *but* free time."

"It's different when I know he's coming home." She turned with a piteous, pleading look. "I've been here two days and I haven't seen the ocean yet. Just the bay. Will you take me. *Please,* Chris?"

They parked at the beach, then stripped off their shoes and socks and stowed them beneath their seats along with their wallets. Julie grabbed a woolen blanket and slung it around her shoulders like a cape. They jumped out and hurried across the parking lot, hobbling on twisted feet over sharp stones toward a separation in the dunes. When Christopher's feet hit the sand, he was pleased to discover that it was still warm below the surface. Blinded by dune-shadow and fog, they slipped through the narrow pass. The path widened and they made out a small, gray house, long deserted, drowned in mist like a sailor's memory of home. Then the ocean. The moon hung low, a gigantic yellow grin on the horizon. He took her hand and sped her as fast as his legs could travel. Then he stopped abruptly, gasping, and cried, "There it is!" She knew he meant the ocean and she laughed. Then she backed up and flung away the blanket.

"Let's go!"

"Where?"

She yanked off her shirt and sweater. She wore no bra. He was momentarily transfixed by her bosoms.

"Hurry!" she laughed, seeing his awed expression.

Christopher undressed. She took him by the hand and they bounded naked into the roaring surf. The shouts they released rang down the beach. They were not cries at the cold. The cold merely released them. They were howls of revolt. In the instant before he dove, his eyes flew to her body and, like a camera, he recorded its glory for his journal. Then he was pelted by a storm of bubbles.

Christopher

"Oh, it's hot!" Christopher screamed as he burst to the surface. "Fantastic! It's a hot bath!"

"What are you talking about?"

"Affirmations! Mind over matter! It's——" But he couldn't finish. He was cut in two by an icy current and his lungs seized. He gritted his teeth and they chattered. She laughed and grabbed him, pressing her bare breasts against his chest.

"Thank you for being my friend!" she said.

She kissed him on the forehead, the cheek, then quickly on the mouth. And then on the mouth again, this time with her tongue. It was warm and salty.

He pushed her away.

"What's the matter?" she asked.

He made a run for it. He strode into the heavy cold. She splashed up behind him. She chased him up the sand. He grabbed the blanket and clutched it madly to his trembling chest. Laughing, she tried to pull it away. When she could not, she contented herself with half. They spun around, rolling themselves into it, then fell to the sand, side by side. Their wet hair lay sprawled in the sand like seaweed.

"Don't move," Christopher began, his teeth clacking. "Or you won't hear what I have to say. Look, I'm angry at Ted, too. He's turned into a materialistic creep. You don't have to convince me he's worth leaving. But it's not right to involve me. He was my best friend. It was a while ago but——"

"Chris," she said, moving her face closer.

He was stopped, not by his name, but by her yielding, sensual tone.

"Are you . . . are you——" he stammered, his heart suddenly stricken with doubt as to what should happen next.

"Make love to me," she whispered, then she relaxed her head into the sand, her lips just inches from his, and waited for him to obey.

"You wouldn't feel guilty *at all?*" Christopher asked, strangely crestfallen, thinking again of Mary and Phillip. She made her eyes lifeless, then shook her head, raking her cheek into the sand. "But he loves you!" Chris insisted. "So much. I know it. He just needs you to show him how to—"

"I want someone who can teach *me* things. Someone like you. Someone who's creative."

Christopher realized with an odd sort of hurt that she did not really know him at all. If she did, she would have known that his creativity was only in its infancy, that for much of the past year he had been worse than blocked, he had been nearly dead. She did not want to make love to *him*. How could she when he was a stranger? She wanted to make love to a fantasy. Just as Mary had. Christopher understood now, for the first time, what he must do, how both this night and his novel must end. He knew his hero's redemption and enacted it:

"Look, if you want to hurt Ted, do it to his face, but don't use *me!*" He had meant it to sound indignant, but it came out as merely hostile. He wrestled himself free, then rose, naked and dripping, suddenly impervious to the cold.

"You're right," she said softly.

He glanced down at her, surprised, vaguely insulted. He had expected her to put up more of a fight.

"Wait," she said, her tone portentous. "I have something to tell you. Come closer."

Was there something he didn't know, some mystery about to be revealed?

He hesitated, then knelt, clutching his clothes against his chest.

"I know—" she said, reaching out and taking his hand, "I know you're right. But I don't care."

She slowly rolled onto her back and opened the blanket.

Her legs eased apart.

Christopher

He had never seen anything so beautiful in all his life. He wanted her with every ounce of his blood. He was not afraid. He remembered Ted. Then he thought of his novel. Nothing was more important than how it ended. His hero simply *could not* make love to Julie.

He climbed on top of her, anyway.

The next morning at ten, Christopher stopped at the hotel to ask Ted what time they would be heading back. The desk clerk informed him that the Palmers had checked out at dawn. Because every bus to Boston was booked, Christopher was forced to stay another night at The Corral (The Dale Evans Room).

His last day was his loneliest, but his most productive. Fed up with crickets and dune grass, he concentrated instead on setting down what he had been too tired to describe the night before: his final two hours with Julie, in which they had made love three times—once on the beach, once in Ted's car, then once more in Ted's car. He did not scribble fragments, either, no mere fodder for haiku; now our young hero constructed actual sentences, groups of which formed something called paragraphs.

The mystery of Christopher's silence was answered for me the next afternoon when I convinced our Maltese super, the sturdy and stalwart, Muscat Xuereb, to use his key to gain entry to Christopher's cell. The ostensible reason for this drastic measure was that I smelled gas. While Muscat crawled on all fours under the sink, I rummaged quickly through the detritus on Christopher's desk, searching for some clue as to his whereabouts. When it seemed that none was to be found, I was struck by an inspiration. I hit the outgoing message button on his answering machine.

Christopher's voice thrummed: "Hi, I'm out of town for the weekend. Leave a message at the beep."

Aha!

And then, only because I was there, I listened to his messages. There were nine in all: one from his sister, one from Daniella (no doubt already plunged into lifelong concubinage), one from an ex-student, one from Julie (left, I later deduced, from a pay phone on the morning of her and Ted's sudden departure), and five from Grace (each the canker of a mind in a savage mood).

"Please forgive me, Muscat," I said, turning to him after I had expertly rewound the tape. "I realize now it wasn't gas I smelled. It was smoke, olfactory residue, no doubt, of the boy's hopeless devotion to the Lady Nicotine. Ghastly habit, don't you think?" The impact of my improvisation was mitigated by the fact that the moment I learned Christopher had taken a vacation without me, I lighted a cigarette. Also, Muscat, while highly industrious, spoke nary a lick of English.

Upon returning to my lair, I paced the floor, trying to imagine where on earth Christopher could possibly have escaped to, and, far more important, *with whom*. My first thought was that he was visiting his beloved Grammy, but four days seemed an inordinate amount of time to spend with an old woman incapable of moving her bowels unassisted. He might be with friends, but I knew that his months-long oscillation between the Dark Unspeakable and the Light Ineffable had alienated just about everyone he had ever known or met.

My meditation was abruptly interrupted when I heard footsteps on the stairs. I ran to my door and peeked out. There he was, dropping his duffel to the floor just three feet away. How I longed to welcome him with a playful, "Yoo-hoo!" and a squirrelly smile, just as though we had never had a falling-out. But, foolish pride silenced me. Instead, I puffed generic tobacco into the hallway, enveloping him as he fumbled with his keys. It was

Christopher

an oblique welcome that said, "Do come in. I have a chilled Cabernet in the fridge. Rude and rustic with a whiff of buckeye and duckling." While such indirection might have worked for the noble Sioux, it failed miserably here. Christopher coughed, dragged in his bag, and slammed his door with a jangling crash.

October

I marked the days of our estrangement like a man jailed, wallowing in the most unattractive of all emotions——self-pity. This based on a fact which even to this day I shudder to confess. *Christopher was thriving.* In retrospect, of course he was; his weekend on the Cape had changed him forever, but, as our reconciliation was still weeks away, I could not have known it. All I had was the evidence of my eyes which was as baffling as it was humiliating. His color was pink, his hair lustrous, and his gaze bright (not, as before, with a manic gleam; now, with the serene glow of self-possession). Plus, he had again quit smoking. I intuited this one morning when he dashed by me on the stairs, wearing shorts and running shoes, bare-chested, clutching a sopping T-shirt. (His gams were lean, shapely, just hairy enough.)

How was it possible? I asked myself. How could he be flourishing without me? Was it merely a false rebound, another manifestation of his erratic brain chemistry? Or had he found God, and, if so, where? Or was it Dr. Geitman's handiwork? My worst fear, of course, was that he had fallen in love while on holiday. But, if so, with whom? The mystery roiled my sleep.

Christopher

Suddenly, the gulf that separated us seemed less a temporary breach than a permanent chasm. I felt like the most irrelevant man in the world, but rather than indulge in even more self-pity, I made up my mind to turn taps to reveille. If *he* could regain his health, then so could I. I rose defiantly from the ashes or, to be uncharacteristically literal, from my dirty queen, and set to work with fierce determination. I hauled my scalpy tweeds to a local Chinaman to be scorched and pressed. I entrusted my soiled linens to the soapy care of a local band of ambitious Koreans. I subjected my dome for the first time in years to a barber. In this case, the Sorrento-born Mario, who ran a kiosk in the guts of the Grand Central Station. I watched with wonder as his hairy-knuckled hand, adorned with a long pinky nail (the traditional symbol of his trade), snipped what remained of my carroty locks into a nifty Late Van Johnson. It cost less than seven dollars, including tip. And last but not least, I opened my mouth to an oral driller, a sadistic Pakistani who, for less than thirty dollars, plugged the holes and scrubbed my enamel from oyster-gray to buttercup.

When I walked home that afternoon, face numb, my metamorphosis was complete. You might wonder how profound the transformation could possibly have been when it had taken only a day and a half to complete and had been solely cosmetic. The answer is *very*. Like, say, Dame Laurence Olivier, I had found my new character not through sense-memory of the morning my boyhood schnauzer had been squished by an ice-cream truck, but in the meticulous alteration of my *external* appearance. Each change to my exterior was like a seed sending long, green roots into the depths of my loamy soul. I had not felt so lovable in years.

Happy to be alive and eager to save bus fare, I cut across Central Park on foot. Demeter, it seemed, was celebrating my renewal, for, despite the fact that it was autumn, it might very well have been summer. It was as if the course of the seasons had been reversed. A hot sun baked the dying leaves, and the flawless grass of Sheep Meadow was alive with scantily clad nubiles—of exactly the sort that shuttled in and out of Christopher's cell. Wealthy and cocksure, they talked and laughed, threw saucers and balls, gargled soda and beer. Their expensive new sunglasses were menacing. These were the heirs of Manhattan Island and they knew it. What they did *not* know was that never again would they be so free of care. Soon college would bore them, jobs mangle them, marriage crush their wills to live. The Fates would bring them unimagined grief and disappointments. All of them would die one day. It made me chuckle.

Perspiring heavily beneath my bomber jacket, I stripped it off and, because it was a bit tattered at the elbows and had been a high school graduation gift from my adoptive father (who had molested me), I tossed it carelessly into the nearest trash container. A magnificent gesture. Like Christopher, I was shedding dead skin, bidding adieu to the negations of the past and greeting, not an instant too soon, the Everlasting Yea. I threw back my head and savored the balmy breeze, letting it dry the patches of sweat that soaked my satin blouse.

I quickened to a trot and looked down at my cordovans. Although they needed mending (the tassels were shot), there was a fresh bounce to their step. Following the course of my previous fancy, I looked around, imagining with great satisfaction all the spring flowers that would grace the park by Thanksgiving and how much younger I would be by New Year's. Then I fell to my knees and eventually found, just as I was ready to abandon the search, a four-leaf clover, which I promptly chewed and swallowed, thinking all the while of my honey.

When I got home, I took off all my jewelry and rushed to the mirror. To say that I looked smashing would be a criminal understatement. I threw on another jacket and grabbed a well-

Christopher

thumbed volume of the poetical works of Mr. A. E. Housman. I had planned since college to pen a tart little parody entitled "To an Aesthete Dying Young." Why not strike while the iron was hot? I ran downstairs to the sunny stoop and settled in. I could barely contain my excitement at the thought of my darling Christopher beholding, for the first time, the new and improved B. K. Troop. At worst, he would be impressed; at best, he would realize that he loved me.

When Christopher got out of his cab five hours later, Helios had long ago ducked for cover and I had yet to write a word. I was intensely cold. I looked up at him more urgently than I would have liked, unable to stop my eyes from blossoming with hope. He stared directly at me, but dully, as though I were a mediocre sculpture, then disappeared inside.

The world reeled and spun.

Suddenly, I was face down on my bathroom floor, sobbing like a Laotian mother who has just watched her only daughter disappear in a scalding vapor. Why had I ever lifted my ban on romantic love? I inwardly howled. Wasn't this exactly why, after my college heartbreak, I had imposed it? Because romantic love, for all its Alpine glory, has a way of wending down, ineluctably, into a vale of snot? Hour upon hour, I writhed on the floor of every room, missing Christopher with the first and last particle of my being. I arose only to use the toilet and press my ear to the living room wall. In my madness, I felt that I was as ugly a human being as had ever lived. A monster really, whose life was a giant sham, a fey intellectual burlesque, designed to distract others and myself from the truth, which was that, although I dreaded loneliness more than anything else, I had come to earth to die of it.

As my agony reached dangerous levels, I ran out of food, but I could not bear to go out, because I knew that wherever I went would be hell, because I *was* hell. I might have killed myself, but for the terrible pain such a selfish act would have caused precisely no one. And yet, despite the fact that I was pitched past pitch of grief, the irony of the situation never eluded me: For all these months, I had thought it was my young neighbor who was destined for a dark night of the soul, when, in fact, it was arrogant I.

As we all know, it is a distinguishing feature of Man that when he is closest to death, he is closest to new birth. On the fourth evening of my trial, I awoke with a sudden shock. I felt inexplicably better. I was drained of mucus and tears, tired of being sick. I crawled to my feet and peered around the room with a wide-eyed, curious look like a freshly hatched reptile. Was this, like Christopher's on the Fourth of July, merely a temporary rebirth or was it a bona fide new beginning?

Eager to test it, I sprinted to the Parnassus. After scarfing down a savory lamb stew with a side of lima beans and a double rum and coke, I vaulted off the curb and flung up my hand. A cab screeched to my feet. A homely Sikh eyed me with envy from beneath his burgundy turban.

"Fifty-ninth and First," I pronounced grandly.

Seven days later, I rediscovered a sobering fact: no amount of liquor, disco dancing, and costly Oriental sex can vanquish love. So I made a stab at more healthful pursuits: I attended an operetta with Wolf; I forced myself into a trendy West Village saloon and made small talk with assorted body builders, actors, and graphic designers; I guzzled wheat grass juice; I even signed up for a trial membership at a local gymnasium. The result? Days later, I trudged back up to my lair, pectorals aching, stomach swimming with chlorophyll, more bereft of vitality than at any point in my long life. I knew then, beyond a shadow of a doubt, that I could not live without Christopher. I loved him with all my heart. I had to get him back, or perish. The question, of course, was how. It was not ethical what I did next, but ethics, I have long held, are a luxury of the secure. Strangely, with all the cunning at my disposal, I did not plan my unethical action at all.

It happened like this: I was descending the steps one afternoon when I heard someone mounting the steps toward me. I stopped and listened. It was Christopher's sneakery footfall, no doubt about it. I wanted to cut and run, but there was no time. Suddenly, there he was, stopped dead, staring up at me, holding two shopping bags bulging with organic produce. He looked lovely. For an instant, we both simply stared. Then it came to me, landing on my brain pan like a cinder spit up from some infernal furnace.

"I have leukemia," I said.

"What?"

"Is there a problem with the acoustics?"

"Is it . . . bad?"

"No, it's *good* leukemia." That was a bit heavy-handed, so I leavened it in with a subtle moistening of eye. "I don't mean to be flip," I said, voice quavering, "but I'm sure you can imagine how awful it must be for me—I have *so* much to live for."

"What are they doing for it?" he asked, setting down his bags.

"Injecting me with toxic chemicals, bombarding me with gamma rays. Only time will tell. Cassandra gives me six months."

"God, I'm really sorry, B.K."

He was sincere. Our eyes locked. And suddenly from the depths of my heart there rose a cry. "*I miss you so much!*"

He looked surprised, then smiled. The smile was hollow, but a drowning man questions not the soundness of the branch.

"Allow me!" I eagerly snatched his bags and scooted up the stairs.

"Are you sure you should be doing that in your condition?" he asked, chasing after.

"The day my disease makes chivalry impossible is the day I *welcome* death."

Then the most awful thing happened. At his door, he took his bags back, wished me luck, and disappeared into his cell. He locked the door behind him.

Skulking back to my lair, I was deeply ashamed of my gambit. It was the retarded spawn of a base desperation. I deserved to be punished for it, perhaps with a dose of *actual* leukemia. But it had at least taught me something invaluable: Even the prospect of my dying was not enough to inspire Christopher to revive our friendship. That night, reflecting on this crushing, final fact, I felt my heart chill. A surge of rebellion stiffened my limbs. My teeth ground. I had reached at long last my limit.

The next night, at the stroke of twelve, Claude, my old Canuck standby from Staten Island, shyly entered my lair. As instructed, he had soaped himself free of bong smoke and was clad in sneakers, faded blue jeans, and a crisp, white button-down.

"I greet thee, my darling," I said from the shadows, my voice hushed and masterful.

He shut the door and came to me. He stopped just a few feet away. I reached out, flicked the button of his denims, unzipped them a bit, then in one quick move yanked them to his knees. I extended a freckled finger and gently pulled down his briefs, revealing his manhood. Uncut! Alas, on several occasions, I had seen the shadow of Christopher's endowment through his pants and it was decidedly manicured. I moved closer to Claude. I swilled wine in my mouth, and, as my teeth slid back his member's pliant flesh, I sluiced its buried treasure with the grape's purple benediction.

I leaned back and studied my handiwork.

"Just as I imagined it," I whispered.

Christopher

I took the puzzled Claude by the hand and led him into the inner sanctum, where for the next two hours I performed several acts of darkness. To wit, I plowed him stupid, all the while growling with an admixture of rage and tenderness, "Christopher, Christopher, Christopher . . ."

As instructed, the lout remained silent.

When he left, I showered, and stepping from the steam I felt, for the first time since that fateful January morning, *whole*. My dignity was restored. I saw my neighbor clearly now. He was not a nice person. I would have nothing further to do with him.

This might very well be the end of my story, but it is not, because three nights later, a miracle occurred. I had passed the evening in quiet bliss, reading aloud to myself, from my morris chair, the works of the last great English poet, Mr. Dylan Thomas. His lilting Swansea rhythms and the copious amount of ale I had drunk in his honor must have gotten the best of me, because the next thing I knew I was waking in my dark bedroom. Standing before me was a shadowy figure. Certain that I was about to have my throat cut, I struggled to scream, but I could not. It took a moment for my brain to clear and my eyes to adjust. I realized with a shock that the intruder was Christopher, wearing only a T-shirt and boxers. My eyes traced down his anxious face to his strong chest to his muscled arm and then to his hand. He held something. A tube. Not what you think. A scroll of papers.

"Are you awake?" he asked.

"Yes," I said. "What do you want?"

"I started my novel," he said, his voice full of fear, which I sensed was really nothing more than curbed excitement. "Would you read it?"

For ten long seconds we simply stared at each other—he knowing that he had had no right to ask; I knowing that I had no reason to agree.

"You've treated me cruelly," I said.

"I know," he said, softly. "I'm really sorry."

"Why have you come to me? Why not someone else? Someone less ridiculous?"

"You're the smartest person I know," he answered.

Pleasing. Quite pleasing, it was.

Then he ruined the effect, by adding, with a crooked smile, "Besides, you live so close."

Despite my lack of appreciation for his jest, I sat up and thrust out a hand. "Give it to me. Return tomorrow at noon."

A classical Greek tale: Man meets Boy, Man tries to get Boy, Man loses Boy, Man gets Boy back. Perhaps you judge me, Stern Reader, for my easy acquiescence to his demand, but there is a calling higher than those trumpeted by our wills and prides. Or even our intelligences. I believe in many Gods, but the one to whom, in my soul's bottom, I pay the most honor is Apollo, and it was he who called me. If the boy was determined to become an artist and I could do something to help, it would have been most impious of me to decline. Denied the privilege of being his lover, or perhaps even his friend, I would serve as his mentor, if not muse. How I *felt* about the prospect was unimportant.

After he left, I splashed cold water on my face and read his manuscript. I was disappointed to find that it was scrawled notes, not typed fiction, but they showed talent. He wrote vividly about the day he had met Mary and the shared idealism that had fueled their courtship. He devoted five whole pages to their wedding day. I suspected that this was a false start, that in the end his novel must begin with their separation, even if only to flash back to the rest of the tale, but a start it was. I removed a blue pencil from a kitchen drawer, ready to begin my cruel

Christopher

work, but then I thought better of it. For now, all the boy needed was encouragement.

The next day at noon, he entered my lair and we began his first tutorial. We discussed in general terms the need for him to structure his tale. I suggested that it would be best, for the time being, if he continued on with his notes, but, as the days passed, to focus his creative meditations on exactly what he wanted to say and the most honest and economical form in which to say it. We chatted for hours, and, as we did, I could feel the gradual return to our previous intimacy. The only difference was an unprecedented reserve in him. Never did he allude to the cause of his renascence, about which I was most curious. Just what exactly had taken place during our long separation? Where had he gone on holiday and with whom? Because he did not tell me, I feared to ask.

One afternoon in his cell, while he was speaking to Grace on the phone, I noticed on his desk a spiral book filled with his handwriting. As you know, I stole it. Once I had made a photocopy and safely tucked it in my night stand, I dashed back to his cell, and, a minute later, as he boiled water for green tea, I returned the journal to its rightful place. Ironically, it was only now that I had the answers I craved that he began to offer them freely.

"Strange, isn't it?" he said. "That you're feeling sick just when I'm finally starting to feel good."

"What do you mean *sick?*" I snapped defensively.

"Leukemia."

Looking back, I wish I had confessed my folly right then and there, but I was stricken with embarrassment. I glanced away and muttered, "Oh, yes, that." Then, I settled onto the couch with a wince, as though my blood ached. I knew he was watching me intently. I batted my eyes. I could not have looked more pathetic. "But *why* do you feel good?" I gasped.

"Well, being miserable for months didn't hurt. And, of course, Dr. Geitman's incredible."

"Yes, I know. I recommended her."

He settled down next to me. "But things really turned around after that last night at Arabia."

"The night you poleaxed me without mercy?"

"Yeah. It was something Patty said."

"Who's *Patty?*"

"Tarek's wife, you knucklehead."

"Oh, yes, of course." As so often happens when it comes to the dumpy, I had forgotten her almost immediately.

"She said she'd dug deep inside and found a golden nugget."

"Come again?"

"Okay, so she's no rocket scientist."

"But she is, it seems, a geologist."

He laughed.

Huzzah—I was appreciated again!

"Anyway, for some reason it stuck with me . . . the idea that she'd found something, some essential part of herself that, no matter what, she was going to protect. That's why she left Tarek. He was beating her, you know."

"Of course."

"You *knew?*"

"Certainly." I was lying. "Go on," I urged with a shaky hand. "What happened? Don't tell me you found *your* golden nugget?"

"I think I did. I decided to be easier on myself. Stop punishing myself for who I am. Don't get me wrong, I'm still miserable a lot, but not like before. Not in the same way. Plus . . . well . . ." He smiled, his eyes dewing. "I sorta got laid."

I sat bolt upright. Having not yet read his journal, I could not have been more surprised. He then told me all about Julie. Most striking to me in the slow-unfolding epic was not that, despite knowing it was wrong, he had made love to her. This carried no greater existential weight than his felonious defiling of little Daniella. It was a breakthrough, certainly, but a redundant one. No, what struck me, thrilled me, in fact (which is probably why I was not at all jealous), was that he had made love to Julie knowing full well that his novel must conclude with *his hero* rejecting her. In other words, he had realized that just because he made love to Julie, did not mean that his protagonist had to. While such a conclusion might be obvious to, say, you and me, for an idealist like Christopher, it was nothing short of momentous. The mooncalf was separating his life from his work, which meant that at long last he could begin to truly live. And write. Strangely, while his sensitive spirit was certainly aware of all this (how else to explain its liberation?), his conscious mind was still in the dark. I ventured to enlighten him, to reveal to him the staggering import of what had taken place:

"My God," I said. "You're free!"

"What do you mean?"

"I mean you're free!"

"I didn't know I was imprisoned."

"You were! Since the day you gazed up into your mama's eyes, looking for God, and found Godzilla." He laughed, but I did not. I was up and pacing now, forgetting all about my terminal condition. "You knew at birth that Grace didn't love you—"

"At *birth?*"

"You sensed that she only wanted to eat you . . . *incorporate* you . . . to satisfy her own selfish needs."

I was reaching him. His mind was working.

"So . . ." he said.

"So you internalized the rejection and aped it, as infants are programmed to do. You rejected your self, just as she had, but then you went even further. You rejected *all* of life, creating a parallel universe deep inside your gorgeous head."

Christopher, mesmerized, sensing where this was going, smiled. "Is that why it's so big?"

"Yes, yes! It had to be, to contain the whole world. From that moment on, you were no longer a human being living a life, but a cripple *dreaming* one."

"Wow."

"But not anymore! You slept with Julie, but your protagonist will not, am I right?"

"That's right. It would ruin the book."

"Yes! Which means that you've separated from your hero. You've entered the world! You're free to do anything you want now, to follow every mad impulse and whim. You're free to be immoral. Free to fail. And from the glorious chaos that ensues . . . the noisy, ambiguous welter . . . the graveyard of mistakes and sins . . . you can later, tranquil at your desk, create something whole and beautiful. You're no longer a saint! You're a man! And you're *alive! There's* your golden nugget! *That's* why you've begun your novel!"

I wanted to hoist him from his seat and give him a congratulatory hug, so that is precisely what I did. And it was at that moment that *I* was set free, as well. Christopher was no longer a prey to be captured or a romantic idol at whose feet to fall, but a friend. Perhaps the first male friend of my life. I knew then that if our bond was to deepen it would be solely on the spiritual plane, and I was content with that. In fact, I was grateful. Good God, what sort of love is this? I wondered (squeezing him tight to my bosom, pecking him chastely on the ear), that accepts a ban not only on sexual intimacy, but on all romantic fulfillment? Could it be—a shock ran through me—of the *true* variety?

Christopher

November

Love is the need to emerge from oneself and that is exactly what I did. I stepped from the shadows of snide disdain and wry aloofness where I had always lived and I engaged another human being as a friend. Freed of all agenda, I no longer manipulated or schemed, which meant that Christopher no longer felt compelled to deflect or defend. Our bond was one of mutual support now, shared optimism. I was able, at long last, to share with the boy the best of Bryce Kenneth Troop. Between tutorials, I sent him into paroxysms of giggles with candid tales of my misspent youth: spitty midnight fumblings at sleep-away camp, the seduction of my summer-school tennis coach, my lifetime banishment from a college cafeteria. From time to time, we actually ventured out together, saw movies and plays, strolled museums, shopped for food, cheered the lesbians at play on the gridirons of Central Park. One night, Christopher read to me from his journal. Of course, I knew it by heart, but that did not diminish my pleasure. I sat back, bathing in the warm light of his confidence.

The only obstacle to our intimacy reaching its full Apollonian potential was that I was still trapped in my foolish and shameful lie. I wanted to be free of it, but it was simply too early for me to announce myself cancer-free, and if, at this late date, I revealed my duplicity, he might never forgive me. In short, I had no choice but to service the lie until it could be safely ditched. So, I borrowed six prescription bottles from an old librarian chum stricken with AIDS and filled them with assorted analgesics and candies which I popped from time to time. Occasionally, I would feign nausea and fire up an oregano joint. (Real pot unhinges me to the degree that I cannot even talk to a person without thinking about his skeleton.) As for the inevitable hair loss, I hired the trusty Mario to hack me to bits with a straight razor (a Red Buttons), then I covered the fiasco with a Mets cap. The charade seemed to work.

And, so, as Orwell's year neared its uncelebrated end, we were so content that we hardly noticed the wind whistling at the edges of our windows, the steam pipes clanging in the corner, or even the landslide defeat of Mondale that sent shivers through the land's few remaining liberals. (Giving in to my friend's insistence that I perform my civic duty, I had accompanied him to the polls. Ever a lover of the Common Man, I voted for Mr. Arvo Halberg—widely known as "that pinko, Gus Hall." Christopher wrote in the Reverend Jesse Jackson.) We were unfazed by all of this, Stunned Reader, because our love bore more marvelous fruit every day.

The *most* marvelous fell on Veteran's Day. Christopher stepped out of the Grand Central Station, having just returned from a painful visit to Grammy. A cruel Canadian wind swept across Forty-second Street. He stopped and bought a scratchy scarf for four dollars from a curbside Nigerian. After walking a few blocks, he wished he had taken the subway. His sinuses were sore, his slow-cleaning lungs still tender. Autumn, which had never really come, was over now and winter was gathering force. Another year was dying, he thought. His tutoring was almost finished. New students wouldn't appear until February. And what a year it had been. Epic. He wondered what he would do now, with so much time on his hands and the burden of so many pictures in his head. Would he leave off his notes and begin his novel in earnest? If so, when, and what would be its shape?

It was then the fruit fell. The words came to him from out of nowhere in precisely this order: *Because every cell contains the blueprint of the entire being, the sketch of a moment is actually a mural of all eternity*. A distinctly Blakean notion, hardly surprising from the well-read son of a geneticist, but almost at once it suggested an approach. What if he told his story of love's sad demise, not beginning, as he had always planned, with the day he met Mary, but much later, after they had already separated, on, say, the first of January? (He was reading my mind.) And what if the novel concluded the following New Year's Eve? Why not? If a sketch of a moment is a mural of eternity, then could not the faithful depiction of a single lonely year illuminate the entire failed romance that had preceded it? In fact, could it not reveal an entire life? The idea sent his heart pounding and before he knew it he was running home to tell me.

I thought it was a fabulous idea. Within hours, the boy was buried deep in *Love's Sad Archery*. The jam was broken. The rat-a-tat-tat of his Smith-Corona fluttered through my walls like birdsong. Every night, his labors concluded, we would sup together in my apartment, then repair to the living area where we would sip the grape (although not in the same alarming quantities as before), and he would read aloud his day's progress. I would listen, head thrown back, eyes closed, reexperiencing the events of his year, but with even more pleasure than when I had first vicariously lived them.

Once his recitals were over, however, I was all business. I

would snap to, whip out my cruel blue pencil, and scribble all over his pages. I soon discovered that I was a superb editor. And this was no easy job! Truth be told, it was positively *Perkinsian* in scope. The lad's prose was talented, but bland and gutless. In no time at all, inspired by my suggestions (actually, governed by them), his style gained brio and panache. By the end of the second week, our styles melded so well that reading over a polished page I could hardly tell which words were his and which were mine. We were like opposing mirrors reflecting each to each.

The pride I felt in his progress brought to mind a masterwork of that great low-country manic-depressive, Mr. Vincent van Gogh. The painting in which a kneeling peasant reaches out long, welcoming arms to his toddler as he takes his first wobbly steps. But I felt pride also in *myself*, because I knew that none of this would have been possible without me. It was I, after all, and not Dr. Geitman, who had given him the intellectual understanding to act on his soul's emancipation.

I do confess, however, that I was a bit put out when, going over the outline of the book, I discovered that I was not to appear, even cleverly disguised, anywhere in the story. I chuckled and told Christopher that this made no sense. It would be like telling the story of 1666 London and leaving out the fire. He agreed, but then argued that a character based on me would strain the credulity of the average reader. "So what?" I replied. But he would not budge. At an earlier date, this might have plunged me into a swivet, but I at last understood the truth of all those time-tested homilies, apophthegms, and dorm-room posters that speak of giving, not taking, being of the essence of true love. I was content to be invisible.

As his work advanced, certain scraps of Christopher's year, as if caught by a fateful wind, obediently appeared at his doorstep, offering chapters of his life precisely the sort of closure they would need if his novel was to satisfy. For instance, one night, Celia, the dog-faced but highly successful fashion model from the Gary Hart campaign, appeared on our landing. Hearing Christopher's voice inside my lair, she poked her muzzle in. She looked so green that I did not even sulk when Christopher cut short our labors and hurried her away.

Inside his cell, she was safe to be herself. She fell prostrate on the couch and sobbed her ugly guts out. Poor thing, she had remained steadfastly loyal, toiling not only for the doomed Hart all the way to the Democratic Convention, but for the coon-eyed Mondale (whom she had previously despised) right up until Tuesday, November 6, when America handed him his head. In the days since, she had staggered the streets, sobbing and drinking, dripping silky cords of snot down the front of her designer coat.

For two hours, Christopher stroked her stringy hair and told her over and over again that everything would be all right, that all she needed was some sleep. Twelve hours later, when she awoke and saw him sitting alone at his desk, typing away, she selfishly patted the cushion and begged him to sit close. When he obeyed, she opened her mouth and lunged voraciously, tongue wiggling. He jerked away.

"What's the matter?" she asked, baffled.

"It's . . . it's just not a good idea."

"You thought it was a good idea *before*," she purred, lacing her fingers into his. "During the campaign. Didn't you?"

"Well, yeah, but that was a long time ago."

"*Six months!*" she cried, alarm flaring in her eyes.

"A lot's happened since then."

Now she was suspicious. "What?" When he paused, she realized the obvious. "You're in love, aren't you?" He emphatically shook his head. "Yes, you are! You're lying! I can see it!" And, of course, she was right. But he was not in love with a young woman, or even with me, but with his work. "You know what, Chrissy?" She sat up and jerked at her filthy duds. "I'm really sorry I bothered you."

He spoke with forceful tenderness. "Listen, even if I were ready for some sort of relationship, I'd want it to be on equal footing. With neither of us looking to be saved. You know I'm crazy about you, but it . . . it just can't start like this."

"*Like what?*"

"Well . . . with you in this condition."

She stared at him as though he had slapped her. "Oh, wow. Thanks a lot. I'm sorry if I have feelings! I'm sorry if I care about the country's future!"

"What about *your* future?"

"Don't you lecture me."

"Why not?"

(He was, after all, a tutor, paid to lecture.)

"At least I *tried!*" she said, her voice shaking with indignation. "I did what I could to get Reagan out! I gave up everything! I worked my ass off! You did *nothing!* So when he drops the bomb on Russia, or——"

Christopher could have let her go on, but he had spent an entire year listening to people. Now he had something to say.

"Look!" he shouted, shocking her into silence. "As long as your life is the way it is, I don't think it really matters *what* happens to the world. You go on and on about deficits, pollution, nuclear this and nuclear that, but the whole time you're in debt, you're not bathing, and your apartment looks like a bomb hit it!"

Inspired by his insight, Celia hurled wild imprecations and vicious anathemata at his head. But for the first time in months——ever?——our young hero was indifferent to the needs of others. He was cloaked in a hard-won selfishness. Serene and inviolate, he was like a pregnant woman who knows that the

Christopher

emerging life inside her renders her exempt from the vagaries and insults of the street. His ears shut down, and he gazed longingly at his typewriter.

In the days that followed, Christopher's resolve only grew stronger. He became ruthless in eschewing all distraction. I dared interrupt him only twice a day: at noon to bring him a home-cooked lunch (ordered in) and at five to knead and pound his aching back. His diligence paid off. With each passing chapter, his prose required less and less of my cruel blue pencil. The pile of his manuscript grew with mushroom speed.

On the afternoon of November 20, I was finishing off the young author with a flurry of expert judo chops, when I cleared my throat. I was about to reveal a gigantic secret: It was my forty-eighth birthday. I had arranged a quiet little dinner for two at the Parnassus. It was Tuesday. The special was beef Wellington. Days before, I had asked Cassandra to set aside a bottle of their finest gin. Suddenly, the phone jangled. His eyes darted, annoyed.

"Permit me," I crooned, picking up. "Hello, what is it?" I snapped into the receiver. "He's very busy."

"Won't take a second! Let me speak to 'im!" The male voice was casual, but very loud, hurled at a speaker phone.

"Who, may I ask, is calling?"

"*Me.*" He broke into peals of full-throated cultic laughter. I covered the receiver. "It's Cameron Jaspar, world-class mama's boy. Do you want to speak to him or shall I tell him to ring back later? Say, during his next lifetime?"

Christopher smiled, thought for a few beats, then reached. I shook my head and hit the speaker function. Two can play at *that* game.

"Hi, Cameron," he said, leaning back in his chair.

"Hey, Chris, how ya doin'?"

"Good. I'm getting a massage."

"Yeah?"

"Yeah. What's up?"

"Well, I'm calling all the people I never see."

"What for?"

"To invite them to a Graduate Seminar. It starts Wednesday, runs six out of the next eight Wednesdays. It's called Getting Unstuck."

Christopher asked him what it was about exactly, and Cameron laughed as though the question were preposterous.

"It's about getting unstuck! It's about moving to the next level. It's about always seeing where you are, telling the truth about it, then seeing the thing that you need to do to move on. It's about drastic measures. It's about having control over your purpose."

"*About* how much does it cost?"

"Two hundred and seventy-five dollars."

"Well, that sounds reasonable, but no thanks."

"What?"

"No, thanks."

"You sound a little serious over there. Take a breath. What's up? What're you attached to? This is an opportunity I'm offering you. Give it to yourself."

Then, like all good salesmen, Cameron left silence.

I watched with anticipation as Christopher considered. I knew only too well that once a person has seen his goal and chosen the road that will lead him to it, the Fates have a way of dishing out roadblocks and scenic detours. This seminar was certainly both. It was, I feared, in the brainwashing process, the Final Rinse.

"I'm *already* unstuck," Christopher said lightly.

"Nope," Cameron snapped with certainty. "The only place you can give this to yourself is here."

"Nope, the place I gave it to myself is *here*." He pointed, not

Christopher

to his apartment, but to his heart. "Thanks for calling." With a quick slap, he cut off the call.

I hopped up and down like a cheerleader. I almost attempted a cartwheel. I was so proud of him that I decided not to tell him it was my birthday. His focus was, and deserved to be, only on himself and his work. That night I dined alone and told Cassandra all about my protégés's emerging novel. She promised to pick it up once it hit the shelves.

One day at noon, I entered Christopher's cell wearing a sneaky look. He smiled quizzically when he saw me, then rose from his chair, expecting me to serve him a tuna salad on whole wheat. Instead, I took him by the hand. His nails were much improved.

"What?" he asked, looking a bit worried.

"What *what?*"

"What's that look?"

"What look is that?" I asked coyly, walking him backward out the door.

"Come on, you nut, what's going on?"

"Close your eyes."

He sighed and indulgently obeyed. I led him into my lair, then ordered him to open up. What he saw on my tea trolley amazed him.

"Whoa!" he ejaculated. "Where did you order *that* from?"

I comically bristled, eyes blazing with affront. "*Order*, lad? Zounds, I cooked it!"

"No!"

"Yes! With these!" I held up my large mitts and wiggled the fingers. And it was true. In an unprecedented display of domestic ardor, I had that very dawn donned an apron and, working to the misogynistic strains of *Annie Get Your Gun*, whipped up, in a mere three hours, a fabulous, traditional Thanksgiving Day feast.

We sat and Christopher watched, spellbound, as I commenced a hasty dismemberment of the fowl. While it is against my nature to boast, it would be the height of dishonesty for me not to tell you, Drooling Reader, that this first foray into the rarefied realm of puritanical cuisine was nothing short of sublime. The bird was pink, the squash soft, the cranberry thin and sweet.

Sadly, Christopher, although he had not eaten anything all day but a bowl of corn flakes, was not very hungry. So he mostly watched while I ate. But it did not matter. Even better than the food was the gratitude we both felt that on this, the second most hallowed of holidays, we were seated not with blood relations, but across from each other. For is it not a fact of our modern age that the family we cherish most is not the one who shares our noses and tempers, but the one with whom we share the minutia of our daily lives?

Hours later, as he read me his day's progress, the telephone offered up yet another roadblock: Mary dash actress exclamation point. Her voice sounded dreamy but grave on the speaker. She wished him a happy holiday, then said that they needed to talk. I smelled a melodrama coming on. So did Christopher. He tried to beg off, but she refused to take no for an answer. He agreed to meet her the next day outside the Port Authority at one o'clock sharp.

Vicious winds whipped around Christopher's legs as he waited. The cold sank deep into his toes. When Mary arrived at 1:32, he was leaning back, rigid against a steel column, his cupped hands pressed down on the stinging burgundy of his ears. She strode up, looking more malnourished than usual. Her hair had been hacked short by a blind gardener. Instead of apologizing for her tardiness, she asked why he hadn't yet purchased a proper hat and coat. Would he never grow up?

On the way to the restaurant, Christopher noticed a new confidence in her step. Head thrown back, arms pumping, she

Christopher

grinned into the gale as she told him all about her new life with Roger, an Actor's Studio disciple whom she had met in the unemployment line.

"He's doing great now," she said. "He's in L.A., shooting a film. I read the script. It's about a group of driving instructors. It's horrid, but money's money, right?"

"Sometimes," he muttered cryptically.

When they got to the trattoria she had chosen, Mary bounded up the stairs. When he entered the restaurant, she was already studying the menu. He sat across from her and for the next half hour she talked without interruption.

"I'm sorry I'm going on like this," she said finally, poking warily at her salad, "but I have something to tell you and I'm doing everything I can to avoid it."

With a pinch of bread, Christopher wiped his plate clean of tomato sauce. When he heard a soap-opera silence, he looked up. Her eyes beamed beatifically at him. She reached for his hand. At the same time, he reached across the table and speared a chunk of her cucumber.

"Chris," she said, her tone lofty and pained.

"Yeah?"

"I'm pregnant." She sat back and waited for him to gasp or howl or weep, but he did nothing. A bit irritated, she added, "I'm going to have a baby."

"I know what pregnant means."

"I knew you'd be angry," she said, shaking her head with dismay.

"I'm not."

"Of course you are."

"I'm not," he said again, spearing a tomato.

"Yes, you are."

He looked her in the eye and chewed. "Actually, I'm disgusted."

His words startled her to such a degree that she began to eat. After a few chews, she said, with a vague air of ennui, "And *why* is that?"

"I don't think you're ready to be a mother."

"Don't be stupid."

"So you planned it then?"

"What? Well, no, but—"

"Oh, so it was only *after* you found out that you were pregnant that you realized you were ready?"

Her eye twitched. "That's right. You think that's so unusual?"

"No, it's pretty common, but don't you think you ought to have figured out who you are before you started having kids?"

"I know who I am!"

"Bullshit!" He spit the word with such force that it occurred to him that maybe he *was* a little angry. "You live in a fantasy world. Which is fine for an actress, but it's disastrous for a mother."

"What are you *talking* about?"

"Maybe you're in love now, but wait till Prince Charming's off on location running lines in his trailer with some gorgeous ingenue and you're at home up to your eyeballs in shit and piss. Then you'll wreak some revenge, and it won't just be against him. It'll be against your kid."

"How dare you?!"

"Let me explain something to you about parenthood."

"Don't lecture me!"

"Why not?"

"Because I'm not one of your students!"

"That's okay, I won't charge you. See, the thing is, I was raised by a self-involved mother, so I know—"

"Don't compare me to that ogre!" She grabbed her purse and got up. "You're insane! I always knew you were an angry person! I'm just surprised it never came out before!"

Christopher

"So am I."

He had said it casually, but she froze and looked down at him, surprised. "Why didn't it? You were *very* passive, you know."

"Not really. I never got angry, but I was never passive."

"You let me go without a fight."

"Yeah, but it wasn't passive."

Now her defensiveness was gone and she was merely confused. "What do you mean?" she asked, sitting again.

In a flash, he admired yet another symmetry: His year had begun with my enlightening *him* on this subject and now it was ending with *him* enlightening *her*.

"I wanted out," he explained calmly, "but I felt guilty. I thought I was a bad person for feeling that way. So I dumped you. But in such a way that you wouldn't even notice."

"*What?*"

"See? You didn't."

"But how——"

"I knew you were in bad shape that night at the party and that you wanted me to fight for you. Play a role. Be your hero. But, instead, I got Phillip to take you home. And then when you fell into his bed, I hightailed it back to the City before you even had a chance to reflect on what you'd done. It was cowardly of me. I practically set you up with him. I should never have put you in that position. I should have ended it like a man. Or, better yet, never married you in the first place."

"Oh, that's very nice."

"It's true. I only got married because I wanted to make my ideals come true. But ideals never come true, that's why they're called ideals and not facts, or plans. But ideals were all I had. I wasn't living in reality."

"And you are now?"

He nodded.

She slowly smiled. He got the uneasy feeling that she found him attractive again, or maybe for the first time. He paid the check and they walked back to the Port Authority in silence. He watched, sidelong, as she tried to make sense of all that he had told her. Then he imagined how he would write this scene. It would end his novel. It had to. But it couldn't go like this. Too grim. Finally, he decided that his hero would slip his arm around his ex-wife's shoulder. Without thinking, she would hook her mitten into a loop of his pants. After a few steps, she would turn to him with a kind smile and tell him almost matter-of-factly that, despite the fact that she was having another man's baby, she loved him as much today as she ever had. And then his hero would peck her bony cheek and, relishing his irony, say that he felt the same way about her.

One afternoon, I received a collect call from Fargo, North Dakota. It was Birdy Olsen, an old classmate of mine from marching band. (He had manned the cymbals; I'd blown the grunt horn.) About to be separated for a fortnight from his loving wife and three towheaded children (a visit to the family seat in Oslo), Birdy had booked, along with three other happily married fairies, a beach house on Fire Island. As the Fates would have it, one of the foursome had just been forced to drop out as a result of a fire-fighting injury. Birdy insisted that I take the empty room free of charge. As the room held two singles, I was even welcome to bring along a friend or a lover, if I so desired.

Because I had no lover who wouldn't cost me an arm and a leg, my mind turned to my dearest friend. I pictured long hikes on the raw, blustery dunes, reciting the poems of Mr. Thomas Hardy to each other. I knew the odds were slim that Christopher would agree, but I did have on my side the pity factor. My cancer had yet to take a U-turn.

Christopher

That night, as he read to me, I cut him off in midsimile with a quick suck of air.

"Are you okay?" he asked.

I snatched at my kidney as though stung by a hornet, then nodded courageously. I allowed him to help me to the sofa. A moment later, I asked if he would do me a favor.

"What? A pillow?"

"Come with me to Fire Island."

He laughed. "*What?*"

I gritted my teeth through the pain, barely able to get out the words. "An old pal. Rented a house. An extra room. Separate beds. Just a few days." Then I inhaled deeply and managed a few complete sentences in a row. "You've worked *so* hard. Wouldn't it be fun? One last getaway, before *the descent of winter?*" These last words I pronounced hauntingly, suggesting my imminent demise.

"God, I don't know," he said, smiling to himself, as though hoarding a joke. "I already went to Provincetown. Now you want me to go to Fire Island? I mean, isn't that, like, the *second* gayest place on earth?"

The pain disappeared. I sat up and spoke fluently. "No, that would be Zurich. Fire Island is third. But the good news is, they've passed a new town ordinance. For the first time in history, it's legal for straight boys to spend the night there without relinquishing their prunes." He laughed. "Honestly, you won't be uncomfortable in the least. Amid the flock of sissies there are *plenty* of heterosexualists—mustachioed ad executives, mostly, accompanied by their husbands and kids. Plus, this time of year it's *exquisite.*"

"It's not too cold?"

"Heavens, no." I huffed. "It's a gorgeous, windswept Eden of low shrubs, feathery reeds, and pastel dune grass. The air is crisp and crystalline. The light is positively *edible.*" The foregoing prose-poem was rather a marvel when you consider that I had never been to Fire Island. "You'll have plenty of time to write," I added, enticingly.

I understood the boy's conflict. On the one hand, it seemed the height of cruelty to deny a friend and mentor (if not muse) what might well prove to be his dying wish; on the other, he had absolutely no desire to see me in casual wear. Finally, he agreed to go, but only from Tuesday until Thursday. I sat up, beaming, and fuffled his lovely hair.

What I enjoy most about weekend getaways is the preparation. It was the eve of our departure and I had just completed an afternoon of risky last-minute acquisitions: cashmere muffler, ox-blood shoe polish, sun screen, *Vogue* magazine, tar shampoo, water-based lubricant (a gift from me to one of Birdy's chums?). As I trotted up the stairs, whistling to myself the latest pop offering of a slim-hipped chanteuse by the name of Mr. Leo Sayer (now entirely forgotten, even by his direct descendants), I had not a care in the world. Imagine, then, my horror, when I sprang up the last few steps and found myself face-to-face with a raging snaggletooth.

"B.M.!" Grace cried happily, as though we were long-lost friends, "Am I glad to see *you!*" And with that she leapt into the air like a fox terrier and planted a wet kiss on my startled cheek.

"B.*K.*," I corrected, stepping back, barely able to wrangle my rising gorge. "What are *you* doing here?"

She flung open the snaps of her down coat. "My birthday is tomorrow, so I thought I'd surprise my favorite and only son. Give him a chance to take me to dinner."

"And then you'll leave?"

"What?"

"Then you'll leave?"

Christopher

"Thursday afternoon."

"No, no, no!" I stammered. "That's impossible! Christopher has vacation plans!"

"Well, he'll just have to cancel 'em. I'm only gonna turn fifty once. Do you have any idea where he is? I thought he was always home. Come on, open up!"

Despite my desire to backhand her with my keys, I found myself numbly obeying. The woman had a power. Once inside my lair, she made herself right at home.

"Yuck!" she exclaimed. "Look at this place. It's a *sty!* And the smell. My God! How can you live like this? Don't you have a cleaning lady?"

"Yes," I lied, "but I was forced to fire her just last week for gross incompetence. He used ammonia on cloisonné."

"Last week? Look at these clumps of dust. They're like tumbleweeds." She saw a frantic flash of gray and shrilled, "Was that a *mouse?!*"

"Was what a mouse?" I replied coolly.

She scuttled to the kitchen. "Where's your broom closet?"

Before I could answer, she found it and removed every cleaning supply. For the next hour I sat by in mute horror as she swept, buffed, and scoured my *Bloomsbury aesthetic* to within an inch of its eclectic life. To add insult to injury, as the blatherskite worked, she prattled on a vast array of subjects, ranging from herself to her *damned* self. Then she moved on to her art. It seemed that the muse Euterpe had been working overtime lately, for in the last two days alone, Grace had penned a dozen feminist odes. I writhed in my morris chair, desperate for a fag, wracking my brain for some way to shut her up. But I knew I was kidding myself. Sooner seek to stanch the Mississippi with a colander.

"It's funny, most women dread fifty, but for me it's been

really liberating. I have my garden, my cooking, my friends, my clients, my books. And I've never been happier! Has Chris mentioned? I'm writing a novel."

"Et tu, Jocasta?" I thought.

"As a matter of fact, he hasn't," I replied.

"Yup. You know, in college my dream was to be George Eliot."

"Not George *Raft?*" I thought.

"Me, too," I replied.

"But I'm not surprised he didn't tell you." She sighed with weary understanding. "He resents my creativity, you know. I guess I don't blame him. I'm where he gets his gift for language, but, boy, he sure doesn't have my discipline. Is he still just sitting around with his thumb up his butt?"

"I have no idea where his thumbs are."

"You know what *I* think? And this is just between you and I [*sic*], but I think Chris should just give up the whole writing thing and go to medical school. He would make one *heck* of a good psychiatrist."

"Well, that would certainly be convenient," I managed. "Then he could move back to Milwaukee and take over your practice while you were off on your book tour."

She smirked and blushed. "Hold your horses! I haven't even finished writing it yet!"

I jumped to my feet and raced to the bathroom. There I sucked deep breaths and clutched at my stomach, wondering whether it was mere rage that twisted my innards or the onset of a *genuine* cancer. When I finally emerged, what I saw stopped me in my tracks like a boot-stomp to the face. I had never beheld a more abominable sight. Grace sat on my desk, skirt hiked, legs agog, pushing her schnozzle into one of my prescription containers. The other five sat open at her side.

"You put *baby aspirin* in here?" she asked. "How come? And

Christopher

what's in this one? It looks like candy. And this one looks like *mints*." She popped a pill in her mouth and sucked it, deriving refreshing wintry pleasure. "It *is* a mint!"

I quickly considered my options. If I held fast to my lie, she would grow suspicious (the aspirins were marked "Bayer," the candies smelled of various fruits, and the mints were clearly mints), and she would certainly share her suspicions with Christopher. If, however, I took the high road, explaining that, as a committed Green, I recycled drug containers, she would no doubt find this eccentric to an extraordinary degree, and, again, would no doubt pass this on to Christopher. My third choice was to throw myself on her mercy. Which is what I did. When I had finished my humble confession, she burst into a trill of giggles, crossed her legs (flashing me in the process; I'll spare you the grisly details) then cracked another mint between her wolverine teeth.

"*Well*," she snipped, "it seems you have a little crush on my son."

She had so entirely missed my point that I felt like reaching over with my lighter and setting fire to her absurdly bleached hair.

"Actually, no," I said. "What I *thought* I made explicit was that it *began* with a crush, but that now it's moved to something else. Something far more meaningful. A Platonic friendship based on mutual affection and a shared devotion to art."

She pursed her lips and shook her head. "Friends don't lie to each other, B.J."

I gnashed my teeth. "B.*K*. And, yes, of course, friends don't lie to each other. That's my point. I regret *terribly* what I've done. I've lost sleep over it. And I intend to remedy it as soon as possible. But cancer must run its course. All I'm asking is that you allow me to undo my own mistake."

"Well, I don't know. He *is* my son."

"And for that you should be mighty proud. He's a *wonderful* boy."

She made a silly, indulgent face as though I were a preschooler and held up two stubby fingers an inch apart. "Are you sure you don't have even a *teensy-weensy* crush?"

I would certainly have lost control here, but at that moment we both heard the tinkling of Christopher's keys in the hallway.

She leapt up. "Well, we'll see."

I vaulted into her path, took her firmly by the elbows, and looked deep into her eyes. Her breath smelled of bullfrogs, mildew, and wintergreen.

"Grace, I *beg* of you! Please be merciful! We've all made mistakes, haven't we? Certainly *you* have!"

Her face changed. Her eyes filled with hate. I had said the wrong thing. In a flash of intuition, I knew that she, as a toddler, had been sexually molested on more than one occasion. I was about to experience delayed retaliation. I staggered back, covering my face. The weapons of the weak are always too violent.

"Oh, have I?" she asked, advancing on me. "What do you mean?"

If only I'd had a cross or a bundle of garlic. My mind scrambled for something to say. I certainly could not mention her heinous parenting. Finally, I blurted, "Well, your mother, for instance. I mean, you couldn't possibly have known what would happen when you urged her toward surgery. Certainly, in *hindsight* it was a mistake, but at the time—"

"I HAD DATA!" she screamed.

Off flew my Mets cap. She grabbed my shoulders and tossed me aside like a rag doll, then rolled to the door. When she reached it, I heard a growling, rusty rumble, and slowly, slowly, her turret revolved until its barrel was pointed directly at my gawping mouth.

Christopher

"I suggest you get some help!" she hissed. "You're obviously a *very* sick man! I mean, look at the way you live! Look at your hair! You're repulsive!" She grabbed her suitcase and coat.

I reached out long, imploring arms. "I'm *so* sorry!"

"Oh, knock it off! I will *not* be told what I can and cannot say to my own son! We don't keep secrets!" With a snort of flame, she was gone, slamming the door behind her.

Three minutes later, I heard from my answering machine Christopher's sad voice: "Well, there goes our trip." My God! Had she told him *already?!* I wanted to snatch the phone and cry out for forgiveness, but I was too afraid. "Talk to you in a few days," he added, then hung up.

I called Birdy, cancelled, then took to my queen. No torture endured by the steadfast Hebrews at the hands of Mr. Tomás de Torquemada could equal by half what I endured in the next seventy-two hours. I was afraid even to crack my door, because I knew that were I to set eyes on Christopher, it would tell me what I could not bear to know, so I clung to my ignorance like a tissue shield, pacing my lonely chamber round, brooding, smoking, picturing the despicable Grace behind the flimsy wall, spitting my flimflam into the boy's face like a mouth of spoiled food.

On the day of her departure, I crawled to my feet at daybreak, starved half to death, delirious with fatigue, spirits shredded, chin stubbly. I hauled my stirbug carcass to the bath. If I was going to lose him forever, then at least let his last glimpse of me be fetching. Once clean and shaved, I stood in front of the mirror, poking at my ill-shorn locks. There was nothing to be done with them. Suddenly, Christopher's door slammed. Muffled voices diminished. I sank to the floor. I felt like a defendant in the docks waiting for the return of the jury. A minute later, when he applied his knuckles to my door, I stood and walked bravely, stoically, toward the sound, ready to learn my sentence. When I revealed him, he was smiling. The Fates had spared me!

"Jesus, you look like shit," he said.

"Yes, I know." I sighed lugubriously. "Chemotherapy. The cure that kills."

"Will you knock it off?" He slapped me on the shoulder and stepped inside. "I know you don't have leukemia. Wow, the place looks great!"

"*The bitch told you?!*" I shrieked.

"The second she walked in." He threw himself down on the sofa and rubbed his eyes. "But I disappointed her. I told her I already knew."

"What?"

"Of course, I knew."

"But how?!"

"Those pills of yours. You *chew* them. A couple of weeks ago, while you were on the toilet, I tried one. It was a lemon Skittle."

"Why didn't you tell me?" I pleaded, growing a bit whiny now.

"I didn't want to embarrass you. Besides, I enjoyed the show. You really should have been an actor, you know. You were hysterical."

Despite my mortification, the pleasure I derived from the compliment was shameless. Beneath my disdain for the acting profession, I had always harbored a suspicion that, in the right role, I might have given Joel McCrea a run for his money.

"Hey, do me a favor?" he said abruptly, grinning. "Take off that stupid hat."

I doffed it at lightning speed, then fell to my knees.

"You forgive me?" I begged.

"Of course." He went back to rubbing his eyes. "I know you just said it because you missed me. You didn't want to keep the lie going. But you were stuck."

Christopher

"That's it! You understand!"

"Now get up and stop being so theatrical. By the way, I'm really sorry about Fire Island."

"So am I. It would have been idyllic!"

"We could still go, but I'm so far behind in my work."

"Don't give it another thought." I clambered to my feet and plopped down at his side. "How was your week? Was it awful? Tell me everything."

"I almost started smoking again."

"Oh, no!"

"Don't worry. I refused to give her the satisfaction. But, yeah, it was horrendous. She was in my face every second. I honestly think if she could find a way to enter my body and have her mail delivered there, she'd do it."

"Who *wouldn't?*" I crooned comically.

He chuckled, then shook his head. "I can't believe she had the gall to turn up at my door like that."

"Well, it *was* her fiftieth birthday."

"Yeah, right. Her birthday was three weeks ago and she's fifty-*four*. No, the real reason she came out was that she's on her way to visit Grammy and she wanted me to come along and ease her conscience."

"What do you mean?"

"Grammy's better physically, but her mind is completely gone. Dementia from the fever. She doesn't remember anything."

"I'm so sorry."

"Yeah, last time I visited, I asked if she knew who the president was. She said no. So I said, 'Okay, I'll give you a hint. He used to be a movie star.' She *still* had no idea. So, I said, 'Okay, here's another hint. His first name's Ronald.' She thought for a few seconds, then her face lit up and she said, '*Ronald Colman* is president?' "

I laughed.

Christopher couldn't. He looked terribly, terribly sad.

"My mom just wanted me to come along because she and Grampy're gonna stick Grammy in a nursing home and—"

"What?"

"Yeah, and she feels guilty about it. Although she doesn't know it, of course."

"How could she? She's a stranger to herself."

"She just wants to dilute the responsibility."

"To make the decision yours, as well."

"Right, so I told her no thanks. I visit Grammy all the time. And I need to keep my writing schedule going. Get this, she said I was selfish."

"As she is a budding novelist herself," I said, leaking battery acid, "I would have expected her to understand."

"Yeah, can you believe that? I started to tell her about my novel and after, like, eight seconds, she starts telling me all about hers. Its working title is *Hot Flashes: Breaking News from Fifty*. It's all about this shrink-poet who has spent her whole life being disappointed by men, only to realize at the onset of menopause the glory of a male-free life."

"It's science fiction then?"

His smile was almost happy. He clearly *had* forgiven me. He was a kind person. Our friendship had enlarged his heart. I told him that he must not let his mother's visit queer his progress, that he must soldier on with his book. The smile he tossed me was appreciative but scared. It conveyed the time-worn idiom, "Easier said than done."

As I have previously stated, it is an indisputable truth that when one is closest to one's goal, the Fates have a way of dishing out roadblocks and detours. Here, at the eleventh hour (and the close of my eleventh chapter), when Christopher ought to have been secure in the completion of his novel (thereby allowing

me, almost a quarter-century later, to commence the denoue-
ment of the work you now hold), the boy's will to live guttered.
Rocked by Grace's visit, he found himself, within hours of her
departure, thrown into the most abject of funks. How it pained
me. The end had been in sight, and suddenly, it seemed, we
were back to page one.

December

Mrs. Norma Payne, a widow, lived alone in the Bronx. She enjoyed a close relationship with her sixteen-year-old son, Johnny, and was known throughout the community as a generous soul who adored children. Taped on her front door was a cardboard sun, part of a PTA program designed to let children know that if they were ever in trouble there was help waiting for them inside. Johnny was the ideal American teenager. Clean-cut, bright, friendly. He was a Boy Scout. He saved every cent he earned from his paper route. His only addiction was to basketball. Yet, one night, early that December, Johnny lifted his father's service revolver and shot his mother in the face.

"He was a Boy Scout until today," noted one detective, from beneath his droopy Italian mustache.

As I read this uplifting story in the *Post*, I imagined how much better Christopher's life would be if he had Johnny's mettle. Killing Grace might prove to be his salvation. Not only would it rid him of her continual assaults on his independence and self-esteem, but it would unblock his spigot. It was almost *worth* being electrocuted for, I thought, the completion of one fine work of art. I even considered killing her myself, as a Christmas gift to Christopher, but I, like most in our anxious age, lack the stomach for homicide.

I turned the page of my newspaper and bowed my head for another slurp of eye-opener. In the days of the Greeks, I reflected, murder was as simple as moving one's bowels. If a husband brought back a new wife from the wars, did the first wife mope around the agora debating divorce? Certainly not. She hunted the rascal down and crushed his skull with a rock. Or if one's mother killed one's father, did one dash off to a support group, desperate to forgive? No. One stuck a sword in her bosom and twisted. And, similarly, perhaps one awoke one day, having lost one's joie de vivre. No need to writhe on the leather. Simply grab a rope, throw it over a beam, and, presto! Yup, I thought, smiling at the naughty play of my fancy and staring out through the window of the Parnassus, those Greeks were really somethin'.

It was only then, Lulled Reader, that, with a flinch, I noticed Christopher standing outside, staring directly at me through the frosty glass. He was crying. I leapt from my booth, rushed to the door, and gestured for him to come in at once. He dropped his head, covered his face with both hands (think Rodin), and obeyed. I threw a protective arm around him and swept him to the vinyl, where he plopped down and began to weep. As one who had been around the block more than a few times, I knew exactly what to do. I sat in silence, drained my cocktail, and waited. I uttered not a single word to distract him from his grief, even when Cassandra came by and removed my only-half-finished paella.

Ten minutes later, Christopher had, for the time being, cried himself dry.

"She's dead, isn't she?" I said.

He nodded. "Last night. Her first night in the nursing home."

"In her sleep?"

"No, actually . . . she choked to death."

"Grace used *her bare hands?*"

Christopher chuckled and sniffled. "No, it was food. I guess it can happen with dementia. Your mind's so far gone, you forget to chew. Anyway, Grammy choked on her dessert. By the time they got to her, it was too late."

He shook his head, enduring a fresh wave of pain. Without thinking, I reached out and touched his hand. Much to my surprise, he took it, squeezed it, and did not let go. Fortunately, we were at the Parnassus, where shows of affection between grown men are actually encouraged. Enjoying the unprecedented moment, I again fell silent. When Cassandra approached with my hot fudge sundae, I waved her away.

When Christopher spoke again it was in fits and starts. He told me for the first time all about his beloved Grammy. Normally, I abhor sentimentality, but not here, not with my best friend. He told me all about the dear little woman, who, because of her childhood accident, was not terribly fond of leaving the house. (A woman after my own heart.) In fact, she had done little in the past few decades but sit at her kitchen table, reading the newspaper, paying bills, answering the phone, and cooking. Her visits from her grandson were among her few worldly pleasures. As she listened to his tales of city life, her eyes twinkled like an elf's. When she laughed, it was from the bottom of her belly. She had to close her eyes and cover her mouth with her wrist to contain it.

"I was always her favorite," Christopher said, dabbing his eyes with a cocktail napkin. "Whenever I walked in, she'd lift up her arms and I'd bend down and she'd kiss me a thousand times."

Weather permitting, in the late afternoon, they would move into the cool of the high back porch—half of it lay in the weeping shade of a willow——and watch Grampy garden. A bandana around his head, his heavy, old Sicilian muscles twitching, Joe mowed and weeded, even transplanted trees, all by himself, refusing help. She watched proudly, but when he trudged up the steps hours later, ready for a beer with his grandson, she yelled at him, telling him that he worked too hard, that his heart would give out one day. At night, they all watched TV together. Perched in her recliner, her little feet barely reaching the footrest, Grammy watched with a look of wonder, as though television were still a miracle.

After an hour of reminiscence, I scraped Christopher off the vinyl and escorted him back to his cell. He understood that he had to board a train at once, but he was so overwhelmed that he did not understand that he would not be coming back before the funeral, which meant that he would have to pack intelligently. He sat slumped on the couch, oscillating between crushed silence and teary reflection, while I filled his duffel for him, a task at which I excel. A half hour later, I lugged the bag down the stairs and found us a taxi.

During the short trip to the Grand Central Station, I was eager to restore the intimacy we had shared at the Parnassus, so I took his hand again. After a few seconds, he gently removed it. This was due not to any lack of affection, but to the Yemenite hack's disapproving gaze in the rearview mirror. Christopher's crying continued intermittently during the ride. As we neared the station, I offered to come along, to function during the ordeal as his rock and pillar. It didn't matter, I insisted, that I was not packed; the outfit I wore would do, as long as I kept to a rear pew. He refused me, saying that it wasn't worth the revenge Grace would exact when she learned that she did not have him all to herself.

As we hurried together across the sticky marble of the terminal, beneath its green sky and spidery constellations, past the

Kodak mural of a tulip garden, I somehow suspected that this meeting between mother and son would be different from all the others that had preceded it. What I did *not* suspect was that he was going to kill her.

When Christopher's sneaker hit the New Haven platform, his sister, Anna, was waiting a few yards away. She smiled bravely, but her hazel eyes were red from crying. They embraced for a long time. Gradually, over her shoulder, Christopher noticed Grace standing ten yards away with Grampy. They, too, were smiling bravely, but only *his* eyes were red. Grace had never looked better, which is to say that she was still a dead ringer for Mussolini, but a burden seemed to have been lifted from her too-broad shoulders.

Christopher walked over and hugged Grampy. The poor old man shook from head to toe. Then Christopher stepped over to face his mother. He wanted to keep the greeting brief, but the moment he was close, she leapt three feet in the air and pressed her ruined bosoms to his neck. She held him there for what felt like half a day.

As they descended to the street, Christopher wanted to ask Grampy a million questions, but Grace, unwilling to surrender his attention even for an instant, latched on to his biceps and regaled him with every nuance of her and Anna's morning flight. She spared him nothing, not even the plot twists of the silly movie or the middle name of the stewardess who had brought her extra peanuts. As the banality of her story and the gulping frenzy with which she relayed it reached a crescendo, she squeezed his arm tighter, tugging and twisting it. Normally, he would have endured it, but, much to his own surprise, he found himself indulging in a rare moment of emotional expression.

"Let go of me!" he cried. "I'm not your *fucking date!*"

Christopher

The only person who looked more shocked than his mother was his grandfather, who had been raised in an era when children were taught to treat their parents with respect, no matter how unspeakable their crimes.

Anna could barely hide her amusement. "Down, boy!" she whispered.

Grace's eyes went damp with hurt, but then, almost immediately, they fell cold and hard.

"*Well*," she snipped, "it's lovely to see you, too."

Christopher opened his mouth to speak, but then stopped.

"What?" she snarled, pushing her face right into his. "*Say it!*"

He couldn't. No words came. Again, the familiar numbness took hold. Anna led him down the steps one at a time, as though he were an invalid. Grace followed, goose-stepping, clutching Daddy's hand. In the car, Christopher sat with his sister in the backseat, listening as Grampy opened his heart.

"Oh, she fought hard!" he moaned. "So hard! So long! And then to die all 'cause of a *lousy piece of cheesecake!* Why would God do something like that? I don't get it, I'll never, never understand it."

Grace laid a hand on his leathery neck and spoke slowly, sweetly, as though to a child. "Ours is not to reason why. The important thing now is *your* health. Life is for the living." Then she leaned over and kissed him full on the mouth, tongue probing. (I exaggerate to make a point.)

Over the next two days, Grace took charge of the funeral arrangements with a vigor barely distinguishable from glee. Although Grammy had requested, before being shoved into surgery, that she be buried next to her family in Brooklyn, Grace felt it made far more sense for her simply to be incinerated. Grampy objected, of course, but in the end surrendered to his daughter's will.

Cremation is incompatible with the Nicene Creed, which

expresses faith in the resurrection of the body, and so, out of respect for the mourners, most of whom, like her parents, were devoutly Catholic, Grace decided that they would *conceal* the fact that Grammy's body had been reduced to ash. They would simply display at the funeral a closed, empty casket, and no one would be the wiser.

Christopher watched her machinations from the sideline, aloof to an almost Hamletine degree. On the surface, he appeared bored and indifferent, calm and disinterested. Whenever Grace spoke to him, hoping for "some support," he answered vaguely or not at all. After all, he told himself, it was none of his business. If Grampy wasn't going to put up a fight, why should he? But beneath this rationalization, he felt, deep in his core, an emerging rage almost Dionysian in its potential for destruction. Watching his mother mince around the funeral home, micromanaging every aspect of the service, down to the precise volume of the Vivaldi, he imagined himself grabbing her by the neck and shaking her hard until something essential *gave*.

The afternoon before the funeral, at the precise hour that Grammy's hallowed corpus was being fed to pagan flames, mourners began to arrive at the Spinelli & Sons funeral home for the viewing, or, to be exact, for a moment alone with an empty box. Many stopped to touch or kiss the waxed mahogany lid. A few were visibly perplexed. Why was it closed? It wasn't as though she had been run over by a truck or the victim of a freak industrial accident. One old man, a former president of the Roma Club, actually dared to inquire. He teetered over to Grace and said, "How come we can't see her?" Grace flashed her snaggletooth and patted his veiny paw with a look of syrupy condescension.

"It's the way she wanted it," she said.

Christopher almost shrieked.

That night, he could not get his mind off the sordid charade.

Christopher

He replayed it over and over again and each time it seemed more despicable than before. Grace noticed his tortured silence, but when she tried to penetrate it with chipper queries, he answered in monosyllables and looked away. After Grampy and Anna had gone to sleep, Grace came into the den, holding a mug of steaming tea, and offered it to him where he lay on the sleeper-sofa, watching the nightly news. He looked up at her coldly. Grinning, she held the mug out. Neither of them moved or spoke.

Slowly, her eyes softened with hurt. Then she exploded: "You bastard! I'll throw this in your face! You've been ignoring me all day! You'd better tell me what's wrong or *I'm* gonna start talking! *I'll* tell you what's wrong with you!"

When he didn't answer, she lost all control.

"You little fucker! Instead of finding fault with me, why don't you look at the way *you* act! Look at yourself! Look at your *marriage!* Look at your faggy friend next door! See if it doesn't add up to something! See if your hostility doesn't start there! See if you're not blaming *me* for your *own* problems! For *what you are!*"

Christopher sat up quickly. She jumped back as though she thought he was going to punch her. But as much as he would have loved to, he could not, because, once again, he was shutting down. His limbs grew heavy. His breathing was labored. He could barely keep his eyes open. He rose slowly and walked out of the room like a sleepwalker.

Christopher turned out the basement light and fell to the sheets and quilt that Anna had laid for him on the cement floor. He closed his eyes and the darkness neared. His hands fell to his crotch. He cupped his manhood, protecting himself as though from a pair of giant scissors. For hours, moving in and out of shallow slumber, he strove to put words to his feelings. He had always known that "hate" was inadequate to describe what he felt for her. In the end, not words, but an image came. He saw a tiny green plant drowning in a black void. Its every living fiber was being killed by the perpetual night that engulfed it. It was doing everything in its power to escape. Then two words came: *cellular aversion*. Yes, that was it. The awful numbness that overcame him in his mother's presence was the feel of his cells tending, braving, away from her, toward light. Or, more literally, toward the fine, healthful things that his mother would not and could not ever be. But because he was firmly rooted and his mother's darkness was infinite and all-encompassing, he was slowly dying. Revolt was futile. He opened his eyes, turned on the lights, and saw that it was dawn.

He knew what he had to do.

He had to kill her.

Upstairs, he set his duffel by the front door, then passed from room to room. He felt like a burglar searching a stranger's house. At the kitchen window, he swiped the cloudy window and saw his grandfather standing in the yard.

When Christopher was just a few yards away, the old man turned, startled, but then, seeing who it was, he opened his eyes wide.

"You're all dressed. So early. What, you didn't sleep too good?"

"Nope."

His grandfather looked across the yard. The grass was dusted with rime. "Me, too. Not a wink." He flashed his perfect dentures and pointed down to what he was wearing—a thin robe and corduroy slippers under an overcoat. "Look at me! But, hey, at least I got my head covered." He put a hand to the funny hat he wore.

When he and Grammy had first moved to the area, their house was surrounded by thick forest and graced with a brook. Once, on its banks, Christopher had dug up an arrowhead and a half-dime. But now all the trees had been felled and their house was just one of dozens along a paved circular lane. But to make up for destroying their brook, the developers have recently doubled their lot. Soon, Grampy would have the largest garden around.

"I figure I'll lay it out like this," he said, walking Christopher to an area marked with stakes. "Tomatoes, peppers, zucchini, pumpkins, some nice cucumbers. Over here by the fence, strawberries, some herbs. Then I'll move that tree over to there and lay down some kinda path."

Christopher heard barking. Behind a wire fence, a black dog that had been sleeping stood tied to a tin doghouse.

Grampy frowned. "She always hated that mutt. It kept her up nights."

The dog bounded forward, and, straining its leash, slapped its paws to the mesh.

"Yeah, I was good to her when she got sick," Grampy mused, "but I coulda been better before. See, I always said that if there were five good points at being a wife, then Rosa had four." He counted on his fingers. "Smart, pretty, good with money, true blue. But if there was one bad point, it was the sex."

His grandfather had never talked to him like this before. He felt like an adult suddenly, which was as uncomfortable as it was pleasing.

"Oh, yeah, she never really enjoyed it too much," he continued. "You know, she had these scars from the operations when she was a kid and they embarrassed her very bad. I never could figure out why. But then, one day, I was helpin' the nurse change her and I saw 'em. Holy Christ! Such bad scars."

It was unfathomable to Christopher that in a lifetime together this was the first time he had ever seen them.

"Yeah, I never understood really," the old man said. "And I

used to say I would rather she had only two of the good points, if one of the good points was sex." He thought about that for a moment, then added with regret, "But now . . . if I had her back . . . I wouldn't care. I'd never look no place else." He glanced back to where his new garden would be. "Yeah, it doesn't matter if you're together ten years or a hundred, you always want more. You read all the time about these tragedies. People dyin' young. A young girl fails to make a curve, hits a tree, and she's dead. Just like that. And you think, hey, I had sixty-one years with Rosa. I should be satisfied, right?" He ruefully shook his head. "But it's never enough. Never, never enough. I should never have let her have that operation. She knew she wouldn't ever come home. She told me so. Told your mother, too. But we didn't listen."

The dog was barking, its leash pulled tight, straining its muzzle through the mesh, trying to reach a robin that had stopped pecking and seemed to be watching it.

Grampy was halfway up the stairs before Christopher found the courage to tell him that he did not want breakfast.

Grampy turned slowly on the top step. "You gotta eat."

"I'm going home."

"What? Now?"

"Yeah."

"What about the funeral?"

"I'm not going. You know how much I loved Grammy. She knew it. I don't need to be there. The casket's empty, anyway."

He seemed more baffled than angry. "Your mother will be very upset."

"I know."

"What, you and her had some kinda fight?"

Christopher looked into the old man's tired, confused eyes, where sadness was beginning to pool. He wanted to explain everything, start at the beginning, but he knew that stories like

Christopher

these have no beginning, unless you go back to Olympus or Eden or the big bang.

Christopher nodded. "Yeah, we had a fight."

In the guest room, Christopher knelt by Anna's bed. The blinds were drawn and he could barely make out her face. He roused her with a gentle hand.

"I'm leaving," he whispered.

"What?" she said groggily.

"I'm leaving."

"What? Now? Why?"

"I can't be around her. Never again."

"Who do you mean?"

"I'm finished. Forever."

Anna raised herself on one arm. Her eyes filled with bewilderment. "You mean— But . . . but you can't. You're her whole life. If you cut her out, she'll— It'll *kill her!*"

"I know."

A few minutes later, he stopped at the den. The door was ajar and he looked in. Grace slept on the couch. She was dimly visible as a ragged pile of rising and falling shadow.

When his train pulled out that morning, Christopher's liberation began. He knew that whatever happened next would be the beginning of something new, a fresh chapter, the tale of a young soul battling toward light. Matricide is a slow and difficult murder, and he knew it. Whether the child shoots his mother in the face or uses more subtle means (as he had, as Grace had with *her* mother), it was just one step. Changes still need to be made inside oneself, changes that can take a lifetime. Or even longer. But if you start early enough, he told himself, get a jump, the changes might be accomplished while the mother is still alive, and then, only then, was forgiveness imaginable. Yes, he had begun to kill his mother. He only wished he had started sooner, before he was born.

In the days following his return, I beheld changes in the young man that were nothing short of caterpillarian. He cracked, once and for all, through the chrysalis of his self-negation, and sprouted bright, wet wings on which he flapped to and fro with merry vim. Once again, he wrote his novel every day, but for not as many hours, because other things brought him pleasure, too. When he laughed it was no longer a tense little cough, but a hearty song, straight from the belly. On his birthday, he bought himself a white mutt and named him Pax. As Christmas approached, he hung twinkling colored lights around his desk.

Eventually, inevitably, his bliss was interrupted by telephone calls and letters from the tenacious Grace, who refused to believe that this was the same person who had sprung a quarter of a century before from her unwaxed haunches. But Christopher was not lured back into her deadly darkness; he screened her calls and returned her letters unopened.

On Christmas Eve, no doubt frustrated by his stubborn resolve, the harridan actually had the gall to contact *me*. I had always wondered whether it had been a mistake to list my phone number, but I had done it in case an ex-lover might want to call me one day, desperate for closure or a nostalgic bout of lovesport. (As yet, none had.) When the phone chirped, my ample frame was expanding in a hot Yuletide bubble bath—a gift to myself.

"Ho, ho, ho," was my unsuspecting greeting.

"B.M.?!" she shouted, as though ours were not a crystal-clear modern-day connection, but a desperate cry between a trapped miner and a burrowing rescuer.

"Speaking," I sighed, braced for the worst.

"I don't understand it!" she whined. "Why is he doing this to me?! It's Christmas Eve!"

"It's quite simple," I said. "He detests you."

"But why?!"

"He believes you to be—and, I must say, I heartily concur— a destroyer of greenery. Like Agent Orange."

"What?!"

"He's in the process of saving his own life. Please leave him alone."

"Forever?"

"Yes. Now if you don't mind, I'd like to ask *you* a question. And I ask it with tremendous compassion, for I, too, am a survivor. Who was it that diddled you? Was it Grampy? An uncle? A neighbor? Well, I suppose it doesn't matter. What matters is that you get yourself some help. Mount the leather, old girl. It worked wonders for me. Remember, just because *your* clients don't get better, doesn't mean you won't."

I am not entirely sure at what point the sorry lady hung up, but I suspect it was somewhere around the word "Grampy."

I never told Christopher that she called.

Adieu

In the words of that second-rate novelist, but first-rate plunderer of Moorish lads, Mr. André Gide, "The promises of the caterpillar bind not the butterfly." No fool, when my young friend sprouted wings, I was fully aware that he might one day use them to escape me. I understood only too well the compulsion in all young disciples to slay their masters. In fact, as a college senior, I had slain Wolf. One evening, deep in my cups, I had called him, in front of a gathering of his colleagues, "a pompous Kraut."

When, as the new year progressed, leaving Orwell's permanently behind, Christopher and I only grew closer, no one was more surprised than I. Was it possible that my superb young protégé was actually an exception to the rule? Never one to question the Fates, I simply decided to savor every moment. Yet, Worldly Reader, as you and I know only too well, there is precious little that time does not eventually get its filthy fingers on.

I began to notice subtle changes. For example, he spent more and more time with other people: with Julie and Ted, who seemed to have survived her infidelity unscathed (aided by the

Christopher

fact that she had never confessed it); with Celia, who had begun working for a Hudson River nonprofit, determined to save an inch-long aquatic creature from extinction at the hands of heartless developers; and with a slew of other friends, new and old, whose names I did not recognize and whose faces I rarely glimpsed. He even began to date a girl whom he considered to be "beautiful" and "his equal in every way." I violently disagreed with this assessment and told him so, but he insisted that I had no right to judge as we had never met. Determined not to perceive a threat where none existed, I offered to host a Valentine's Day dinner, to which he would be free to invite his new girlfriend and any of his other friends. Unfortunately, he declined, explaining, in dreadful New Age parlance, that they would not "get me." My feelings were hurt, of course, but there was nothing I could do about it.

By March, I was down to one night a week, and no longer did he share his pages with me, preferring instead to share them with something called a "writer's workshop." He was slipping away right before my eyes. Beginning to panic, I sought to lure him back. I cooked a vegetarian lasagna and let the aroma waft into the hallway. At great personal risk, I picked up gifts for him (a Mark Twain first edition bound in vellum, sterling cuff links, a cabinet card of Mr. Ralph Waldo Emerson). One night, hopelessly cockeyed, I foolishly hired an ex-lover of mine, retired from the Peking Ballet, to call Christopher, introduce himself as Dr. Pearlman, and inform him that I was secretly suffering from a nasty case of lupus. When he pronounced it "rupus," the jig was up. I will not bore you with how I regretted this foolishness in the morning.

The *coup de grace* came even sooner than I had expected, when one afternoon in April he bounded up the stairs, grinning ear to ear, holding up a letter, announcing his admittance to a graduate program in English. (I did not even know that he had applied.) I did my best to hide my horror as he gushed about the faculty and the idyllic location, because, as everyone knows, graduate school is to the artist as a hospice is to the ill.

A few months later, the removalists arrived and emptied his apartment. I stood on the stoop and watched with him and Pax as the van drove away, then I turned to face him. We parted stiffly and dryly, shaking hands like two insurance salesmen after a particularly exhausting convention. I was in pieces, of course, but I couldn't bear to burden him with it. I smacked his shoulder, grinned like a cretin, and told him to be well. Watching his taxi drive away, I waved. Only Pax turned back and saw it.

I wept away the long afternoon, but it was not the sort of crib-suffering that had marked our earlier separations. If I may be permitted a momentary lapse in modesty, it was a more mature grief, born of wisdom. I was proud of myself. Ever since my first and only heartbreak, I had feared that if I ever loved again, I would never, should events conspire to separate me from my beloved, find the generosity of spirit to let him go. And yet here the worst had happened, and not once had I tried to stand in his way. I had merely kissed the joy as it flew by.

As you may have already guessed, having never seen the title *Love's Sad Archery* or the name Christopher Ireland in the fiction section of a megastore near you, our young hero never published his novel. Or any novel at all. Alas, he lost his way, as so many of our best and brightest do, among the stacks of academe. I know this, because, over the long years he sent me sporadic Christmas cards (no return address), keeping me abreast of his gradual rise from teacher's assistant to full professor.

During the final Christmas week of the second millennium, my shivering mailman, Benjamin, handed me in my foyer (Sasha had died and left me her brownstone), a padded envelope with no return address. Inside, I found a thick paperback book. It was published by an obscure university press and it was entitled

Christopher

Love's Sad Archery: The Allure of Heartbreak in Byron's Don Juan. I turned it over and saw a black-and-white photograph of Dr. Christopher Ireland. He looked much older, of course, but he was still pretty, and, it seemed, quite happy. His smile struck me as bright and sincere. Below, a two-line biography told me that he lived in Palo Alto, California, with his wife, Jill, and their three children. Studying the photo, I grew more pensive than moved, because his clear, untroubled eyes told me, conclusively, what I should have known sooner: Christopher was not now, and had never been, an artist. The fact was, he loved life more than he did his dreams. He was a normal fellow.

Flipping idly through the book, knowing already that I would never read it, I lugged my guts up the creaking stairs to my boudoir. I heard from the basement one of my lodgers wailing on his alto saxophone. As I reached the door, I stopped dead. My eyes had landed, almost by accident, on the following words, sitting on their very own page:

For B. K. Troop, who asked for nothing in return

I stared at it for a very long time, then smiled. He remembered me, after all. I walked into the shadows of my bedroom and stopped at Sasha's Victorian dresser. In the bottom drawer lay a great chunk of Christopher's old manuscript, its margins still etched with my cruel blue ink. I wondered, as I removed it, if its beauty could be saved, plucked from the oblivion toward which all things tend.

THE END

© Charlie Lieberman

ALLISON BURNETT is a writer and film director living in Los Angeles. This is his first novel.